Even pregnant, Jill looked good.

No, she looked incredibly sexy.

He'd never found pregnant women a turn-on, at least not until Jill. Maybe it was just her. Maybe he was just nuts.

Just the thought of the life growing safely beneath Jill's heart brought a lump to his throat. He wanted to wake up Saturday mornings to a little body jumping on the bed and falling into his arms. He wanted to rub his beard-stubbled chin into a warm neck just to listen to a happy squeal. He wanted Little League games and dance recitals.

He wanted to be a dad. And he wanted Jill for his wife—in every way.

Dear Reader,

This is it, the final month of our wonderful three-month celebration of Intimate Moments' fifteenth anniversary. It's been quite a ride, but it's not over yet. For one thing, look who's leading off the month: Rachel Lee, with *Cowboy Comes Home,* the latest fabulous title in her irresistible CONARD COUNTY miniseries. This one has everything you could possibly want in a book, including all the deep emotion Rachel is known for. Don't miss it.

And the rest of the month lives up to that wonderful beginning, with books from both old favorites and new names sure to become favorites. Merline Lovelace's *Return to Sender* will have you longing to work at the post office (I'm not kidding!), while Marilyn Tracy returns to the wonderful (but fictional, darn it!) town of Almost, Texas, with *Almost Remembered.* Look for our TRY TO REMEMBER flash to guide you to Leann Harris's *Trusting a Texan,* a terrific amnesia book, and the EXPECTANTLY YOURS flash marking Raina Lynn's second book, *Partners in Parenthood.* And finally, don't miss *A Hard-Hearted Man,* by brand-new author Melanie Craft. *Your* heart will melt—guaranteed.

And that's not all. Because we're not stopping with the fifteen years behind us. There are that many—and more!—in our future, and I know you'll want to be here for every one. So come back next month, when the excitement and the passion continue, right here in Silhouette Intimate Moments.

Yours,

Leslie J. Wainger
Executive Senior Editor

Please address questions and book requests to:
Silhouette Reader Service
U.S.: 3010 Walden Ave., P.O. Box 1325, Buffalo, NY 14269
Canadian: P.O. Box 609, Fort Erie, Ont. L2A 5X3

PARTNERS IN PARENTHOOD

RAINA LYNN

Silhouette® INTIMATE™ MOMENTS®

Published by Silhouette Books

America's Publisher of Contemporary Romance

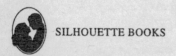

SILHOUETTE BOOKS

ISBN 0-373-07869-2

PARTNERS IN PARENTHOOD

Books by Raina Lynn

Silhouette Intimate Moments

A Marriage To Fight For #804
Partners in Parenthood #869

RAINA LYNN

is married, the mother of three, mother-in-law of one and grandmother of two. She lives in a peaceful, secluded corner of paradise in Sierra Nevada. To her unending joy, not even the U.S. Postal Service comes out there. Her favorite way of unwinding at the end of a long day is to disappear into the forest on her horse for a couple of hours, then curl up with a good romance novel. She would love to hear from her readers, at P.O. Box 739, Foresthill, CA 95631.

To my son-in-law, Travis,
one of the world's true heroes.

Prologue

It was one in the morning when Mason Bradshaw flipped on the stairwell light and trudged up the steps, grateful to be home. Exhaustion burned through muscle and bone. After the day he'd had, he wanted two things—a hot shower and the chance to sleep like the dead until noon.

As he stepped through the open doorway to the master bedroom, shock and agony nearly buckled his knees. He grabbed the doorjamb for support, still not believing his eyes.

Across the room, Karen—his Karen!—writhed in the arms of another man, the pair so caught up in the frenzy of lust that neither noticed him. Clothing had been dropped on the way to the bed like a trail of bread crumbs. Sheets and blankets hung to the floor, torn loose from the mattress.

Pain congealed into rage, creating a dangerous stew of emotions boiling out of control. On the night table sat a bottle of wine—his wine!—two glasses and a cheeseboard. The knife had bits of brie stuck to its polished blade. Odd how the trivial detail registered with such stark clarity. In his mind's eye, Mason watched his fingers close around the polished mahogany handle. So tempting. So easily done.

A tiny voice of reason screamed above the din of burgeoning insanity. He could kill them, yes, but he'd destroy himself in the process. Jealousy roared at him to cross the room, pick up the knife and end her betrayal, but reason countered that it would change nothing, that he needed to survive. Mason couldn't think of a single reason why survival was relevant or even desirable at that point, but he kept his place by the door.

Beyond speech, he forced badly needed air into his lungs and announced his presence by clearing his throat. If a bomb had gone off, it couldn't have had more impact.

Karen whirled around, her dark eyes huge with shock. "Oh, God, Mason, no!"

Her lover leapt from the bed and backed against the wall. Raking his long pale hair from his face with one hand, he grabbed his pants from the floor with the other and covered himself. Karen scrambled for a blanket. Neither dared take their eyes from the dangerously still husband standing in the doorway.

Devastated and nearly blind with fury, Mason stepped forward. Karen's lover cringed, lifting his hand in a warding-off gesture. "Let's not overreact here, man."

His young voice quavered and Mason, for the first time, took a good look at him. He couldn't have been more than twenty-two or twenty-three, and was as fair as Mason was dark. He was a good head shorter but had the physique of a bodybuilder and the advantage of a dozen or more years. Mason wondered if he could take the guy in a straight-up fight. God, how he wanted to find out.

Wild-eyed, Karen's boy toy looked to her for help. "Talk to him!"

The outburst turned the tide. If the bastard had shown any backbone at all, Mason would have beaten him to a pulp—or at least attempted to. But what would it accomplish? Inside, a dam broke, and the urge to fight drained away.

Deliberately, Mason turned his attention to his wife. "I suggest you both get dressed. We have some things to discuss." The dead cold in his baritone was a strange companion to the howling grief in his soul, but the control pleased him. He'd always taken comfort in his ability to withdraw behind a cool facade when trouble threatened to upend his world. Never before had he needed that ability as he did now; never before had he been so grateful for it.

Unable to watch any longer, he left the room. In a fog of shock and disbelief, he wandered down to the kitchen, sagged against the counter and stared blindly into the sink. Willpower alone kept him upright.

Love was something he'd never had much experience with growing up. And as an adult he'd been reluctant to open himself to that kind of vulnerability. Being a loner wasn't comfortable, but it was, at least, familiar.

The day he'd met Karen, her beauty had staggered him. Women often pursued him, a nuisance he preferred to avoid. When she'd expressed an interest in him, he'd tried his usual evasive tactics, but this time his brittle, barely adequate responses to attempts at conversation had lacked their usual conviction. She'd seemed to view getting beneath his guard as a personal challenge. Gradually, over several months, she'd worked her way in. Once she'd reached his heart, he'd fallen hard.

Muted voices sounded from the entry. He heard the front door open, then close—but he stayed where he was. Then Karen stepped into the kitchen alone.

"Mason, please," she whined. "I'm sorry."

Slowly, he turned to face the death of his marriage, of his dreams. His wife of seven years stood in the doorway, her lion's mane of pale blond hair in sensual disarray and looking as if she'd been doing exactly what he'd caught her doing.

He sighed wearily, too angry and hurt to raise his voice. "Where's your friend?"

She squirmed and wrung her slender hands, her big brown eyes liquid. "I didn't know how civilized you were going to be about this, so I asked him to leave."

"Civilized!"

Flinching, she stepped back. "Don't make it worse," she protested. "This isn't my fault. You weren't supposed to be here."

He blinked at that. "You've never been one to take responsibility for your actions, Karen, but blaming me for this is outrageous, even for you."

"That wasn't necessary," she snapped. A heavy silence widened the distance between them. Her gaze skated across the room, and she asked softly, "Why aren't you at the conference?"

The pain ripped him up so badly inside, each breath came hard fought. "I blew the transmission halfway there. By the time the shop replaced it, I'd missed all of today's meetings, so I drove straight back to Los Angeles." He didn't know why he bothered to explain. His reasons for being home weren't relevant, not anymore. "A divorce won't be a problem."

She paled. "I don't want a divorce."

Silently, Mason studied the woman he had loved beyond all reason. For the first time, he noticed the sullen lines around her seductive mouth, the unbending selfishness in the aristocratic line of her jaw. Before he had married her, he'd truly believed he'd found an end to the loneliness he'd known his whole life, found a woman with whom he could settle down and have a normal family—something he'd craved since childhood.

Before he'd proposed, Karen had gushed over the prospect of a house full of kids, but it hadn't taken long after the wedding for her tune to change. For seven years she'd invented one excuse or another why babies weren't a good idea right then. Now he saw how badly he'd been duped, realized how many of his own dreams he'd buried or killed for her.

He grabbed her purse off the counter and stuffed it into her hands. "Go now."

Karen recoiled, and the designer bag dropped to the floor. "I'm not going anywhere."

"Oh, yes, you are." He took a step forward. "You have two minutes to gather enough clothes to last until your lawyer can contact mine."

Her expression opened into an incredulous smile. "You can't be serious."

Deliberately, he looked at his watch. Staring at the digital readout certainly beat looking into her deceitful face. "You're down to a minute and forty-five seconds."

At the low menace in his voice, her smile faltered. Cautiously, she backed away from him and darted up the stairs. Mason choked down a bourbon as he listened to her slam closets and drawers. The liquor sat in his stomach like lead.

By the time she had packed, better than twenty minutes had passed, but he didn't comment. She pulled open the front door to leave, glowering at him over her shoulder. "I'll come home when you've calmed down and decided to stop acting like a dinosaur." The door slammed behind her so hard the windows shook.

Mason wasn't sure how long he stood in the silence before soul-deep fatigue forced him upstairs. He didn't want to look in the master bedroom, much less go in there, but he couldn't seem to help himself. The room was as he remembered it—disheveled and smelling faintly of heated bodies and sex. It was also as silent and empty as all the secret hopes he'd had for his life.

Taking another large swallow of bourbon, he dropped the glass beside the bottle of wine. With a vicious jerk, he tore the sheets and blankets from the bed and stuffed them into the laundry hamper. Then he trudged woodenly to the guest room and spent what remained of the night stretched out fully clothed on a twin bed far too short for his tall, lean frame.

"Never again," he vowed into the dark. "No one will *ever* get that close again." Mason stared at the ceiling until the sun came up, then mechanically changed clothes and left for work.

As usual, the L.A. traffic was gridlocked for miles, and as he sat inhaling carbon monoxide, something deep inside snapped. He was sick of the smog, the crowds and the cold-blooded attitude of the people he knew. Surely, there had to be another way to live.

Chapter 1

Jill Mathesin swept into the *Stafford Review-Journal*, feeling rested, sassy and considerably younger than her thirty-two years. After two weeks of decadent luxury, it was time to return to the real world.

Vicki Haynes, the struggling newspaper's secretary, came from around her desk and enveloped Jill in a fierce hug. "You look fabulous, girlfriend!"

"Amazing what the vacation of a lifetime will do," she chirped. With no one else in the reception area, Jill impulsively slid her blouse off one shoulder to flaunt her new tan. "Not bad, huh?"

Vicki gave the darkened skin exaggerated scrutiny then compared it to her own mahogany tones. "Well," she drawled in mock disdain, "if one's not born with it, one must compensate, I suppose."

Jill latched onto the familiar byplay and arched an eyebrow. "Seems to me you coveted my hair until you went to braids."

"Yes, but now I'm perfect."

After being gone for so long, Jill's wit had lost some of its razor edge. Left without a retort, she groaned in defeat, and the pair dissolved into more hugs and laughter.

"A cruise," Vicki breathed. "I still can't believe it." She leaned back on her desk and crossed her arms. "Tell me *everything*. I want details, girl."

Jill chuckled. It had been years since she'd felt this good. The pain of her failed marriage still nagged at the shadowy corners of her heart, but after eighteen months, it was more scar than open wound, and no longer ruled her life. The cruise had been a declaration of independence, a celebration that she'd exorcised most of the mangled dreams. Life held promise again.

She didn't quite feel like her old self yet, but close. Loneliness was an all too frequent companion in the night now. Maybe that was a good sign. During the worst of her divorce and its aftermath, being alone had been comfortable, like a warm blanket on a winter night. Now it chafed. "Vicki, I'm broke. You wouldn't believe how much money I went through."

"Meet any interesting men?"

The thought of taking that kind of risk again still didn't hold much appeal, but her best friend believed the best cure for a broken heart was finding someone new.

Jill shrugged. "A couple, but none I wanted to wrap up and take home." Before Vicki could ask if she'd actually looked, she rattled off a rapid-fire account of her time of self-indulgent bliss, ending with, "So, what's new around here?"

"Hang on to your bikini. Ralph sold the paper."

Jill felt herself gape. "He can't have. My charge card is maxed out. I can't afford to be unemployed."

Vicki sighed in contentment. "I'm so glad you're back. This place isn't the same without you."

"I should hope not," she retorted, feigning an air of injured hauteur. Fear of the unemployment line gripped her. Granted, the new owner would need a bookkeeper. But he—or they— might not want *her*. "Seriously, what's the deal?"

"Ralph said enough is enough. Believe it or not, the paper sold three days after he put it on the market. The new publisher takes over this morning."

"Are our jobs okay?" Jill had no one to depend on but herself. More to the point, she liked her job and didn't want to lose it.

Now it was Vicki's turn to shrug. "That's the impression he gave when he went through here to check things out."

"What's he like?"

Vicki looked thoughtful. "Hard to describe. Mid- to late-thirties. Tall. Built like a runner. In the looks department, he's no Denzel Washington, but not bad for a white boy."

"I'm sure he'll appreciate your noticing," Jill said dryly. It was good to be home and back with friends again.

Vicki's expression turned inward, all trace of humor gone. "The thing I noticed most about him was he's very reserved. Almost defensive. Like he's carrying the weight of the world on his shoulders."

Jill mulled that over. A new employer was not designed to ease her concerns over her uncharacteristic spending binge, especially one who had all the earmarks of being vain and moody. That type tended to hire and fire at the slightest provocation. "What's his background?"

"Managing editor of a special-interest paper in L.A."

She groaned. "Just what Stafford needs, another Los Angeles squirrel. Those people are nuts." Shuddering with distaste, she headed for her office and called out over her shoulder, "Who did the books while I was gone?" Then she saw the grotesque pile of assorted invoices, receipts and expense account vouchers on her desk. It looked like something from a comic strip.

"Nobody, girlfriend," Vicki called back. "Welcome home."

Mason parked his car, got out and allowed himself to inhale the pine-scented air. Then he stared—not for the first time—at a sky so blue it looked painted. One drive through the small rural town of Stafford, Washington, with its clean air and cleaner streets, and he'd been hooked. Warm, friendly people. No gang shoot-outs. Houses with only one lock on the door. The idea that this was home washed a little more of California from his system.

What pulled at him most, though, was the ancient brick building at the intersection of Main and Washburn—and all it represented. He'd always wanted to own a small-town newspaper, but Karen had demanded nothing less than the nonstop excitement of Los Angeles. Out of commitment to their marriage, he'd bowed to her wishes.

Contentment pervaded his soul as he buttoned his suit coat and cast a possessive look at the unassuming building. This, at least, was one dead dream that he'd resurrected and made reality. The seller had been so desperate to retire, he didn't even care that Mason wouldn't have the down payment until the house in L.A. sold. As long as Mason made regular payments, Ralph Everett would be satisfied. So was he.

Flooded with pride and hope, he opened the door—his door—and stepped inside. The familiar odors of machine grease, paper and ink scented the air in the simple reception room. A staggering wave of nervousness nearly overwhelmed him. In buying the daily, he had risked everything. If he failed, it would mean bankruptcy and starting over from scratch. Even if he succeeded, it would be years before he could afford to buy another home and return to his previous standard of living. He took another breath, catching once again the familiar smells of a newspaper office. His confidence returned. He might not do relationships well, but *this* was solid ground. *This* he knew.

"Good morning, Mr. Bradshaw." His new secretary smiled warmly. Ralph had said Vicki Haynes had been with the paper for years, ran his life like a well-oiled machine and wrote "damn fine freelance" if the mood struck. Mason had liked her on sight. Her friendly openness seemed to typify everything he'd ever hoped a small town could be.

After they exchanged pleasantries, he said, "As soon as everyone arrives, I'd like to call a staff meeting, something informal to get acquainted."

"Certainly, Mr. Bradshaw."

He winced. That made him sound like his father, a man he had few occasions to see and less desire to emulate. "Call me Mason, would you?" At her affirmative reply, he headed down the hallway for another look around.

"By the way," she called after him. "Jill Mathesin, the bookkeeper, is back from vacation. If you'd like to meet her now, she's in her office—first door past yours—swearing at the mess the guys made of her desk. On second thought," she added, a grimace in her voice, "you might want to wait until she calms down first. Otherwise, you might get hit by shrapnel meant for somebody else."

He felt his face grow tight. Ralph had assured him Jill could "squeeze a dollar till the eagle screamed." Mason had been around bookkeepers like her before. Their souls were made out of ledger paper, and everyone was assigned a line. Nothing existed for them except the totals at the end of the month.

"Oh, well," he murmured under his breath, "everyone else here seems to be human."

Steeling himself to meet the crone who'd pass judgment on his abilities to keep the *Journal* afloat, he stepped through her open doorway. A slender woman stood hunched over the desk, her back to him, muttering. She clutched a wad of receipts in one hand and pawed through a stack of invoices with the other.

Jill had a head full of short blond curls barely reaching her tanned neck. Her sleeveless white blouse was tucked into a western-cut denim skirt, the hem of which hung in feminine folds below her knees. And she was barefoot—

barefoot!—her leather sandals haphazardly stuffed under her desk.

"Jerry is dead meat," she growled, slamming down the stack of papers. "I'm taking him out to the parking lot. Then I'm going to run over him a few—"

Gratefully revising his opinion of a middle-aged battle-ax, Mason laughed. "Jerry Williams? Isn't he in charge of advertising? Seems to me we need him around here."

She whirled around and stared at him as if he were a ghost who'd materialized from nowhere. Mason had been prepared to fire off another snappy remark, but his brain suddenly shut down.

Jill Mathesin looked so much like Karen it made his skin crawl. Her eyes lacked the calculated sophistication of his estranged wife's, but they were the same shape and same rich, chocolate brown. Doe eyes. The high cheekbones and sensuous mouth were identical, as were the pert nose and elegant jawline.

The woman's surprise gave way to a frank perusal of her own, and her eyes lit in startled appreciation. He didn't want to see it, but he wasn't blind. Nor did he miss the darting glance to the band of pale skin on his finger where his wedding ring had rested.

Her eyes clouded with indecision for the briefest of moments before she stuck out her hand. "Jill Mathesin, Bookkeeper Extraordinaire. I take it you're the new Head Honcho around here?"

Still not completely recovered from the innocent blow she'd delivered to his midsection, Mason numbly shook her hand. Her grip was confident and honest.

His brain seemed to have short-circuited, and the best he could do was mumble something about the staff meeting he wanted that morning. She just stood there smiling at him with open interest. Given the circumstances, he enjoyed it even less than usual.

"Umm, who's in charge of making coffee?" he asked. *Lame,* he castigated himself. *Very lame.*

If she sensed how threatened she made him feel, it didn't show in her cheerful voice. "Coffee's like everything else at the *Journal*. Whoever sees something first is in charge of it. Job descriptions don't really work around here." She smiled impishly, and he recoiled. "While we're at it, we only have one bathroom for everybody. It's in the back of the pressroom. The door's marked The Titanic. In case Ralph conveniently forgot to tell you, it floods frequently.

"We also have a *standing* rule. Any male who leaves the seat up is in serious danger of immediate bodily injury. That includes you, even though—technically—you own the throne."

Mason's mouth sagged open. If her looking so eerily like his estranged wife wasn't bad enough, he felt like he'd just been hit by a cyclone. He stood staring at her, and she cocked her head expectantly. With her huge brown eyes, she looked like Disney's Bambi. The whole thing was too much, and he beat a cowardly retreat to the break room, a cubbyhole with a hand-painted sign on the door designating it The Closet.

Vicki poked her head around the corner. "Well? Still think we've been overrun by a Los Angeles squirrel?"

"Don't know yet. You're right about one thing, though. He's no Denzel Washington." Jill forced a grin. Vicki would want to know if any chemistry had sparked, and the best course of action would be to feign interest and let her friend get it out of her system. The problem was, Jill had found herself all too attracted, and it scared the stuffing out of her. "Definitely Alec Baldwin. Best of all, he appears to own a newly naked ring finger."

Vicki stepped in and leaned a shoulder against the door-jamb, her smile fading. "Honey, that man is USDA Choice, so I hate to throw up any caution signs—but I've seen that haunted look in a man's eyes before. Unless I miss my guess, he's been hurt *bad,* and not long ago."

"I noticed," Jill murmured, relieved. There wouldn't be

a sales pitch this time. She could figure out on her own why Mason Bradshaw had swept away ninety percent of her battle scars just by walking into her office. "I don't know what his story is, but I'll bet my last pair of panty hose he's still in shell shock from whatever hit him." She shook her head. "Too bad. Not only is he extremely easy on the eyes, but that baritone of his is sexy enough to melt concrete."

Vicki chortled. "No argument there." Then her pencil-thin eyebrows lowered. "But if he just made your 'A' list, and if we're right, the timing couldn't be worse. The last thing you need is a man on the rebound."

"Yeah, I know, and I think I scared him somehow."

"Came on a little strong, did we?" Vicki asked drily.

Jill rolled her eyes. "No, seriously. He gave me the strangest look. Like he expected one thing and discovered the Bride of Frankenstein."

An hour later, the dozen or so men and women who worked at the *Stafford Review-Journal* crammed into Mason's tiny office and jockeyed for a place to see. Mason leaned back on his desk, his weight braced on his hands, one ankle crossed over the other. The pose looked casual enough, but the coiled tension in his eyes told Jill the truth. She didn't like *anyone* feeling like he was on the hot seat—not even a new boss—so she gave him an encouraging grin.

He stared at her, then blinked as if he expected an apparition to vanish under the cold light of reality.

Forcing a polite smile in return, Mason turned his attention to the group. "I imagine learning that the former publisher sold the paper without warning gave all of you a few sleepless nights."

Nervous chuckles rolled through the staff.

"Even though the sale went through in very little time, I investigated the *Journal* thoroughly. You people do good work, and no one is being downsized or otherwise replaced."

He'd hit where the rubber met the road, and Jill sensed

the pent-up apprehension flow from the room like a soft breeze. Something seemed to take hold that moment, too. The beginnings of loyalty. If this man intended to play fair, they'd all work their little tushies off for him. A Los Angeles squirrel might not be so bad, after all.

The man in question seemed to notice her again. This time when he blinked, he looked as though he were trying to keep from shaking his head to clear it. Weird.

"I realize profit isn't a word normally associated with the *Review-Journal*—"

Everyone laughed.

"—but I think we can do a little better if we concentrate on what we do best and not try to compete with the bigger papers out of Seattle and Vancouver."

We. Jill liked the sound of that. Her opinion of him went up a notch. He outlined his plans and asked for feedback, but she only half listened. Every time their eyes met, he looked at her so strangely. Why?

As the meeting broke up, he made small talk with the reporters and scheduled a production meeting, but his scrutiny never left Jill until she walked from the room.

Once out in the hall, she cornered Vicki. "Are my clothes on inside out?"

"What?" Her head snapped around, making the beads in her hair rattle softly.

"Bradshaw is acting like I'm some sort of hallucination."

"You're imagining things." Vicki waved a hand dismissively.

"No, I'm not. If I'm not his answer to Demi Moore, fine. But I don't think anything about my appearance is particularly shocking, do you?"

Vicki put an arm around her and steered her into the break room. "You know what your problem is?"

Jill poured coffee into her favorite mug, the large one with two handles. "Well, according to you it's lack of—"

"Don't be crude."

Jill snorted. "Okay, Dr. Ruth, what's my beef with the world?"

"While you were gone, your desk was defiled by heathens who don't understand the concept of an 'in' basket. After two weeks of pampering, the reality of this place fried your brain."

"Must be it." She took a tentative sip. The coffee at work often tasted so horrible that she tried to give her stomach fair warning. Not bad today. Ben, the press supervisor must have made it. "If I get organized this morning, how about we celebrate and go to lunch?"

They firmed up plans, and Jill headed back to her desk. As she passed Mason's open door, he looked up. There was no mistaking it. He looked bewildered. It hurt.

"Three-piece suit types aren't my thing anyway," she muttered, taking a swallow and closing herself in her office.

On Friday, she had a question about payroll. She didn't have a clue what the man wanted to draw as a salary—not that he could have much. Just as she reached his door, she heard his voice raised.

"If you have anything further to say, Karen, it had better be to your lawyer about signing the property settlement." There was a short pause. "I told you, I'm not interested. Goodbye." The last was punctuated by the slam of a telephone receiver hitting its cradle.

Helen Armstrong, who'd been a *Journal* reporter since the Civil War, came out of the newsroom and gave Jill a puzzled look. Jill realized she'd been holding on to the doorknob, eavesdropping. Blushing, she barged in.

Mason's skin was pale. He looked a little like he'd just been run over by a garbage truck.

"Everything okay in here?" she asked. Immediately, she could have kicked herself. Nothing like prying into a man's personal life to make a good impression. Then again, she cared about people. Couldn't help it. If there was something she could do, she would.

"Perfectly, why?" His body tensed defensively.

She knew she could lie and say her question had been nothing more than a smart remark. But that wasn't the truth, so she crossed her arms and leaned on the doorjamb. "I accidentally overheard the tail end of your conversation. It sounds as if you're going through a divorce." Which, in Jill's mind, explained his shell-shocked appearance on most days. "If you need someone to talk to.... You know—one combat veteran to another? Whatever you tell me won't go any further."

His marvelously kissable mouth gaped open. "Thank you, but that won't be necessary. I'm fine."

"You don't look fine, but my offer stands. Half the staff have been in that spot, too. All I'm saying is that you have friends here if you want them."

Mason pursed his lips and squared his shoulders in a vaguely insulted posture. The body language did not invite open communication. "Thank you, again. I'll remember that."

She couldn't tell if he was genuinely annoyed or just trying to project that impression. Either way, it didn't matter. She'd made her pitch. What he did with it was up to him.

"Then we need to talk about something only mildly less personal." She pulled up a chair. "Payroll. Specifically, your niche in it."

To her surprise, the tension visibly drained from him, and they got to work.

A month later at the employees' annual July blowout at Memorial Park, Jill paused in serving up a glob of potato salad and glanced at the edge of the picnic area. From a distance, Mason stood surveying the scene, hands stuffed in his pockets.

Since he'd taken over the paper, Jill had discovered a whole new dimension to the term "reserved." What she saw in him mirrored too closely the basket case she'd been after Donald left her. Mason's eyes held that same haunted look, and she'd repeatedly caught him staring off into space, apparently lost in dark thought. The idea of anyone trying to survive all that pain alone overcame her sense of self-preservation. The initial spark of attraction had grown into full-fledged awareness, and until she could sort through her emotions, she'd have preferred to avoid him. But he needed a friend, and she intended to be there. How could she live with herself, otherwise?

"Nobody but Mason Bradshaw would come to a park wearing a suit and tie," she sighed to Vicki, who was busy getting hot dogs down her toddlers, ages two and four.

Vicki followed her gaze. "Well, at least he showed up. How did you manage that?"

"Two weeks of badgering and harassment followed by a healthy dose of guilt and shame."

"Oh?" Vicki chuckled.

"I told him Ralph never missed one, and that everyone would be really hurt if he snubbed his lowly peons."

"You're bad."

"Yeah, but he looks like a little boy who wants to play but doesn't know how to join the fun."

Resolve roared in like a flood tide, and Mason didn't stand a chance. Jill finished filling her plate, crossed to where he stood and shoved the plate into his hands. "Welcome to the party, Bradshaw." She pointed exaggeratedly to the fried chicken and all the trimmings. "This is called fun food. Proper eating attire is church jeans and a T-shirt, not your best suit."

He blinked at her. "*Church* jeans?"

"Yeah," she answered as if speaking to a particularly dense child. "You know, holey ones?"

He groaned, a grin twitching the corners of his sensuous lips. "The more holes, the better, I suppose?"

"Absolutely."

Their eyes met and locked, warming her. Here was a kindred spirit—strong, but wounded and in need of a little support to get him through. She swallowed hard and turned her back. "Hurry up and eat. Then go home and change. You're needed on the volleyball court in forty-five minutes." She marched halfway back to the food-laden tables before pointedly glancing over her shoulder to see if he'd followed.

He hadn't, but he watched her intently. Within the clouded depths of his hazel eyes, she saw puzzlement, speculation and a hint of turmoil she could only guess at. Her heart drummed slowly in her chest, and she fought back the urge to dive into her Volkswagen and leave. Fortunately for her sanity, he dropped his gaze to his plate and experimentally poked at the homemade chili beans. Something told her he was debating more than whether or not to eat lunch. A moment later, his breath eased out, and he took a bite. Chewing, he walked over to her.

"Very good, Bradshaw," she said, mentally sighing in relief. "I suspect that letting your hair down is an alien concept. So I'm giving you a choice. You can fire me now or get used to being hounded until you learn how to relax."

He gave her a baffled look. "Are you always like this?"

"Only with people I care about," she answered softly. Impulsively, she took his hand to drag him to the picnic area. A jolt of sexual awareness shot up her arm straight to her soul, and she bit back a gasp. She wished she could tell if the sudden tension in his body was the result of the heat ripping through him, too, or whether she'd thoroughly offended the man.

Oh well, kiddo, you've got both feet planted in it now. Might as well see it through. With a gentle tug, she got him moving, relieved when his attention was diverted by the warm greetings from the rest of his employees.

Mentally, she groaned as she discreetly watched him walk the rest of the way to the tables. Mason moved with an innate grace she could watch all day.

Mason ate until he could hardly move, and he couldn't remember having laughed so much. Jerry, the head of ad-

vertising, Ben, the press supervisor, and Vicki's husband
Wilson had conned him into taking off his suit coat, tie,
socks and shoes, and filling the empty place on the volleyball court. Now Jill stood on the far side of the net, looking
like a cat who'd found the cream. In his experience, man-
agement didn't mingle to this degree with employees. Then
again, the people who depended on him for their livelihood
didn't treat him like a boss. Instead, they'd welcomed him
as a new member of their extended family, another novelty
he hadn't been prepared for.

Without warning, Jill fired a vicious serve. He and Wilson dove for the ball, both managing to miss. It hit the sand
between them, and the two men exchanged sheepish looks.
Wilson Haynes was fifteen years older than his wife and
the light frosting of gray at his temples added to the image
of the respected high school principal that he was. From
the sudden glint in his dark eyes, Mason suspected that the
man wasn't in the habit of losing at anything, not even
volleyball.

"Gettin' old, Haynes?" Jill taunted. "As for you, Bradshaw, if you think that little display of physical prowess
impressed your devoted underlings, think again."

Anything remotely resembling decorum abandoned the
group at that point. By the end of the day, Mason was
exhausted, foolishly content and convinced he'd discovered
something touchingly priceless.

While everyone loaded dirty plates, leftover food and
tired children into various cars, he made it a point to carry
Jill's basket to her fully restored, canary-yellow Volkswagen, the most preposterous-looking contraption in the parking lot.

"Thanks," he said low enough so that no one else would
hear. "How did you know what I needed today?" His unexpected openness startled even him. There was something
about Jill that invited trust, despite the fact he doubted he'd
ever get used to her eerie resemblance to Karen. Every time

he saw her, stopping himself from staring took every ounce of willpower.

He expected one of her usual crazy comments. Instead she turned to him, compassion smoothing her delicate features.

"I've been there," she said simply. "It's not a pretty place. Alone is insufferable."

Thanks to Karen's frequent calls, everyone who worked for him knew about his personal problems.

"Remember, Bradshaw, if you ever need to talk, my coffeepot is always on."

He gave her a tentative smile. "I'll think about it." That he was actually considering it startled him, too. The pressure had begun to eat him alive. His stomach hurt most of the time, and he wondered how close he had come to an ulcer.

Indecision tightened Jill's expression. Then she bobbed up on her toes and kissed his cheek. "See you Monday."

With that, she took her basket from his hand, tossed it onto the passenger seat and fired up her VW. She didn't look back, and her gentle, undemanding kiss stayed warm on his cheek the rest of the weekend.

Jill looked up as Vicki stormed into Mason's office, her eyes snapping with annoyance. "Mason, you've got another call from L.A."

Jill watched the color leach from his face as his gaze swiveled to the blinking light on his phone. "Thank you," he said tightly. Vicki went back to her desk, and Mason gave Jill what he probably thought was a passable smile. To her, he looked as if he'd just been slugged from behind. "We'll tackle the rest of the budget later," he said.

Studying the haggard lines of his face, she nodded and backed toward the door. "When you say hello, sound like you're having the time of your life. It'll drive the bad guys insane."

Winking, she left then, but engraved on her mind was

the image of him staring at her in surprised gratitude, his hand poised above the receiver.

Dejected, she returned to her own office, sat down at her desk and dropped her head into her hands. "Do you have any idea how much pain you're setting yourself up for?" she asked herself. "Falling in love with a self-centered creep like Donald was bad enough. Falling for Prince Charming in the middle of an ugly divorce is emotional suicide."

"Talking to yourself isn't a good sign, either, girl-friend," Vicki drawled as she walked in, purse in hand.

Jill looked at her watch. Time for lunch. The last thing she wanted right now was to put food in her stomach. "What possessed me to kiss him at the park Saturday, and in *front* of everyone, too? Facing him this morning was awful. Please tell me he doesn't think I'm a complete idiot. Lie if you need to."

Vicki's face crumpled in shared pain. "Did he say anything about it?"

A lump formed in her throat, and she swallowed past it. "Mason? Mr. Good Breeding himself? Of course not."

"Why *did* you kiss him?" Vicki asked. "You're impulsive, but that's just not like you."

"That man needed a good smooch more than anyone I know, so I gave him one." The lump in her throat got bigger, but she put on a brave front. "How about we hit the pie shop over on 'B' Street? I'll smother my humiliation in meringue and listen to you whine about the calories."

Chapter 2

Jill swung through the pressroom on yet another search for Mason. In the two months he'd been here, they'd all learned he worked like a man possessed, and she never quite knew where he'd be at any given moment. As bosses went, he was fair, appreciative of everyone's efforts and made them all feel that the lowly *Stafford Review-Journal* was as prestigious as any big-city daily. Maybe, she suspected, because that's how he saw it.

She finally found him checking inventory, engrossed with the figures on the clipboard in his hands. She took a moment to study him. The set to his finely chiseled features seemed more strained than usual. In fact, he looked absolutely gaunt. Her silent questions as to the reasons were endless, but he never seemed willing to confide in anyone, always kept the world at arm's length. Maybe it was just her. Even so, she wondered if he knew any other way to live.

In Mason she found all the things Donald lacked— warmth, strength and consideration. Every nuance of his personality yelled "Good Guy Here." No matter how hard she tried, she couldn't find one single significant flaw to latch onto. Frankly, she was beginning to feel doomed. If she couldn't find a way to put a lid on the hormones that had begun to make themselves heard, she knew she'd end up getting hurt. Maybe if she ignored them long enough, they'd go back to sleep where they belonged. *Right, and ducks walk south.*

Finding the right man at the wrong time was hell. "You got your check-signing pen out, Bradshaw?" she asked, forcing as much cheer into her voice as she could.

Startled, he raised his head. As usual when she came upon him when he didn't expect her, something painful and defensive flared in his deep-set hazel eyes. And as usual, it hurt.

If he didn't find her attractive, fine. She was a big girl and could live with the rejection. But she couldn't help wondering what it was about her that bothered him. And why couldn't he get past it? Ordinarily she'd ask, but it struck her as too much like wearing her emotions on her sleeve. So she kept up the protective facade that she had no interest in him other than friendship. That approach also struck her as the best way to keep her job.

"You straightened out those invoices already, Jill?" A softly incredulous smile warmed his face. He smiled so rarely. But when he did, it chased away the haunted cast to his features. At those moments, she believed she saw the man he *should* be. If it were up to her she'd make sure he smiled like that all the time.

"Bradshaw, I keep telling you, I'm the hottest bookkeeper on two feet." She winced at the accidental double entendre.

Instead of pretending he hadn't heard, he seemed to recoil further into himself. Without a word, Mason took the proffered stack of checks, braced them on the clipboard and went through the pile. His signature was an elegant script—something else she found fascinating. The voice of disaster

told her that when a woman became infatuated with mi-
nutiae such as a man's penmanship, she was in serious
trouble.

Then she noticed the deeper shadows under his eyes. Her
heart turned over in her chest, and common sense deserted
her. "Okay, out with it. What's eating you?"

His gaze snapped to hers, and he froze. "Beg your pardon?"

Groaning, Jill shook her head. "You're falling apart."

He gave her another incredulous look. Come to think of
it, over the weeks, she'd gotten used to them from him.
"You looked bad enough the day you bought this rock pile.
I doubt you're sleeping right, and it's getting worse, not
better."

A twinge of panic raced up her spine. She'd really
jumped in with both feet this time. If he didn't fire her on
the spot, it would be a miracle. Swallowing hard, she
plunged on. "Bottled-up garbage ferments. That's bad for
humans."

He pulled himself up to his full height, which was con-
siderable, and gave her a decidedly cool look. "I don't
think my personal life is any of your concern."

True, except I care about you too much to let it alone.
"Bradshaw, your divorce is killing you. You'd better talk
to somebody about it before your stomach lining commits
mutiny."

Color blasted his cheeks, and his gaze shot to somewhere
across the room.

Uh, oh, she thought. *How close to home did I hit with
that one?*

The guilty flush turned into a cold glower. Jill crossed
her arms and held her ground. After a tense moment, he
returned to signing checks. *Had his anger been all bluff?
A defense mechanism?*

The fact that his signature changed into something tighter
and less flowing did not escape her notice, either. Instinct
said she was far from standing on solid ground, but it might

not be too dangerous to give one more nudge. When he finished, she still stared at him, arms crossed, making no effort to take the stack of checks he held out to her.

"Why are you doing this?" he blurted out.

The question made her ache with empathy for him. It also confirmed her suspicions about his show of anger being nothing more than a ploy to get her to back off. Her voice softened. "Because you need a friend."

Mason shot her a look of total bafflement.

"Come on, Bradshaw. When you walked in here that first day, that white strip of skin on your ring finger looked like shark bait. You'd probably had your wedding ring off for a week, maybe two. Every time your soon-to-be-ex calls, your face turns a sick shade of gray. You can't tell me this isn't destroying you."

Unrequited hormones aside, Jill empathized so much with the horrors of divorce that all she wanted to do was to wrap her arms around him and make the ugliness go away. Her voice lowered, and lacked the steadiness she would have liked. "You need to talk to someone. I've got two ears, no waiting."

"I'm not sure that employers and employees should—"

"Cut the bologna." Jill cringed the moment the words left her lips. Once again, the unemployment line loomed large in her mind's eye. Then, beyond conscious will, she reached out and laid her hand on his coat sleeve. An electrical storm of awareness arced between them, and she could hardly breathe.

"Oh, Mason, you can't live this way," she whispered. "It's not healthy to build a fortress around yourself, then fill the moat with alligators and pull up the drawbridge. People here care about you. Talk to me."

Mason didn't exactly pull away, but he shifted his weight enough that she either had to make an obvious reach to maintain contact, or let her hand drop away. She chose the latter, holding her breath as he weighed her words.

Then unexpectedly, he hooked his hip on the corner of

a packing crate. His shoulders slumped. "My divorce goes to court tomorrow." Pain radiated from him in a solid mass, and she grieved for him.

"Is that why you won't be in? You're flying down to L.A.?"

His eyes closed on a nod. "My wife finally agreed to sign the property settlement if I promised to meet with her before the hearing."

Something didn't sit right. He had all the symptoms of a man who'd been dumped, and dumped hard. Yet the implication was that Karen was the one doing the foot dragging. "You don't sound like a man looking forward to his freedom."

"I'm not."

That really confused her. Jill wanted him free and ready to find someone new. Everyone deserved that measure of happiness. Maybe he would even find it with her—provided she could get past her own misgivings about taking the relationship plunge again— but he apparently still had a lot of feelings for his estranged wife.

An entirely inappropriate twinge of jealousy lanced her chest. What kind of idiot would let a man like Mason Bradshaw get loose? Convinced she was slitting her own throat, she asked, "Is there any chance of an eleventh-hour reprieve?"

He frowned. "What do you mean?"

"A reconciliation." She shrugged. "It does happen sometimes."

In a rush of agitated motion, Mason jerked to his feet. "There's no going back."

"Look, Bradshaw," she said firmly. "It sounds to me like you still love her. Maybe with counseling—"

He turned on her then, his eyes bleak with fury and memories. "I caught her in bed with another man."

Old, barely scarred-over memories of her own surfaced, and Jill wanted to weep for them both.

"She's done everything but spin cartwheels to get me to

forgive her. At first, I tried to tell myself maybe I could—
eventually. But I can't. It's like what I saw is permanently
burned into my brain.'' The rage seemed to drain out of
him then, and his tall, lean body sagged.

Tears burned behind Jill's eyes, tears for his wounds and
tears for herself. No one had ever cared for her as deeply
as Mason loved the woman who'd betrayed him. Loneliness
had become a pronounced part of her existence, and she
wondered if she'd ever experience that kind of devotion.

''She's the only woman I ever wanted, and it's over. But
I can't seem to get on with my life.'' Raw emotion boiled
out with such force and he seemed so consumed by it that
Jill doubted if he even remembered her presence. ''You're
right about the lack of sleep,'' he added softly, more to
himself than her. ''I haven't slept more than four hours a
night since I walked in on her.''

Jill knew putting her arms around him was a stupid thing
to do even before she did it, far worse than kissing him in
the park. But she could no more stop herself than she could
stop the sun from rising. He tensed as her slender arms
encircled his ribs, but then the pent-up breath eased from
his chest, and he wrapped his own arms around her shoulders.

His embrace was genuine and comfortable and seemed
to fit in all the right places. A tingling warmth started in
her soul and trickled through her veins. Everything within
her wanted to stay like this forever, but the unwanted voice
of reason said that wouldn't happen. *Why is it I'm drawn
to emotionally unavailable men?*

The hoarse clearing of his throat signaled the end. Jill
accepted it and turned loose before she suffered the indig-
nity of being pried off him.

''Jill, I'm sorry. I don't know what came over—''

''That's what friends are for,'' she whispered, trying to
keep the sexual hunger and frustration out of her voice.
''You're supposed to dump on us, impose on us, and generally make a nuisance of yourself.''

One side of his mouth twitched in a smile, but his natural reserve aborted the effort. "I'll remember that." Then he walked away, and she wondered if he had even a clue where he was headed. Probably anyplace she wasn't. "Well, as the old saw goes, you can lead a horse to water, but...."

At nine sharp the next morning, Mason walked into his attorney's office. He hadn't realized until he'd been away from Los Angeles for a while just how bad it smelled, how much everyone lived like rats in a maze. Mentally, he shook his head. No, southern California held nothing for him anymore.

A moment later, Karen and her lawyer arrived. Echoes of what he'd thought he once shared with her reverberated through him. He hadn't seen her since the week before he'd left L.A. Secretly, he'd hoped she would look as horrible as he felt, but she didn't.

Her pale blond hair hung down over her shoulders in heavy, seductive waves, and she wore a navy blazer and straight skirt that gave her a touch of class. She looked good. Too good for the occasion. Suspicious, he braced himself the instant before she threw herself into his arms.

"Mason, I'm so glad you agreed to meet with me." Her voice cracked.

He held himself rigid, praying she'd let go. He didn't dare try to extricate himself. If he put his hands on her at all, he might end up pulling her closer. Then again, he might strangle her. He honestly couldn't tell which. The implications scared the hell out of him. "You said if I came to this meeting, you'd sign the property settlement."

She leaned back and gazed up into his eyes. How many times had he seen that look? It promised so much and delivered so little. He stepped away, and her face fell, the picture of devastation.

"I didn't know any other way to get you to hear me out."

Both attorneys shared uneasy glances. The audience embarrassed him, too, but he couldn't do much about it. "Then you never intended to sign anything?"

Moistening her full lips with the tip of her tongue, she glanced at him through lowered lashes. He saw pain there, and something else that surprised him. Could it be genuine remorse? With Karen, he could never be sure.

"Not signing would only give you more cause to hate me." Each word resonated with emotion.

Stunned, he stared at her. "I don't hate you, Karen. You are what you are, and we just don't belong together."

"I love you." She drew a finger down his cheek.

Mason caught her hand and pushed it away. "Our lawyers really don't want to hear this. Frankly, neither do I."

He motioned for her to take a chair. Both of the other men sat down, but Karen remained standing. The fiery set to her shoulders cooled. Tears glistened in her eyes, and she reached into her purse for a tissue.

"Whatever you want, Mason," she said, blotting her eyes. "Ending this marriage might be something to consider. Once the pressure is off, maybe we can start fresh. Would you give us a chance to work out our problems when there aren't any ties?" She perched on the edge of her seat and leaned forward in entreaty.

Did she honestly expect him to forget seeing her tongue trailing wet circles down that punk kid's chest?

"I don't want to lose you." The tears spilled over. "I'm so sorry for what I've done to us."

That rendered him speechless. Had she begun to grow up? Had she learned to consider other people's feelings? For a moment he wondered.

Her attorney pushed his glasses higher on the bridge of his nose and glanced at his counterpart. "Perhaps your client and mine would like a chance to discuss this in private."

Mason's attorney turned to him, a silent question arching one eyebrow. People put their marriages back together after far worse, but Mason couldn't see him and Karen being among them. Her indulgences had gone too far.

Her expression became imploring, and she slid to her knees at his feet, reaching for his hands. "Please, Mason?"

Reality slapped him hard. No one did remorse like Karen when she'd overreached her grasp. Suddenly, he felt more hollow and alone than he'd believed any human being could. But he knew her—finally. He'd fallen for her histrionics for the last time. She loved him as much as she was capable of loving anyone, but it wasn't enough.

Levering himself out of his seat, he stepped around her. Deliberately, he kept his gaze on his attorney and off the shocked-looking woman clinging to the arm of the chair he'd just vacated. "I'll meet you at court in an hour." Then he turned and walked away.

That night back at his apartment in Stafford, Mason poured himself bourbon, lifted it to his lips, then set it on the coffee table in disgust. Booze never accomplished anything except to make him maudlin. And he felt enough of that right now without any help.

Karen had tried to corner him outside the courthouse just before the hearing. From the looks of her, she'd been crying at least long enough to cause her makeup to run and her face to develop that appealingly vulnerable cast. He didn't know how the woman did it, but she actually looked cute when she cried. Unfortunately, she knew it.

Both confrontations left him unsettled, but at least he had ended the legal ties. Now, maybe, he could begin to heal. He took a mouthful of bourbon and swallowed. Grimacing, he decided to pour the rest down the sink. While on his way to the kitchen, someone knocked on the door.

He pulled it open, and as he caught sight of his visitor a distant portion of his mind became aware that he was gaping. He couldn't seem to help himself.

Jill stood on the landing outside his apartment, a small grocery bag in her arms. "I've got a six-pack of soda, a bag of chips and a friendly ear.'' She offered a tentative smile. ''It's not exactly uptown, but I picked 'em out with my own two little hands. Except the ear. That I was born with.''

Jill Mathesin had the biggest brown eyes he'd ever seen—much more expressive than Karen's, and rounded now in self-consciousness.

The last thing he wanted was company, particularly the woman who, with innocent tenacity, reminded him of Karen just by walking into the room. Except the hair, he amended. Karen had every man's fantasy—long, thick and sexy as hell. But like everything else, Karen flaunted that attribute to the world. Jill's hair, on the other hand, was wash-and-wear. It fit her. So did her smile and her natural unadorned beauty. In short, she was *real*.

Common sense told him to send her away, but he found himself stepping back and motioning her inside. A tiny breath of relief escaped her, and she swept in with her usual aplomb.

When she spotted the half-empty bottle of bourbon on the coffee table, she frowned. ''That does *not* look like a celebration, Bradshaw.''

''It's not.'' Despite himself, depression got the better of him, and the melancholy edge to his voice came through with embarrassing clarity.

She gave him a shrewd look. ''People who get miserable when they drink shouldn't indulge.''

''You have no idea.'' Further discomfited by her far too accurate observation, he gathered up some dignity. ''I owe you an apology. Friend or not, I had no business dumping all that on you yesterday.''

''Right,'' she muttered drily. ''Why don't you park your-self on your couch and tell ol' Jill all about your day's battles with the legal system and other people. We'll call it round two.'' She gave him a Cheshire cat grin. ''At least you're calling me a friend now. Does that mean you've lowered the drawbridge and taken a few alligators out of the moat?''

Mason blinked, wondering if he'd ever get completely used to her. She barged into his life—whether he wanted her there or not—and had the damnedest ability to make him feel as if he were the single most important person in her world. Did she treat everyone that way? He wished he could think straight.

She popped the top on a soda, stuffed it into his hand, then commandeered his recliner chair—the one piece of furniture he'd taken with him from the house. "Come on, Bradshaw. Take your cola like a man and spill your guts.''

His mouth gaped open again. So much for dignity. "The concept that employees shouldn't pry into their employer's personal life doesn't mean much to you, does it?''

"Of course not." She took a long pull on her drink. "Time's wasting, Bradshaw. Start spinning your my-baby-done-me-wrong tale, so I can sing the praises of all your bright tomorrows." She ripped open the chips and held out the bag. When he didn't make a move to take any, she shook it at him in comical, wide-eyed invitation.

For no other reason than fascination with her, he took a few. Nothing ever seemed to faze this woman. How did she do that? By some chance, did she give lessons? "Are there any more like you in your family tree?''

"Nope. I'm an original." She dropped the chip bag on the coffee table between them and leaned back. "Easy, since I'm an only child. I was a change-of-life baby. Mom thought I was menopause. They never wanted kids, and I pretty much had to depend on myself. It made for a strange childhood. They're both gone now." She popped a chip into her mouth. "What's your family tree look like?''

Mason's composure slipped another notch. He hadn't realized his innocent comment would sponsor a dissertation on her background. The idea of discussing his own upbringing made him slightly ill. Intellectually, he knew that thirty-six-year-old men had no business hanging on to old baggage, but he'd also accepted the fact that he didn't know how to let go—of anything. Childhood scars—like knowing his parents' only concerns were their high-powered careers—didn't disappear on their own. He couldn't imagine discussing it with anyone, much less his bookkeeper.

"Well?" she prompted.

"I appreciate what you're trying to do, but I'm a rather private man."

"No kidding," she retorted. "Would you like me to describe the moat around your private fortress? To make it worse, you've got a seven-year marriage down the tubes. The idea of *any* kind of tomorrow probably sounds obscene."

"How did you find out how long...." He strangled off the rest of the question. He really didn't want to know.

She cocked her head. "How about this, instead? We'll sit around, cry in our colas and swap marital war stories."

It startled him to realize she had no intention of dropping any of it. Then again, this was Jill. It had been eight weeks since he'd taken over the paper. That meant eight weeks of daily doses of Jill Mathesin. Nothing she did should surprise him anymore. "I appreciate your offer, but why don't I just see you at the paper tomorrow?"

"Come on, Bradshaw," she cajoled. "I bet my exmarriage beats yours. I'll even spot you ten points." Challenge glowed in her dark eyes.

From somewhere deep within the hollow pit his heart had become, temptation nudged. Maybe he did need this, a friend who cared enough to invade his space and stay there. Warily, he seated himself across from her on the couch. "What's the scoring system?"

Victory flashed across her face. "Irresponsible money handling, inconsiderate behavior and being a slob are worth one point each. General rattiness and outright betrayal are double and triple bonus points depending on the infraction."

"Are you making this up as you go along?"

Her generous lips curved in a smile. "Yep. The best games in the world are invented that way. Didn't you learn that as a kid?"

"Apparently, I missed that one." His entire childhood had consisted of rigidly structured boarding schools and equally demanding summer camps, all designed to keep him away from home and out of his parents' lives as much as possible. They'd loathed Christmas vacations when he was home and underfoot. At the time, he remembered empathizing with young Ebenezer Scrooge.

During his college years he'd begun to crave sharing a true Christmas with children of his own. He wanted a tree decorated by love, not a work of art created by a professional. He wanted wrapping paper strewn all over the house. He wanted quiet family conversation over a cozy meal, not a catered feast for two dozen. Toys and laughter and, yes, he'd even welcome the worry of how to pay for it all.

"You never made up games?" Jill asked, staring at him like he'd just sprouted an extra head. "Pathetic, Bradshaw. Really pathetic." She shook her head, then grinned suddenly. "Did I mention each point is worth a buck?"

"Why doesn't that surprise me?" he mumbled, fighting the smile forming deep in his chest. He dragged out his wallet and checked the meager contents. "You're on." Leaning forward again, he braced his elbows on his knees. "Who goes first?"

"Me. It's my game."

"Of course."

"Donald and I met at a party. He treated me like a princess on a satin pillow—until after the wedding. Then, I guess, he thought his part in the relationship was over. The male had conquered the female. That type of thing. Now married and victorious, it was time to get back to his life. He made no effort to be home at a regular time, yet he expected me to have dinner on the table the moment he waltzed in. And I held down a full-time job, too."

"Definite rattiness," Mason pronounced. "Two points." The idea anyone would treat Jill that way annoyed him more deeply than he thought it should. "You're going to lose, though. Karen's self-centeredness approached epic proportions."

Jill smiled in apparent approval at his answering salvo, and hunched forward. "Now you're getting into the spirit of the thing, Bradshaw. Spill it."

The ease with which she'd sucked him in amazed him. For some reason, that didn't bother him at all. "Karen wanted to redecorate. The furniture she wanted wouldn't fit in the rooms, so she thought it made perfect sense to buy a bigger house."

Jill's face smoothed with disbelief. "You're making that up."

"Am not." He raised his right hand and solemnly folded thumb and little finger across his palm. "Scout's honor." The spontaneous gesture was so out of character that he smiled. Despite her eccentricities, Jill was good for him.

"That would be worth four points all by itself, unless, of course, you knuckled under to the bi—" she cleared her throat "—brat. In which case you lose all your points for being a sap."

Deep within him, a long-dead spark came back to life, and for the first time in months, the weight eased from his chest. Yes, Jill was definitely good for him. "The day escrow closed on the new house—"

Jill groaned and dropped her head into her hands.

"Karen announced she'd changed her mind about the furniture. Everyone wanted that look, and she didn't like the idea that people might think she'd turned into a herd follower. She envisioned herself as a trendsetter."

Karen had never truly understood why they'd had to scrimp to raise the money for the new house. In her mind, since his parents were well off he should have asked them for the funds. She'd come from struggling middle-class parents who'd indulged her every whim. To her, the idea that wealthy in-laws wouldn't be proportionately more generous made no sense whatsoever. And Mason knew he'd never understand how she'd managed to convince herself that journalism was a hobby, not a profession that just happened to be his means of putting food on the table.

"Bradshaw, you're so far in the hole on points, you'll never dig yourself out."

"Your turn," he countered, eager to get off the hot seat. "What's the dumbest thing you ever did to keep peace in the home?" Inside, he froze. That much confession had slipped out without permission.

Jill's expressive eyes widened in absolute incredulity. "Keeping peace? Is that what you were doing?"

Feeling stupid and foolish, he shrugged. He'd left out all the tantrums Karen had thrown, and he would never admit to anyone that he'd swallowed her favorite lie—again— that if he'd give in to her latest whim she'd be ready to have kids.

"Bradshaw, in that case, I nominate you for the Good Guy Hall of Fame."

The open awe glowing on her face made him feel like all his efforts hadn't been for nothing—that someone appreciated what he'd tried to do, even if he'd failed. All he'd wanted was a home filled with simple pleasures and love. And for all his sacrifices, he'd found neither. "Still your turn."

"Hmmm." Thoughtfully, Jill looked at the ceiling. "Definitely time to haul out the big guns. Otherwise, I'll never catch up. How many points do I get for marrying a man who never loved me?" Her voice caught on a smothered gasp.

It would seem he wasn't the only one making unexpected confessions. Had they lived through similar heartaches? Apparently so, and the shared agony of it struck deep in his chest. "Is that what you did, Jill?" he asked with a tenderness that startled him.

Her large chocolate-brown eyes glistened. "We'd been

married two weeks when Donald said he only married me because he hated being single."

The depth of Mason's disgust at the man came as another surprise, and he bit down on a pointless commentary on her ex-husband's lack of character.

"He said women were only good for a couple of things and that he'd had better." Determinedly, Jill blinked a few times, her jaw set.

Somehow, Mason found himself across the room, crouched beside her. Without taking the time to think about it first, he cradled her head against his shoulder and held her tight. Her arms crept around his ribs, and he held his breath, afraid to break the spell. How long had it been since he'd experienced the touch of a woman who cared, who understood? Thinking back that far hurt too much, so he shook off the question. "We make a great pair, Jill. The walking wounded of Stafford, Washington."

She offered a thready laugh and burrowed her face deeper into his neck. "No argument there, but how are we on points?"

"Exactly even." The scent of her hair filled him, and the softness of her skin tempted. He hadn't wanted to kiss anyone in a long time, but an undeniable need coiled within him now and he wasn't quite sure what to do about it.

"No good, Bradshaw. I hate ties." She pulled back and swiped at her eyes with the heels of her hands—such unpretentious honesty in the gesture. "One of us has to win."

Forget points. The game's over. This is for real. "Did he ever cheat on you?"

For an instant, the reminder cast a stricken look deep in her eyes. Then she conquered it. "This was a dumb game."

Tenderly, Mason tilted her chin toward him. "Tell me."

"Yeah, he cheated on me," she whispered brokenly. "How often is anyone's guess."

Answering echoes of her misery reverberated from the depths of his soul. When she looked into his eyes, vulnerable and alone, Mason saw himself and knew he was about to drown.

"Bradshaw, I only wanted his love. Nothing more. Nothing less. I tried everything." She swiped at her eyes again, pulling a mien of anger around her like a protective shield. "I was such a jerk. All he wanted was an available body when he couldn't find someone better."

Mason didn't say a word. How could it be that the two of them—strangers—had spent a lifetime fighting and losing the same wars? They might be wounded and bleeding inside, but they were both survivors.

Her lips trembled slightly, shattering what little common sense he had left. Need ignited and roared out of control. He tunneled his fingers through her short, silky curls and pulled her to him, covering her mouth with his own. In a quiet rush, her warmth and sweetness filled his emptiness in a way the bourbon never could. When she molded her body into the contours of his embrace and kissed him back with equal ferocity, the wildfire destroyed all rational thought.

Words would have intruded, so neither spoke as the passionate storm mounted. Mason was only half aware of carrying her to his bedroom. Letting her feet touch the floor, he kissed her cheeks and lips, then crushed her to him. Her small breasts pressed tightly against his chest, and his body throbbed.

She looked shyly around the room, taking in the double bed with its mahogany headboard and earth-tone print comforter.

"Are you okay with this, Jill?" he whispered. The willpower it took to give her some space nearly brought him to his knees. Never in his life had he wanted a woman this badly. If she was having second thoughts, it might very well kill him. He brushed disheveled blond curls from her eyes and tilted her face up, spreading feathery kisses across her mouth and cheeks.

She trembled, then swallowed hard.

Oh, God, she's going to say no. He groaned under his breath, but couldn't bring himself to move away. "Change your mind?"

Her cheeks pinkened, and she lowered her eyes, playing with the button on his dress shirt. "It's just that I don't normally do this kind of thing." She gave him a darting glance. "It's been a while—" she swallowed again "—since Donald."

Nothing she could have said would have made him want her more. She might have a freewheeling approach to life, but that didn't include the bedroom. Whatever was happening between them meant serious consideration on her part—his, too, for that matter.

Basic decency told him to back off until she'd made up her mind, but the gnawing ache in his body made honorable intentions about as practical as suggesting they sit down and chat about the weather. "I understand." His brain might, but his body was a screaming mess.

Then she surprised him by undoing the top button of his shirt. Her fingertips brushed the skin beneath his throat. It felt so good it burned. The ability to breathe vanished, another complication he didn't need.

"No, I don't think you do understand," she said softly, not quite meeting his gaze. "Being nervous isn't the same as changing one's mind."

Jill always took life as it came. He had never suspected she had an insecure side. A wave of tenderness overtook him, tempering the urgency. He cradled her face in his hands, then slowly kissed her lips, taking care to invite, not demand. After a few tentative explorations of her own, she opened to him with quiet trust.

One button at a time, they undressed each other, hands reveling in the discovery of naked skin. When he pulled her against him again, he knew what they would experience with each other would be something special. "You okay?" he murmured.

"You talk too much," she complained against his lips.

He pulled her down onto the bed and the fire raged. It seemed only moments—then again, it felt like forever—before he buried himself inside her welcoming body. He hadn't intended to rush, but it seemed right, and she was more than ready for him. The explosion that rocked his body came without warning, its suddenness embarrassing.

"Jill, I'm sorry. That wasn't what—"

She clamped her hand over his mouth. "You're wonderful, Bradshaw. Now, shut up and kiss me."

The second time, he found with her a completeness to lovemaking that he never suspected could exist. They held each other in the darkness, alternately sleeping and loving. Together, they kept the loneliness at bay.

Chapter 3

Jill woke at three, a glorious feeling of well being infusing her with warmth. She braced her elbow on the pillow and rested her head in her hand. The moon had risen, and soft light filtered in through the window. Self-indulgently, she watched the man she loved as he slept. And she did love him, too. She wasn't sure when she'd crossed the line, but, win or lose, she had definitely crossed it.

Mason slept soundly on his back beside her, the sheets shoved erotically down to just below his waist. He had very little body hair, mostly a thin, dark patch across his chest and a matching fine line down his abdomen. It seemed to invite her touch, and she had the almost irresistible temptation to trace that line with a fingertip. Smiling in the dark, she kept her hands to herself. If she woke him, she'd no longer be able to watch him unobserved, no longer be able to savor the way the moonlight glowed on his satin skin or the way his heavy lashes shadowed his cheeks in sleep.

Could this night really be happening? Or was it all a delightful dream? Had she really made love with a man she had assumed would never want her? And what love, she sighed. She hadn't even known she was multi-orgasmic. With her ex-husband, whatever dissatisfaction she felt during sex—she refused to call it making love, not after what she'd experienced tonight with Mason—Donald had always blamed her. With Mason, they'd experimented, learning each other's preferences and needs. There'd been no self-consciousness, only absolute trust.

Still asleep, he flung one arm above his head. The empty place by his side became more temptation than she could deny. Careful, so as not to wake him, she snuggled against him and closed her eyes.

The Prince Charmings of the world gravitated toward educated women of elegance and success, not self-taught bookkeepers. But maybe, just this once, the rules had been set aside.

When his alarm went off at four o'clock in the morning, Mason dragged his eyes open and tried to force his fuzzy brain to function. Beside him, a warm body stretched languorously and rolled over. *Jill!* The electric shock of denial raced through him as memories of the night crystallized.

Sleepily, she reached for the lamp. The light's brutal glare somehow fit the moment, and he squinted against the pain blasting through his eyeballs. Smiling as only a woman thoroughly sated can, Jill scrutinized his face. What she apparently found there fractured her contented glow into shards of uncertainty. Regret flooded him. One night stands definitely weren't his thing, and as he fought for something to say, she pulled the sheet protectively around her naked body.

Jill appealed to him. Obviously she did, or they wouldn't have spent the night together. But he wasn't any more ready to begin a new relationship than he was to fly.

Her body tensed with apprehension. "Mason, are we okay?"

NOW, she calls me by my given name. He needed time

to clear his head, needed time to think this through. Dealing with problems before breakfast and his first cup of coffee wasn't one of his strong points.

"Are we?" she insisted, sitting up and clutching the sheet just above her breasts.

"I don't know."

She flinched, and he wished he'd lied. Then again, lying ran as contrary to his nature as did casual sex. He tried to find something comforting to say, but as he struggled for the words, an accepting disappointment dulled Jill's expressive face. Her body wilted, saying more than he wanted to hear.

"Don't sweat it, Bradshaw." She swung her legs over the far side of the bed, putting her back to him. Even in the harsh light, her delicate skin invited touch. "I'm pretty unscrupulous. I knew you were drunk when I got here."

"I was not!"

"Taking advantage of you in a vulnerable moment got me a no-ties roll in the sack."

He'd thought only Karen could bring his temper to the flash point with such speed or accuracy—apparently something else he was wrong about. "Don't cheapen what happened between us with flippant remarks!"

Keeping her back to him, she took so long in answering that he wondered if she intended to speak at all. Finally, she stared off at nothing, and her voice wilted with resignation. "Now I know why God frowns on sex outside of marriage. I guess since He created us, He knows it has a good chance of backfiring and making us miserable." Agony rolled from her like summer heat. "I can't believe I'm so stupid."

"Jill, don't." Things were happening too fast. Mason didn't know how to handle it. Relationships weren't his strong suit. He reached to her, but the moment his hand closed around her arm, she shot off the bed and out of reach.

"I don't know about you, Bradshaw, but I feel like hell."

She snatched up her clothes and disappeared into the bathroom.

In the pit of his stomach, regret and guilt churned violently. The last thing Mason had wanted was to hurt her. Pulling on his pants, he knocked on the bathroom door. Not a sound came from within. "Jill, come on out." He knocked again. "Please? We've got to talk about this."

A moment later, the door whipped open, and she stood before him fully dressed. That in itself startled him. Karen took twice that long just to find the right shoes.

Her lips were pursed tight against bloodless skin, her dark eyes glistening with haunted humiliation. "You still love your ex-wife, right?"

Mason wouldn't have touched that question if his life depended on it. In the first place, he didn't know what he felt for her. In the second place, just thinking about Karen turned him inside out, which meant he still hadn't laid her adultery to rest. That didn't bear close scrutiny. Lastly, opening that can of worms right now would only complicate the problems between himself and Jill. "It's normal to have morning-after—"

She clamped her hand over his mouth, exactly as she'd done the night before. "Both of us were a little too emotional last night. Hormones got out of hand. Don't sweat letting me down easy, Bradshaw. You're a terrific guy and a great lover, but I rushed my fences on this one. Sorry. Despite what you probably think, I don't have much experience chasing men."

He took hold of her shoulders and drew her to him—the only thing he could think to do. She jerked free and brushed past him.

"Look, Bradshaw, I have just enough time to get home, do my hair and still be at work on time." Then she checked her watch and whimpered. "Actually, I have enough time to read *Wuthering Heights* first." With that, she darted down the hall. The sound of her opening the front door short-circuited his stunned immobility, and he rushed after her. By the time he reached the living room, she'd stepped out onto the porch. Her expressive, pain-filled face made him feel like he'd just shot Bambi.

"It's been fun, Bradshaw." The door shut softly and with soul-jarring finality.

Jill cried during the entire drive home. At that hour, few other cars were on the road, a small blessing but an appreciated one. Then she cried again while she showered and picked out her clothes for the day.

"You always thought you were a reasonably intelligent human being, didn't you?" she muttered, putting on her makeup. She used a heavier hand than usual to hide the carnage of her face. "If you thought facing him after a kiss in the park made you squirm, wait till you get to work today!"

She hurt so badly from throbbing heartache that even swallowing was painful. She curled her short blond hair and scrutinized her appearance. The redness had begun to ease from her eyes. She saw no trace of her usual spark, but maybe if she didn't break down again, no one would think anything of it.

On the drive to work, she had a couple of close calls when the burn behind her eyes almost got the better of her, but by the time she swung into the break room, self-control had a fighting chance. She poured herself a cup of coffee, scalded her mouth on the first swallow and nearly swore.

"Today's going to be hell," she whispered. "But you're a survivor. Keep telling yourself that, and everything will be okay."

The muffled voices behind Mason's closed door told her that the daily production meeting was in full swing. With luck, a newsworthy disaster had happened that would keep him busy enough to ease past the first few awkward encounters. Frankly, she dreaded the thought, particularly when the memories of his touch were still so raw, and her body still tender from his ardent lovemaking. With a heavy sigh, she flipped on her computer and got to work.

Thirty minutes later, the reporters filed past her office, still discussing the approach they wanted to take on assorted stories. Helen and Bobby waved at her, and she hunted for anything out of the ordinary in the way they looked at her. They kept walking. Apparently nothing registered, or they were too polite to comment.

Jill breathed a sigh of relief, looked down at her desk and picked up the next voucher.

"Can we talk?"

She jumped out of her skin at Mason's voice. Tears blasted to the surface, and she turned away, blinking them back.

"I'm awake now, Jill. I've had coffee, breakfast and my morning run. We need to discuss what happened."

"I thought we already had." She stared hard at the papers in her hand, without a clue as to what they said, but making a good show of scrutinizing them anyway. "We're both over the age of consent, so there's nothing else to say."

He closed her door and walked to her desk. Jill's pulse pounded in her veins. He hooked his hip on the corner of her desk, drew the papers from her hands, then hit the "off" button on her monitor.

"I owe you an apology."

She knew better than to glance up at his beloved face, but refusing to look at him would have been an even bigger mistake. If nothing else, she needed to give the impression she'd shrugged off being upset. Despite how little sleep they'd managed, Mason looked surprisingly rested. Maybe a good roll in the sack was what he'd needed all along. The worried tension around his eyes and mouth had apparently come later—like after he'd awakened, found her in his bed and realized what he'd done.

"You're a nice man, Bradshaw, but you have this irritating tendency toward apologizing for things that don't need—''

"Jill, we can't sweep last night under the rug. We have to find a way to put it behind us so it doesn't destroy our working relationship. Either way, the next few days will be hard enough."

Jill hadn't realized until then that deep down she'd been hoping he'd say something about wanting to take things one step at a time, about seeing what they could build, about feeling last night had been the most wonderful night of his life. *So much for stupid hopes and dreams.* "Okay, Bradshaw, if that's what you want to do. Since I had my say before I left your bedroom this morning, I'm done. Your turn."

He stared at her, his handsome face bleak. "You don't make it easy on a man, do you?"

She crossed her arms, hoping she looked irked. "I'm trying to. You're the one who wants to beat this to death."

He glanced at the floor and rubbed the tension from his brow with the fingertips of one hand. From what Jill could see, he really didn't know what to say, and was floundering. If they'd been swimming, she'd have thrown him a life preserver.

"Jill, I value your friendship."

She flinched. That had no more finesse than "you're a great girl, and someday you'll find a man who really appreciates you." Yadda, yadda, yadda. *Just get it said and out of your system, Bradshaw, so I can go back to licking my wounds in peace.*

"I don't want to lose that. I don't want to lose you as a bookkeeper, either."

"That's good, because I like it here."

He sighed, pausing to weigh his words. "Can we move forward? Or did last night ruin everything?"

"Depends on how fast you forget things, I suppose."

Swearing under his breath, he paced the room. "I will

never forget last night, Jill. You were incredible." He swore again. "*We* were incredible—together."

"But?"

"But I'm not interested in becoming involved right now."

She blinked, deliberately projecting a picture of serene innocence. "I know that. It took me a year and a half to get to a place where I could even think about starting over with someone new. The ink on your divorce decree isn't even dry yet. A man on the rebound isn't somebody I want." That was not quite a lie. Why did he have to still be tied in knots over his ex?

"But I hurt you," he said. His voice sounded as bleak as his face looked.

"No, Mason." Jill sighed. "We hurt each other."

He just stared.

"Bradshaw, if we want to continue on as before, we'll have to accept that it will take time to put this behind us. Like you, there are some things I handle better alone. Let me work through my half by myself, and maybe one day we can dance at each other's weddings. But for now, please go back to work. The deal Jerry cut the Happy Mart people on their advertising campaign won't give us the operating capital to expand the Community Events section like you wanted. I need to figure out someplace else to rob funds. Okay?"

Suspicion radiated from him like a furnace, but she held her ground, saying nothing more. "Jill, are you sure you're okay?"

"Positive. Now get lost before I throw you out and you have to fire me for insubordination."

A ghost of a smile played at the corner of his mouth. Nothing in his body language said she'd convinced him, but they were surviving the first horrible face-to-face meeting. In another few seconds, it would be over and she could breathe again.

Silence stretched out longer than she thought she could bear. Then he spoke.

"You're special, Jill."

"Glad you noticed. Now scram."

With one last look, Mason nodded, then left her office. His retreating footsteps sounded like a death knell to her heart.

At noon, Vicki dragged Jill from her desk. "I'm taking you to lunch."

"But I'm brown-bagging it today." Making a fancy lunch had given her something else to do that morning after she'd gone back to her apartment and had hours to kill.

"So? Eat it for dinner. We're going to the seafood place downtown. The atmosphere is cozy and private. Just perfect for you to tell me all your darkest secrets. Like why you look like something the cat dragged in."

Reflexively, Jill pulled back. "I'm fine."

"Okay, we'll talk here."

She glared at her best friend. "You're as bad as Mason."

Vicki looked thoughtful for a moment. "I've been compared to worse. *Now* are we going?"

"Are you sure you're buying?"

"That's the spirit, girlfriend. Never turn down free food."

At the restaurant, Vicki waited until they had their entrees before she pounced. "Okay, your wine should be hitting your brain cells about now, effectively loosening your tongue." She stabbed a shrimp, popped it into her mouth and moaned with delight.

Jill picked at her salmon, trying to convince herself she really wanted to eat. "What do *you* think is wrong?"

"Is this twenty questions, or are you trying to weasel out of answering me at all?"

"Both." Despite her lack of hunger, Jill began eating

her meal. Starvation really didn't do much for unrequited love. "So start guessing already, and I'll tell you if you're hot or cold."

Vicki snorted. "Well, Mason only looks marginally better than you do. So offhand, I'd say something happened when I turned my back."

Jill hadn't expected Vicki to hit the nail on the head with her first swing. "You're good at this."

"Of course. My youngest child is two. That means I have to be part mind reader. Now how warm am I?"

"You could fry eggs on that answer." Keeping this mess from her best friend really was pointless. "But at the moment, I don't want to talk. I want to curl up in a nice dark bomb shelter until my life finishes exploding around me."

"That does *not* do good things for my curiosity level."

Jill sighed. "I went to his place last night and things got…complicated."

"As in 'two bodies, one bed' complicated?"

"How do you do that?" she sputtered.

"I told you. Mothers are psychic." The teasing edge left her voice, and she laid a hand on Jill's wrist. "The morning after can be a killer. Especially if lightning strikes from nowhere, and both people are left to wonder what hit them."

The philosophy worked. It just didn't fit this particular situation, at least from Jill's perspective. Maybe Vicki ought to be having this conversation with Mason.

By the time the dessert tray arrived, Jill had talked until her throat hurt. She'd analyzed her actions, grieved over what could have been, then waxed poetic on her regrets. Nothing had changed, but the first round of the healing process seemed to have gotten off to a good start.

Absently, she glanced at her watch. "It's two o'clock!"

Vicki shrugged. "Don't sweat it. When I mentioned to Mason I planned to take you to lunch, he looked like I'd lifted something really horrid from his shoulders. Said to take as long as we needed. All afternoon if necessary."

Jill bristled. "Oh, so that's how you figured things out. So much for psychic powers."

Rolling her head back, Vicki chuckled low in her throat.

Mason kept a close watch on Jill. Despite her nonchalant air, he worried about her. One morning they arrived at the paper at the same time.

"What are you doing here at this hour?" he asked, holding the door for her.

She shrugged. "I have a dentist appointment today. I figured if I do my work first, I won't have to catch up tomorrow."

The wounded longing in her eyes told a different story. The break room was empty, and he took her by the arm and guided her in there. He hadn't touched her since the night they'd made love, and the intensity of the instant fire stunned him. It took an inordinate amount of fortitude not to pull her into his arms and kiss her senseless. Making love with her had been the most incredible experience of his life, one he wouldn't mind repeating. But she deserved more than sex, and that's all he could offer now.

"Jill, it has been a month. Things aren't any easier between the two of us than they were that first day."

Panic flashed across her face, and her chin came up. "Are you asking me to leave?"

"No!" How could she even think that? "I'd be absolutely lost around here without you and Vicki."

She stepped back, casually removing her arm from his grip. Holding her had seemed so natural, he hadn't noticed until just then that he'd let go.

"I'm glad we're appreciated. Now, whose turn is it to make coffee?"

Her insistence on pretending that their night together meant nothing irritated him to no end. "I didn't mean to hurt you, Jill."

Tears sprang into her eyes, and her chin came up again.

"You're awfully arrogant if you think my sun rises and sets on one roll in the sack with you, Bradshaw."

The retort would have flayed him alive if her obvious pain didn't pulse around him. He wanted to hold her, to undo what he'd done. When he'd first taken over the paper, she'd been perky and bright, with a kind word for everyone—including him. One night of self-indulgence had killed it, at least between the two of them.

They stared at each other a while longer, words impossible. All the words had been said.

"I'll make the coffee," he murmured.

"Fine by me." With a shrug, she headed to her office.

Jill sank onto the edge of her bed and stared numbly at the trash box where she'd thrown the home pregnancy test. It couldn't be. It just couldn't. Fate wouldn't be this cruel.

She walked into work in a fog, unable to come to grips with the implications of that little pink dot. When she walked past Mason's office, she couldn't quite make her feet move any farther. He looked up and forced a smile. Regret clouded his eyes to one degree or another whenever he looked at her. It seemed particularly pronounced today.

Frowning, he stood up. "Jill, are you all right?"

She opened her mouth to speak, but nothing came out.

"You don't look well. Are you coming down with something?"

She cleared her throat and tried again. "I think I already did."

He crossed the room and stopped less than an arm's length away. To touch him, she need only to reach out. The temptation to fall into his arms swelled over her. It was on the tip of her tongue to blurt out, "Mason, I'm pregnant," but the words stuck in her throat.

The future course of their lives depended on how she handled this. That required clear thinking, a skill momentarily beyond her. Pessimistically, she wondered if she'd ever be clearheaded again. Oh, Lord, how could one mistake have such long-reaching implications?

"Jill?" He tipped her face up and gazed into her face. His touch was torment, and she closed her eyes. Then his hand came to rest on her forehead. "You're not feverish, but you don't look good at all. Come in here." He guided her to one of the extra chairs in his office and sat her down. Then he filled a paper cup from the water dispenser in the hall. "Here. Drink."

She wished passionately that something as simple as a cool drink would fix the problem. One thing was certain. She needed to pull herself together before she did something even more stupid than getting pregnant—not that she could imagine what that might be.

Mason knelt before her, frowning in concern. "Is that helping?"

She took another sip and rested one hand over her stomach. Over her baby. Mason's baby. Tenderness and terror swept through her, and she began to shake.

"That does it," he said, getting to his feet. "I'm driving you home."

"But I—"

He waved her off. "You're sick. You need to be in bed. Do you have any chicken soup?"

The world tilted completely out of control. She blinked at him. "Probably."

Letting him believe she had the flu seemed to be the path of least resistance for now. She needed time to figure things out. As he stuffed her into his sedan and drove her to her apartment, she stole furtive glances at him. An incongruous blend of thoughts swirled through her mind. How would he react? What would their child look like? Mason had beautiful eyes. Would the baby inherit them?

Jill shook her head, hoping the fog would lift. Her life had crumbled down around her ears, and she was counting fingers and toes!

"Feeling worse?" he asked, unlocking her door. "You look like you're chilling again."

"I'll be fine. Thanks." She smiled into his worried face. He really was something special. "It's probably just a twenty-four hour bug."

"Would you like me to buy you some orange juice?"

She wished his concern ran in deeper veins. "Bradshaw, just because we had sex and you feel rotten about it, doesn't mean you're responsible for me for the rest of my life."

He looked irked. "If you're sure you'll be all right."

"I'm fine, thank you." She wanted to rise up onto her toes and kiss his cheek, but decided against it. He'd probably think she'd exposed him to God knows what. Worse, she didn't think her battered emotions could stand it.

She closed the door, then stood in the middle of the living room, staring into space for a long time.

"Morning, Bradshaw," Jill chirped as she swung past Mason's office.

His head snapped up. As sick as she'd been the day before, he really hadn't expected her to come in today. "Feeling better?"

"Yep. No flu. I'm doing great." She stopped, back-tracked, then leaned through the doorway. "Actually, I had a thought."

"About what?" There was something different about the way she stared at him. Intense. It made him feel like a bug under glass.

"Are you doing anything Saturday night?"

His defenses kicked in. "No, why?"

"Would you like to take in a movie?"

The question effectively kicked the wind out of him. "A what?"

"My treat. I owe you for taking me home yesterday."

He took another look at her eyes and decided that bug under glass had been too mild a comparison. She'd just put him on trial for something. But for what? "You don't owe me anything."

"Yes, I do, but that's not all of it."

"Oh?" His skin started to crawl.

"I thought dinner and a movie might give us a chance to get to know each other, see if anything develops."

She couldn't be serious. "Jill, I'm very flattered, but the one time we got together, things became…well…."

"Complicated?" Her impish grin didn't match the heightened scrutiny in her eyes.

"That's putting it mildly." Even after a month, he couldn't look at her without castigating himself. Letting emotions run out of control was bad enough. Sleeping with an employee had been an inexcusable lapse of judgment. "Jill, you're an incredible woman, but the timing and circumstances aren't right. I need to put my divorce behind me. Dating is—" *The most repulsive thing I can think of* "—not in my plans."

"I'm not proposing that we make love again. Just see if we have the ingredients for something worth pursuing."

"Jill, we have to *work* together."

"What if I didn't work for you anymore? Would that help?"

The words seemed straightforward enough, but the undercurrents were all wrong. "Jill, what is this conversation really all about?"

Squaring her shoulders, she sighed. Her gaze dropped from his face to somewhere on his desk. "I thought we established that, Bradshaw. I'm a woman asking a man out on a date."

He felt every muscle in his body knot up.

"Well, Bradshaw, since you look thoroughly revolted, I'll take that as a 'no.'"

"Jill, office romances beg for trouble. Haven't these last few weeks been bad enough?"

She inhaled a trembling breath. "So there's no chance you could ever be interested in me? None at all?"

Lord, why was she putting him on the spot like this? "I'm sorry."

The intensity left her eyes, replaced by the pain of yet another wound he'd inflicted.

"It's not you, Jill," he said, his eyes imploring her to understand. "Please believe that."

"Don't sweat it, Bradshaw." Her voice sounded strained. "I understand."

She pushed off the doorjamb and headed down the hall. Mason knew he'd missed about ninety percent of that conversation and rose to follow her. Halfway across the room, he stopped. If Jill was that interested in him, he needed to pull back and let it end on its own. Despite his attraction to her, no good could come of it. Every time he looked at her, he saw Karen. With a heavy sigh, Mason turned around and went back to his desk.

Mason's reaction had been no more or less what Jill expected, but she closed herself in her office and trembled anyway. Her world had tilted on its axis, and she didn't know how to right it again.

She'd thought the horror of her loveless, first marriage had faded, but the pink dot brought it all back with demonic intensity. She'd adored Donald, but he'd thrown her heart back in her face. Mason didn't have a self-centered bone in his entire body, but that still didn't mean he loved her. Just the *idea* of deliberately stepping back into a one-sided relationship was enough to make her want to run screaming into the night.

Jill tried but didn't get much work done for the next couple of weeks. Mason seemed to be hiding from her. The worst time to make a life-altering decision had to be while sitting on an emotional powder keg, and she couldn't think of a more volatile one than this. She knew there was no way on earth that she could make good decisions right now. But how would she support a baby alone? Mason had a right to know. Yet how could she tell him when she knew he didn't want her?

Oh, she knew exactly how he'd react. His first response would be, "We're getting married." That was the problem with men of integrity: They tended to make personal sacrifices. And this was one Jill knew she couldn't live with.

One thought gave her a lifeline to hang onto. She had time. Nothing needed to be done yet. Once the shock passed, maybe another option would present itself. She wasn't past hoping for a miracle, either.

One week crawled after another, and nothing changed.

Chapter 4

Jill eyed the jumbo employee coffee pot longingly, then settled for an unappealing fruit juice from the vending machine. Her obstetrician had come unglued over her blood pressure and yanked her off every vice she'd ever considered having. She didn't smoke, had never touched drugs and she'd quit drinking the occasional glass of wine the moment she'd failed the pregnancy test. That left taking away the only things she had left—coffee, donuts and fast food. Losing them for the duration really stung.

"For someone who insists they don't like coffee anymore, you sure grieve over that pot every morning," Vicki drawled. The break room had one table, and Vicki motioned for Jill to pull up a chair.

She shrugged and sat down. She'd worked hard at hiding her pregnancy, even from her best friend. Fortunately, the way she carried the baby, not much showed. Even so, at four months bulky sweaters weren't going to cut it for much longer, and life was about to get very sticky.

"Coffee's bad for you, Vicki. It'll put hair on your chest."

The other woman laughed. "At least you're putting some meat on your bones. Thin may be fashionable, but the waif look offends me." She sobered. "Truthfully, what's rattling around in that head of yours? The last few months you've had all the spark of a dead battery."

"Thanks for worrying, but I've got some personal issues to resolve."

Vicki looked wounded. "Ouch."

Jill took her arm apologetically. "It's not you. It's me. You know how I am with a problem."

"Unfortunately, yes." Vicki shook her head in sad disapproval. "Girl, you turn into a one-woman island."

Jill gave her a chagrined smile. "Sorry, but this is bigger than a bread box, and I need a little space."

She resisted the urge to wrap her arms protectively around herself in the telltale maternal gesture. Never had she imagined it possible to love anyone as deeply as she loved this baby. At times, she ached from it.

Before Vicki could utter the comment that obviously hovered on the tip of her tongue, the door swung open and Mason trudged in. Dark stubble shadowed his cheeks and throat, and he headed for the coffeepot as if navigating on autopilot. Jill's heart did its usual painful lurch.

To Jill, he was the epitome of the tall, dark, handsome male, a tender man with warm hazel eyes that twinkled every time he parted with one of his rare smiles. Over time, she'd noticed his features were a little too sharp, a little too well defined to fall under the category of perfection. But to her, the overall effect just made him more appealing.

Lately, his demons appeared to haunt him less. She could see it in the more relaxed set to his brow and jaw. That didn't mean he'd finally gotten over his ex-wife, or that he had suddenly become interested in her. For months, she had waited patiently for some indication that as he healed from the battle wounds of his marriage, he might change his mind about her—but he never looked her way. The miracle she'd hoped for hadn't happened, and time was no longer on her side.

"Bradshaw, are those the same clothes you wore yesterday?" she demanded bluntly. Most men wouldn't want a business that routinely required fourteen-hour workdays. Then again, Mason Bradshaw wasn't most men.

He gave her a sheepish look over his shoulder as he filled his mug. "Would it do any good to plead the Fifth?" he asked in his gentle baritone.

An almost irresistible urge swept through her to smooth his rumpled hair and rub the exhausted tension from his shoulders. One-sided love hurt, but she had no intention of ever letting him learn how she felt. Her emotional stupidity wasn't his fault or responsibility. *Damn you, Mason! Why can't you be a self-centered louse like ninety-nine percent of the other men I know?* "Did you work all night again?"

"Last I heard, it's not a crime."

Jill made a scoffing sound low in her throat. "In your case it ought to be."

He snorted.

"News flash, Bradshaw. Normal people sleep each and every night."

His sensual lips quirked into that aloof half smile that kept walls securely between him and the rest of the world. It broke her heart. Taking a slow, obviously fortifying pull on his coffee, he headed toward the door. "I'll be in my office if anyone needs me."

Jill squirmed as Vicki intently watched the byplay. When Mason left, Vicki stuffed the last bite of yogurt into her mouth and skewered Jill with a look.

"By the way," she said in a tone far too casual for Jill's peace of mind. "Are you ever going to put some more moves on that man? Or do you intend to keep drooling over him forever? Sparks flew once. No reason they can't again."

Jill blushed purple. "Who said I still want sparks?"

For a moment, Vicki looked stunned, then disgusted to the core. Slowly—and with entirely too much force—she tapped her spoon on the rim of her empty yogurt container. "Girlfriend, whenever Mason walks into the room, you look at him like he's the dessert your diet won't allow."

Having her best friend catch her in a lie, then call her on it, humiliated Jill. But she feared if she said even one word, the whole disaster would come tumbling out. Hiding behind walls gave her the only protection she had. Besides, lifelong habits weren't easy to break. *And you had the nerve to criticize Mason?*

"Come on, Vicki. Every woman breathing looks at him like that." She stood up and dumped the rest of her unwanted juice in the sink. "His wife's affair scarred him pretty badly. Just because he's single doesn't mean he's available."

"Well, there's nothing wrong with being first in line when he's ready to step out again."

Jill stifled a pain-filled shudder. "I had my shot at him and lost. Let it go. *I* have."

For once, Vicki took the hint and changed the subject. "Are you still job hunting?"

Jill turned around a little too quickly. "Yeah, did you hear of anything?"

The other woman frowned at the too-desperate reaction. "Unfortunately, yes. I don't like the idea of you leaving the paper."

"Mason pays us as much as he can, but someday I'd like to buy a house. You know, build a future." And, she added to herself, I can't hide this pregnancy much longer.

"So you've said." Vicki gave her a shrewd look. "Somehow, I think the real reason just walked into his office."

Tears seemed particularly close to the surface today. Stupid hormones, she thought. "What job did you hear about?"

"Casey's Home and Office Furniture is looking for a full

charge bookkeeper. They're pretty desperate, from what my neighbor said. He's their warehouse manager.''

"Great!'' Relief flooded from every pore. "I'll check it out at lunch.'' Looking at her watch, she got up. "That is, if I don't get fired first for sluffing off.''

As she cleared the doorway from the break room, Vicki added, "Jill, the only time you do your one-woman island impersonation is when you're in over your head and scared to death. It always comes crashing down around your ears. I think I'll come over this weekend and twist your arm till you start talking.''

Jill shuddered. She opened her mouth to lie and say she had plans, but changed her mind. God knew, she'd been there for Vicki and Wilson during that horrible year when they'd come half a breath from divorce. She needed to talk, needed reassurance that she'd made the right decision in keeping her pregnancy from Mason—at least until she had a new job and wouldn't be around him day after agonizing day. It would ease the pressure and keep her co-workers' noses out of a hot piece of gossip that would do neither Jill nor Mason any good. "You're the best friend I've ever had, Vicki.''

"I'm trying to be.''

She swallowed hard. "Tomorrow's Saturday. How about we go out for late breakfast?''

Vicki's victory sigh didn't escape Jill's notice. "Whatever it is, girlfriend,'' she said quietly, "we'll get through it together.''

Choked up past speech, Jill nodded, then headed down the hall.

The door to Mason's office stood open, and she caught sight of him at his cluttered desk, poring through mail he hadn't gotten to the day before. No matter how painful or stupid, she couldn't seem to resist the chance to watch him when he wasn't looking. She liked to pick out little details about him that she might have missed before, or get reacquainted with familiar ones. Like the way he tapped his pen in an uneven rhythm when wrestling with a particularly vexing problem. Or the way he raked his fingers through his hair when at wit's end.

This morning, as usual, classical music drifted from an ancient stereo on top of a battered file cabinet. How anyone could listen to that depressing stuff boggled Jill's mind, especially at this hour of the day. Give her a snappy Brooks and Dunn tune any day—real music to get the blood moving.

Their eyes met, and remorse flashed across his face, perhaps not as pronounced as usual, but she saw it nonetheless. She'd have thought after four months he'd have forgiven himself and moved on. But Mason—being Mason—hadn't done either.

Those realities were almost beside the point. The misery had become unbearable, and a nagging voice whined continually that he'd had a right to know about the baby long before this. She swallowed past the sudden lump in her throat. *One day soon. I promise. But not today. I know how you'll react. I'm just not strong enough to tell you 'no' when I'm this emotional.*

Taking one more look at his cherished, exhausted face, she stormed into his office and rummaged through a desk drawer.

"Jill, what are you up to now?" He shoved his chair back out of her way, his lips pursed together in exasperated incredulity.

She dragged out his cordless razor and dropped it on his blotter. "Shave, Bradshaw. You look like a scrounge. Not good for the paper's image."

That coaxed a tenderly amused smile from him. His smiles shredded her, but anything beat seeing the regret.

His expression turned gently probing, and he set his coffee mug down. "Jill, are you all right? Lately, you seem so…I don't know…distracted."

She snorted in what she hoped sounded like disgust. "Talk to Vicki. She compared me to a dead battery. When you two decide what my problem is, let me know." Then she gave him a fierce smile. "Just remember, though, I get ten minutes of rebuttal time."

"Are you sure nothing's wrong?" The whisper softness of his concern nearly proved her undoing.

"Positive." The lump in her throat doubled in size, and she nearly gagged. "I'm just rallying the courage to attack the morgue. Yesterday, Helen needed some research she'd done for a story a couple of years ago, but couldn't find it. Piecing everything back together cost her all afternoon. I promised I'd reorganize that disaster zone as soon as I finished the expense accounts this morning. I'm not looking forward to it."

She turned and walked away, tossing over her shoulder, "Rather than shaving, Bradshaw, go home and get reacquainted with the inside of your eyelids. It'll be good for you." Jill couldn't quite hear his laughing refusal as she headed down the hall. Then again, she didn't really want to.

After lunch and the interview at the furniture store, Jill typed up her letter of resignation. The Caseys had been euphoric over her resume. How soon could she start? Did she *really* have to give her current employer two weeks notice? Being welcomed with open arms did a world of good for her battered emotions, but her heart belonged to the *Journal.* The staff were her friends. How could she say goodbye?

Knowing she had no other choice, she carried the letter to Mason's office. He wasn't there. She laid the paper on his blotter and went looking. No luck. Depressed, she trudged into the break room for another godawful fruit juice.

A minute later, Mason's horrified voice sounded from behind her. "What is *this?*"

She cringed, then turned around. He stood in the doorway, her letter of resignation crumpled in one hand.

"I'm sorry." Her voice wobbled. "I'd hoped to tell you

in person, but I couldn't find you. You shouldn't have any problem finding a replacement for me.''

"You're leaving? Why? This is because of what happened between us four months ago, isn't it!''

"Don't be ridiculous. The *Journal* has a very loyal bunch of readers, and subscriptions are coming up. But I need more money than you can pay me. I'm tired of living in a one-bedroom apartment.'' Truthfully, she could afford much better, but the complex where she lived had nice neighbors, an indoor pool and a terrific gym. Unfortunately, it was adults only, and she needed to start looking for someplace baby-friendly.

"Jill, I need you.''

Inside, she grieved at the entreaty on his face and at his words, even though she knew the context of both was strictly professional.

"Thanks, but it's time to go.''

"I'm not kidding. You run everything around here but the presses. How much of an increase do you need? I'll look at the books. Maybe I can tighten the belt.''

Sad laughter filtered up through the torment. "Bradshaw, I'm your bookkeeper, remember? There's nothing there to cut.'' Jill detested crying, but the pregnancy had made her disgustingly weepy. Tears welled up, and she blinked them back.

"There's more to this than money, Jill. What's wrong?''

Swallowing hard, she did what she'd been wanting to do for months—she stood on her toes, stroked his satin-soft hair and kissed his cheek.

He sagged, but he didn't pull away. "I knew it. We had the beginnings of a good friendship before that night.''

Time to tell him part of the truth at least. "I didn't mean to fall in love with you, Mason. It just happened, and I can't turn it off any more than you can forget what Karen did to you.''

Most of the color in his face drained away, leaving him deathly gray.

Jill sucked in a breath. "Vicki and I go to lunch every Wednesday, so you and I will still see each other from time to time." *Boy, will we ever! Once I have my finances and living arrangements settled, we'll talk. Then we'll fight. I'm not sure how I'll stop you from dragging me to the altar, but at least you won't be in my face every day, and we won't provide an unending source of gossip for an entire newspaper staff.*

He raked his hand through his hair in that characteristic gesture of frustration and half turned away. "You have no idea how much I wish that night had never happened."

Gallows humor took over. "That bad, huh?"

His skin flushed an angry dark crimson, and he spun back around. "That's not what I meant, and you know it!"

"True," she whispered. Not for the first time, she toyed with the idea of never telling him about the baby at all. Wouldn't a clean break be so much easier? But her sense of fair play rebelled loudly at the notion. No, she'd tell him. In her own time. "But I'm still leaving on the fifteenth."

The abrupt pounding on the front door caused Jill to jump even though she had been expecting it. When she didn't immediately answer, Vicki's muffled voice came through the wood.

"I hope you're not hiding in there, girl, because I'm not going anywhere."

"You'd better not," Jill hollered back, "because I need all the friends I can get." As she opened the door, Vicki muttered something disagreeable and swept inside.

Dropping her purse on the couch, she gave Jill a warm hug. "Okay. I want the truth *now*. All of it," she growled, clearly miffed but never loosening her hold. "No frills. No stalls. And you'd better include the 'bigger than a bread box' part. I don't believe for one minute you're leaving the paper because of money. Now what *exactly* happened between you and Mason?"

Jill held tight. "Do you remember the night things got 'complicated' between me and him?"

"Hard not to."

"I'm pregnant."

A frozen silence descended, then Vicki stepped back to look at Jill's stomach. "Pregnant?"

She nodded. "Isn't life fun?" She'd intended to deliver the comment with her usual flippant air, but her voice cracked.

Vicki stared at her in horror. Jill stretched her bulky sweater across the slight bulge at her abdomen.

"Girlfriend, you really pulled one over on me," she said, dropping onto the couch beside her purse. "Seeing your cheeks filling out pleased me so much that I never noticed your tummy."

"You weren't supposed to." Tears gathered again. "This whole pregnancy business really stinks." Jill pulled back and swiped at the embarrassing moisture.

"Does Mason know?" Then she answered her own question. "Of course not. He'd be a raving maniac right now if he did. Instead, he calmly asked me to plan your farewell party."

"Calmly?"

"Sort of." Vicki shook her head as if to clear it. "Why haven't you told him he's going to be a father?"

Jill sagged into a chair across from her. "He doesn't love me. I can't go through that again."

Vicki scratched her brow with a manicured fingertip. "Back up and pretend I don't know what you're talking about."

"Remember what I went through with Donald?"

"What does that slug have to do with Mason?"

"I thought the scars had healed. I even flirted a little on that cruise last summer. It was really nice. No threat of anything permanent. Just some lighthearted fun. Then I came home and got hit in the face with Mr. Perfect himself.'' She took a shuddering breath. ''Vicki, I fell like the proverbial ton of bricks.''

''So? What's the problem?''

''He doesn't want me.''

Vicki's face scrunched up in bafflement. ''Girlfriend, from your condition, I'd say he wanted you at least once.''

''A temporary aberration, believe me.'' Jill gently stroked her tummy. ''If I tell him about the baby, he'll go through all the right motions. We'll have a quick wedding, and I'll be right back in the same horror show that tore me apart before.''

Vicki sighed thoughtfully. ''Donald was emotionally abusive and cold. Mason would never treat you that way.''

''Not on purpose, but in his own way, he'd be worse. I know him, Vicki. He wears honor like a second layer of skin. He'll hound me until hell freezes to marry him. Think about it. As much as you love Wilson, how would you cope if he was still torn up over an ex-wife and married you only because it was the decent thing to do? Wilson's like Mason. Honor demands a specific course of action. He'd even make love to you if you wanted him to, *not* because he cared.''

Vicki mulled that over, then grimaced. ''I'd probably go a little crazy.''

''That's why I found another job. I can't have him camped in my back pocket day after day until I say 'I do.' Once the baby's born, the illusion that marriage is the only answer won't be so larger than life. Then, we can approach our parental responsibilities in calmer, more sane frames of mind.''

''There are worse things, girl,'' she said softly. ''Single parenthood is rough.''

''Not as rough as another crummy marriage.''

Vicki shook her head hard enough to make the beads in her hair click together. ''I understand what you're saying, but keeping this from Mason isn't right.''

Jill leaned back and closed her eyes. ''I will tell him in my own time.''

"Are you absolutely sure marriage to him would be so hopeless?" From her tone, it was clear Vicki was grasping at straws and knew it.

"Vicki, I've never loved any man as much as I love Mason Bradshaw. Being his unwanted, unloved wife would kill me."

"But what if you accidentally run into him somewhere? He'll find out before you're ready."

Shaking her head, Jill took a long breath. "Stafford is small, but not *that* small. I won't have any trouble avoiding places he's likely to be. And as uncomfortable as he is around me, he'll be doing the same."

"To Jill Mathesin, Bookkeeper Extraordinaire."

Jill closed her eyes at Mason's toast. He'd deliberately used the words she'd used to describe herself the day they'd met. His presence seemed to penetrate muscle and bone, and Jill fought back a shudder at the thought of how badly she would miss him.

Cheers and applause swelled in the banquet room he'd reserved at a modestly priced restaurant. She'd have preferred to have the farewell luncheon in the break room, but people called the tiny room The Closet for a good reason. They'd have had to eat in shifts! So this two hours was brutally cut from her last precious day at the *Stafford Review-Journal*.

Mason towered over everyone else at the tables, and when he looked down at her seated beside him, he didn't quite succeed in hiding the remorse in his eyes. "I wish circumstances were different," he continued, "and she didn't feel the need to leave us."

Jill's eyes snapped open. Talking on two levels really was hitting below the belt.

"Even so, I hope she finds everything she's looking for. She deserves it."

More applause and murmured agreements met his words.

"Speech! Speech!" The last came from one of the reporters.

Jill forced a smile. "You're the one with the words, Bobby, not me."

Mason sat down and gave her a challenging look. Not even the first time she'd discovered Donald cheating on her had she hurt this badly. She wondered how much of the misery would go away after she gave birth and her body chemistry returned to normal, and how much she'd be stuck with until she worked Mason out of her system. Provided she ever could.

"Come on, Jill," he encouraged.

Reluctantly, she rose to her feet, but she couldn't begin to know what she said after that. Apparently, it went over well, if the scattered "ohs" and "ahs" meant anything.

Shortly after she sat down, the waiters served lunch. The steak came medium rare, exactly the way she liked it. But with Mason's eyes on her the whole meal, she could hardly choke down a bite. Frankly, he looked as bad as she felt, even though he managed to eat. Maybe food consumption in pressure situations was a guy thing.

"You didn't drive me away, Bradshaw," she said back at the paper as she cleaned out her desk.

"Looks like it to me." He eased out his breath in a long sigh. "Jill, I—"

Her head shot up. "If you apologize one more time for sleeping with me, I swear I'll string you up by your shoelaces. Is that clear?" She waved her finger at him.

A shadowed smile flickered across his face and faded away. "I'm going to miss you."

If he'd kicked her in the stomach, it couldn't have hurt worse. She zipped her bag shut, gave him a brave smile and tried one more time. "We could always take in that dinner and a movie. I won't even be here for the office romance complications to be a factor."

Typical of Mason, his reaction was controlled and discreet, and if she hadn't been watching closely, she probably wouldn't have seen how every line of his lean body tensed. But she did see it, and it tore her up. So much for last minute miracles.

"I'm sorry," he murmured.

She glared at him, and he held up a placating hand.

"Jill, I know you don't want to hear it, but it's the truth."

He took her by the shoulders. His warm touch eased the chill that had crept in unnoticed. She couldn't meet his eyes.

"For what it's worth, what we shared that night meant—"

If she couldn't bear looking at him, hearing whatever he intended to say was really asking too much, and she rested her fingertips over his mouth to silence him. His lips were warm and firm and every bit as sensual as she remembered. The fire ignited as her body remembered his touch and burned with want. Pulling back, she picked up her bag.

"Like I said, Bradshaw." Her voice rasped with emotion. "It's been fun."

"Mr. C., you can't take money from the cash drawer every time your pocket money is a little low." Jill truly liked the Casey family. They sold good quality furniture at affordable prices. Unfortunately, their idea of sound business had little to do with making ends meet. By the end of her first week, she wanted to tear her hair out in clumps. "And about the overdue accounts. If you don't let me lean on some of these people, you'll never see another dime."

The older man shrugged. "We've been doing business like this for thirty years, Jill. What's the fuss?"

She longed to be back at the *Journal* where Mason had a solid business head on his shoulders. "The fuss is that you have a choice. You make payroll, or you cover bills. The bank balance won't let you do both."

"Oh." He sounded like a small child who'd just found

out that Christmas elves didn't make all the toys Santa delivered. "What do you recommend?"

For the umpteenth time, she rattled off a budget that would get the store out of debt, and solvent again.

"If you're sure."

Latching onto the concession, Jill sagged into her chair with a heavy sigh. On her new desk sat her farewell present from Vicki, a customized coffee cup that read "Property of Jill Mathesin. Free refills anytime in The Closet." She could hardly look at it without crying.

Stupid hormones.

"Are you okay, Jill?" he asked. "You look a little blue today."

"Fine." She took a sip. "Decaf was invented by a sadist. That's all."

He gave her a grandfatherly pat on the shoulder and wandered off. She pulled up the list of the most delinquent accounts and started making phone calls.

Mason shoved the caster back into the chair leg. One wheel had developed the tendency to fall off at the most inconvenient of times. Like just now, when he'd been on the phone with a reporter in the field. Being dumped onto the floor while trying to hold a reasonably intelligent conversation hadn't done his disposition many favors.

Vicki came in with some letters for him to sign. Shaking her head at finding her boss kneeling on the carpet, she looked down at him. "That chair was old during World War Two. Replace it."

"Vicki, for three months you've invented every excuse imaginable why I need to go to Casey's Furniture," he said tiredly. He rolled back on his heels and reined in his irritation. "I assume Jill told you about our…aborted relationship. I admire your loyalty to your friend, but I'm not going over there." He flipped the chair back around and set it on its wheels. "Not now. Not ever."

She visibly wilted. "Fine. I've done my best to be a good

friend to both of you without betraying any confidences.
I'm washing my hands of this whole thing.''

"Thank you."

Glowering at him, she mumbled something under her
breath about stupid people. "I'm going to lunch."

"Have fun."

An hour later, Mason found himself staring at the letters
stacked on his desk. He tried to read the one in his hand,
but he couldn't focus on a single word beyond "Dear Editor." How much longer would he be reminded of one mistake? As Jill pointed out, they'd been two consenting
adults. People had casual sex all the time. No guilt. No
looking over shoulders afterward. So why couldn't he do
the same? Why after seven months couldn't he let go?

He reflected on that a moment and came to the same
conclusion he had about other problems in his life. He
didn't know how to let go of anything. Karen's betrayal ate
at him as intensively as it had the night he walked in on
her. Only the initial shock had worn off. Acidly, he wondered if he was redefining the term "anal retentive."

Bobby Creamer tore down the hall, grabbed the doorjamb and skidded to a stop. "Hey, Mason! Does anyone
know if Jill still works at Casey's Furniture?"

"Without a doubt," Mason drawled. "If Vicki weren't
at lunch, she could give you her work schedule, I'm sure."
When Bobby cocked his head in confusion, Mason realized
how sarcastic he'd sounded. "Why? What's up?"

"Armed robbery in progress." He shoved his arms into
his coat sleeves. "The cops rolled in just as the suspect
tried to leave, and they've got a hostage situation. The dirt-
bag has a gun to a pregnant woman's head. I'm on it." He
said the last as he turned and left, the photographer on his
heels.

The bottom dropped out of Mason's stomach. It was
Wednesday. Jill and Vicki always went to lunch on
Wednesdays. Still did. What if this had come down before
they'd left? Like an automaton, he reached for his coat and
pulled his car keys from his pocket.

Chapter 5

Jill rubbed her bulging stomach in a soothing gesture, praying her baby understood she was trying to protect her as best she could. Just after Vicki had arrived to take her to lunch, a gunman wearing a red ski mask barged in and rounded up employees, customers and Vicki. Then he'd robbed everyone and locked them in the storage room. Jill had hit the silent alarm the moment she saw him clear the door. He'd dismantled the back office looking for cash. There hadn't been much—something he should have realized. Anyone who would rob a furniture store in the middle of the week wasn't exactly a mental giant.

The police arrived, and the situation became really ugly.

She supposed her obvious condition had made her an attractive target, because he'd separated her from the others, dragging her onto the sales floor where he could keep an eye on the plate-glass windows and the door. Then he'd shoved her into a wing chair where the police could see her, the snub-nosed barrel of a revolver pressed to her right temple. The click of him pulling the hammer back would haunt her for the rest of her life.

"Stop stalling, man!" he screamed into the phone. The police negotiators had been talking to him regularly for the last two hours and had gotten nowhere. "I won't say it again. I want a helicopter and twenty-thousand dollars in cash. And the pilot better not be a cop, either. I want a *real* pilot."

Jill took a long, slow breath. After hours of living moment to moment, her thoughts had become strangely detached. The chances of her dying were all too real. She was due in six weeks. If the bullet struck only her, neonatal care might pull the baby through. The idea that a petty criminal could risk that tiny life infuriated her.

The thought occurred to her that getting shot was a hell of a way for Mason to find out, but Vicki—safely locked in the back room—would make sure he'd know about the baby. The knowledge made for dark comfort.

"Yeah, well you'd better find a way." The gunman slammed the receiver down, and Jill flinched.

He bent to her, leaning heavily on her shoulder. Jill closed her eyes. "They say they can't let me just walk out of here. What do you think?"

She swallowed hard, and tried not to move.

"No answer, Little Mama?" His breath reeked of stale beer and bad teeth.

A shudder rippled through her. He laughed, and turned his full attention back to the dozen or so cops watching him from outside. The police had cordoned off the parking lot, and spectators lined the barricade. The gunman adjusted his ski mask and glanced at his watch, nervous gestures that fueled Jill's terror.

The phone rang. His lips curled into a parody of a smile. The phone rang a second time.

"Think I ought to answer it?" he asked, leaning on her again.

The muscles across her shoulders knotted to the point of pain.

"I asked you a question, bitch!"

Jill recoiled reflexively. A sob escaped, and that made her mad, madder than she'd ever been in her life. Her insides went dead cold. "Depends," she said with an unnatural calm.

"So," he drawled. "You can talk."

"Only when I have something to say."

"I like that." Standing behind her, he pressed his cheek against hers. His breath came uneven, like a cornered animal on the verge of taking reckless chances. "So, what do you think? Should I let them lie to me some more?"

"You haven't killed anyone," she said, each word spoken with care. "If you turn yourself in now, you'll live long enough to get out of prison."

"Been there before, Little Mama. Not some place I want to go again."

"A good lawyer might pull that off for you."

The phone's shrill ringing had begun to get on her nerves. The gunman didn't even seem to hear it anymore. The ringing quit, and her pent-up breath eased from her chest. Then the police negotiator dialed again. If the man held true to past patterns, he'd keep trying until the gunman answered.

The robber snatched the receiver off the hook. "What!" He listened a long time. "Maybe I ought to just shoot a hostage or two. Think that'll make your day?" He ripped the phone from the wall.

Given his state of mind, Jill took the threat as truth. "I have a question."

Through the eyeholes in the red mask, she saw his surprise.

"How did you plan to get out of here in the first place?"

"Why?"

"Well, they won't give you the helicopter and the

money. You need another plan. I figured it might be a good idea to start with your original one and go from there.''

"My car's outside.''

She invented as she went along. "A driver or just you?''

His eyes narrowed in suspicion.

"If you had a friend, he's long gone by now. But if you came alone and you're parked in a regular parking space, then they might not know which car is yours. They might not have tampered with it. You could—''

"Why are you trying to help me?''

Swallowing hard, she turned her head to look at him squarely. That meant staring down the bottomless barrel of the gun. Somewhere in that darkness rested a bullet. "Because I want this over. Because I want to go home.''

The gun never wavered as he mulled over what she'd said. "I'll take you with me, you know.''

Keeping her gaze level on him took everything she had. "I assumed as much.''

"Then let's shake them up a little.''

Terror coursed through her veins. *Hold on, sweetheart.* She laid her hand on her stomach. *Mommie's trying.*

In the nine months Mason had been in Stafford, he'd established a fairly good relationship with the city police chief and was allowed inside the cordon. The chief made it very clear, though, that civilians had to stay at a safe distance. On the way through, Mason had walked past Vicki's car. Fear sang through his veins. Wilson had gone to the state capital for a school administrator's conference. Mason tracked him down by phone and promised to stay until the man could get back.

As the afternoon dragged by, he kept telling himself both women were fine. The police believed the suspect hadn't harmed anyone yet, that everyone except a pregnant woman was safely locked in the storage room and not in any immediate danger. As evening approached, the suspect had broken off negotiations, and the police were getting nervous. The longer the standoff lasted, the greater the chance that someone could get hurt.

Then the door to the furniture store opened, and everything changed.

A single gunman emerged, his arm locked around his pregnant hostage's throat, a pistol to her head. She held perfectly still, one arm laid protectively across her belly. Her captor surveyed the scene, a dozen rifles trained on him.

On second look, a vague familiarity about the woman caught at Mason. From this distance, though, he couldn't be sure of anything. She had shoulder-length hair about the color of—

"My God! That's Jill!" Shock rooted him in place.

The head negotiator had opened his mouth to say something to the suspect, but at Mason's outburst, he turned around. "That's your former employee, Mr. Bradshaw?"

Dumbfounded, Mason could only nod.

"It would have helped if you'd told us that's who he had." The man's censure barely registered. "The more information we have to work with, the better our chances of getting people out."

"I didn't know." Not since the night he'd walked in on his wife had his world come apart with such speed and thoroughness. He couldn't breathe. At that moment, everything narrowed down to two images—Jill's distended abdomen and the gun against her temple.

"What are you doing now, buddy?" the negotiator asked, his tone conversational.

Mason braced his hand on a patrol cruiser's trunk lid to keep from falling over. *Jill was pregnant. Very pregnant. And that scum might kill her. And their baby. Their baby.*

"We're going to my car. Little Mama here thinks you won't risk shooting her to get to me."

The singsong quality to his words made Mason's blood run cold. That psycho might do anything.

"I think she's right," the gunman answered himself. "How about you?"

"I think you need to let the lady go. Do you have any idea what a judge and jury would do to you if you killed a woman and her unborn child? You'd never see daylight again. Right now, things aren't so bad."

He laughed. "Maybe from your end of things. Not mine." He said something low to Jill, who nodded. Together, they began a sideways shuffle down the sidewalk.

"Where's your car, buddy?" the cop tried again. The gunman stopped. "Let the lady go, and we'll clear a path to it. You don't want to hurt anybody." With a jerk of his head, he indicated the crowd of reporters and onlookers.

Mason couldn't take his eyes from Jill. Raw emotion flooded through him with such ferocity that he couldn't begin to sort out any of it. Her point of focus narrowed, and he watched her find him in the crowd. Her lips parted, and he could have sworn she mouthed his name.

"I just want out of here, man."

"We all do. Now which car is yours?"

"The beige two-door."

The negotiator scanned the parking lot. "I don't see it. Could you be more specific?"

At first the man tried to point with the arm around Jill's throat. He jerked her back and forth like a rag doll. She stumbled, and he dragged her back to her feet. Mason lunged forward, but men on either side of him hauled him back.

"You're a civilian, Mr. Bradshaw. Stay put!"

Mason clenched his fists by his sides and hung onto every word of the gunman's exchange with police.

"It's the car by the light pole."

"Next to the gray Ford?"

"No, you bastard. That's brown. I said *beige*." He swung the pistol away from Jill to point at his car.

Time dropped into a tableau of slow motion. Jill grabbed

his gun arm and shoved it into the air. Cops surged forward in a black-uniformed wall.

The pistol went off. One group of cops ducked, while others made flying tackles on a single point on the sidewalk, burying Jill and the suspect behind and beneath it all. There were shouted orders. Other voices lifted in warning. Mason fought against the hands that restrained him, then forced himself to regain his composure. He could do nothing except get in their way—but standing idle was miserable. More officers poured into the furniture store, guns drawn. Then two cops half carried, half dragged Jill from the tangle of bodies to the protection of the police cars.

Questions peppered her from all directions. "Yes, I'm fine. Yes, I think everyone else is all right, too. Somebody needs to let them out of the back room. Mr. C. is a heart patient. Could one of you get a paramedic to check him over?"

Mason nearly demanded to be let through, but he shook so badly he could hardly stand. He needed time to think.

Jill was safe.

Jill was *pregnant*.

Someone threw a blanket around her shoulders and led her toward a police car. Dazed, she scanned the crowd, looking for what, he didn't know. He didn't mean to step forward out of the crowd. His feet just moved. Hers stopped.

Their gazes met and locked. From the hysteria in her eyes, she didn't fully comprehend that her ordeal had ended. Her shoulders hunched forward as if she wanted to hide from the world—him in particular—for a while, and one hand came to rest again on her stomach. Her lips moved around his name.

The rest of the hostages ran from the building. Only then did Mason notice the cuffed suspect being marched toward a cruiser. Two of the hostages tried to attack him and had to be restrained by police. Reporters jumped to cover the action. The professional part of his brain registered that his people were on it. They knew their jobs, and he left them alone with it. He had one thought—to reach Jill. But he couldn't get through the sea of uniforms.

The cop who'd given her the blanket helped her sit down on the back seat of a patrol car. Mason's gaze locked onto her stomach. She recoiled and turned away.

"Other than being scared, I'm fine," she told the officer. "I just want to go home." Her body trembled.

"Just as soon as we get a statement, ma'am. Do you have family that can come pick you up? In your condition—"

"No." She shook her head. "There's no one."

"She has *me*," Mason growled loud enough for people on the next block to hear him. A path to her opened. Closing the distance between them, he realized vaguely that his own shock had passed. Rage replaced it and battled with relief that she'd made it through unharmed.

When Jill saw him towering over her, she visibly shrank into herself. A distant part of his mind observed that he needed to back off. After what she'd survived, she didn't need a confrontation right now.

"What are you doing here?" she squeaked. "How did you find out?"

"I'm the press, remember?" Glancing at her belly again, he told himself that just because he learned the real reason she left the paper didn't mean he knew it all.

Then Vicki was there, laughing and crying and rocking Jill the way she would a small child. "It's okay now, girlfriend," she crooned. "It's over." Then Vicki gave Mason a heated look. "If you'd come down here months ago and bought yourself a new damned chair, she'd have been back at the paper where she belongs. Nothing like this would have happened to her!"

Mason exploded. "Why didn't you tell me straight out that she was pregnant? It would have been a lot easier on everyone!"

Jill hunched down in the seat, out of the line of fire.

"What did you expect me to do, Mason? Break my word? If you weren't so pigheaded—"

"Where's my wife?" Wilson's bellow split the crowd in half. It hadn't been all that long since some of the younger police officers had been students dragged into Principal Haynes's office for one infraction or another. Reflexively, one of them let him through. A moment later, he pulled Vicki into his arms.

"Fine time for you to show up," she snapped. "I've spent all day locked in an oversized closet with a bunch of hysterical white people who—"

Wilson kissed her into silence. Slowly, her arms crept around him, and she drooped into his embrace.

"It's okay, baby," he murmured into her hair, caressing her back and rocking her gently. "I've got you now."

Vicki buried her face in his neck and sobbed.

Jill watched the devoted couple a moment, loneliness clouding her dark eyes. Then she glanced at Mason. She tucked her feet inside the car and shut the door. But the cop trying to get her statement pulled it back open and began writing on his clipboard.

Mason listened as she described her ordeal. Her voice cracked and shook. Several times the cop had to repeat the questions, but her responses were clear and concise. Not many people would come through a threat on their life as well as she had. He admired her strength. Always had.

What he didn't admire—much less understand—was why she'd kept the pregnancy from him. The Jill he thought he knew would be more inclined to storm into his office, and announce, "Bradshaw, the rabbit died and you killed it." Then she'd cross her arms and wait to see what he intended to do about it.

That's not what happened, though. Didn't she know him well enough to realize that he'd want to know? They had created a life together! Did she believe that since it was her body, he had no right to even common courtesy?

Vicki had apparently known all along. He glanced at his

secretary and her husband, still holding her and talking softly. She caught him watching her and gave him a questioning look.

"Why don't you take a day or two off?" he suggested. "Pamper yourself a little."

"Are you sure?" she asked, her gaze darting from him to Jill.

"Positive." Then Mason swallowed some of his indignation over Vicki's subterfuge. "Regarding Jill. I'm sorry I yelled at you just now. You were in an impossible situation and took the only course you could."

Still clinging to her husband, Vicki shuddered. "All I want is a bubble bath."

"How does a rubdown sound?" Wilson murmured. "We'll even leave the kids at your sister's for a while." As they left, he told her how much he loved her, how he wouldn't have been able to go on without her. Mason was convinced she'd be living life on a satin pillow until they got through the worst of the shock.

Mason turned back to Jill. She'd suffered more than any of the other hostages, yet she seemed to be in the best shape.

"Is that it?" she asked the cop.

"For now," he assured her. "The District Attorney's office will be contacting you soon. Are you going to be all right?"

"Yeah," she sighed, sounding drained. "Just give me a couple of days." Stepping from the patrol car, she eyed Mason standing a few feet away. Her chin came up, but her lips quivered, spoiling the defiant gesture.

He took her arm, and she wilted. "Did you want to go back inside and get your purse and coat?"

Her head snapped around to the building, and she shook her head convulsively. "I don't think I can go back in there today."

Understandable, he thought. She handed the blanket to the paramedic. Mason draped his suit coat over her shoulders, and she huddled into its warmth. The symbolism struck deep, and he clenched his jaws to keep from saying anything possessive that he'd have to apologize for later.

"My car is three rows over."

She nodded but wouldn't look at him. They walked in silence, Mason very aware of the generous bulge that peeked from the open lapels of his coat.

In monotones, she gave him directions to her apartment, and he helped her into the car. Neither spoke until he'd pulled onto the freeway.

"How mad are you?" she asked into the silence.

He swallowed back most of it. "More so than you need to hear right now."

She leaned back in the seat and closed her eyes. The temptation to reach over and touch their child nearly overwhelmed him. They were having a baby, and she'd deliberately kept it from him! Taking a deep breath, he forced his attention back on the road. The rush-hour traffic kept his mind occupied and off the rage that boiled up with annoying persistence.

Once at her apartment, Jill climbed out of his Buick and laid his coat neatly on the seat. "Thanks for the ride. Maybe you can come over tomorrow and we'll talk." She had sensed his fury the entire trip, and knew he had bided his time until he'd gotten her home. Without answering, he killed the engine and got out.

"Really, Mason, I don't want to talk about it now."

"You haven't wanted to talk about it for the last seven months, so that's not surprising. Tonight, you actually have a legitimate reason." His face could have been carved from concrete for all the warmth she saw there. Holding that much anger in check took tremendous willpower, and she doubted he owned an inexhaustible supply.

Wrapping her arms around herself against the spring chill, she said, "Go home, Bradshaw. We'll talk tomorrow."

He ignored her and stepped around the car. "Do you lock your apartment?"

The question confused her. "Of course, I do. Why?"

"Unless that maternity dress has a pocket in it—"

"My keys!"

He nodded. "Get back in my car where it's warm, and I'll see if I can find the manager."

She wanted to take issue with his high-handed attitude, but she just didn't have the strength. The process of getting her apartment unlocked dragged out getting him to leave. Once she stepped inside, she turned around to make one more attempt.

Mason's glower darkened to lethal proportions. "May I come in?" The far-too-polite request sounded more like an ultimatum.

The baby moved within her, and she nearly wept. Keeping her life her own was a thing of the past. Resigned, she stepped back and let him barge into her home.

Then, wrapping protective arms around her belly, Jill took a deep breath for courage. "Would you like something to drink?" If she had to go down, it would be fighting and with her dignity intact. "I have fruit juice, ice water and milk. Soda gives me heartburn, and anything with more kick to it has been banned for the duration."

His flint-like hazel gaze swept the cramped living room as he turned full circle. His eyes then focused on her face. Her knees trembled under the force of the burning fury he held barely in check. Mason reminded her of a hawk the moment before it folded its wings for an attack dive. Suddenly, she felt very much like a field mouse caught out in the open.

"Why?" he demanded in a low voice. No more, no less.

For a panicked second, she nearly pretended to misunderstand and comment on her diet. Then she saw the devastation beneath his fury, and she sank into an overstuffed chair. Two victims—not one—had been created the night they'd conceived a new life.

"Jill, what reason could you possibly have for keeping this from me?" His breathing came labored, uneven. "Don't you think I have a right to know?" His voice fractured under the strain of holding back that much raw emotion.

Tears dripped onto her cheeks. Crying in front of people always made her angry, and she swiped at her face with the heel of her hands. Between being pregnant and nearly being shot, she found holding the tears back impossible. "I really hate this."

He looked stricken and started to reach for her, but stepped back, visibly hardening himself. "Well?" he repeated, his own misery barely tempering his anger. "I've got to know that much. Then I promise I'll leave."

Her stomach churned, and the tears picked up speed. He towered over her, hands low on his hips.

"Mason," she began, her voice a thready whisper, "I don't know what to say."

"What's wrong with the truth?" The agitation shifted the pain lines on his face. "For God's sake, Jill, that's my baby, too."

"I know," she said gently, trying to find a way to make him understand. "Mason, what do you want your involvement to be?"

His eyes widened as if the question constituted a mortal insult. Then the emotion cleared from his eyes, and he went into the kitchen.

"Bradshaw, what are you doing?"

He didn't answer.

"Bradshaw, I don't need this right now."

He came back into the living room with a glass of milk. "Here. You probably haven't had anything to drink since this morning, right?"

Nodding, she took the glass. The first sip tasted better than the finest wine, and she downed it with uncharacteristic speed.

"Thought so," he grumped. Then he wandered into the

alcove that passed for the hallway between living room, bedroom and bathroom. He rummaged through the cupboards until he'd found two large, fluffy bath towels and a wash cloth.

"Please leave me alone. I'm not up to this."

When he didn't answer, what little remained of her sense of control over her life drained away. He moved into the bathroom, rolled up his shirtsleeves and turned on the tub faucet. "How hot do you want the water?"

"I don't want a bath."

"Wilson's getting Vicki a bubble bath." His bland tone allowed for no argument. "Sounds like a wise move to me. Do you want bubbles or plain?"

"Plain," she murmured.

He stuck his head out of the bathroom. "What did you say?"

"I said you're a pain, Bradshaw."

Apparently he didn't feel the remark warranted answering, because he returned to the bathroom and banged through the vanity drawers.

The robbery and Mason's presence had bled her reserves dry. She huddled on the couch, too weak to do more than sit there. She didn't know how many minutes passed, but before long, Mason once again stood over her. This time the implacable lines had eased a tiny bit. Had drawing her bath blunted the knife edge of his anger?

"Come on. I'll help you undress," he whispered. The tenderness in his voice didn't match the glitter in his eyes, but he had his temper under wraps.

"I don't think so, Bradshaw. My body isn't for public viewing."

He just stared at her, hand outstretched, waiting.

"Did you hear me? Go home!" Something snapped inside. Tears came from nowhere, shocking in their speed and intensity. She groped for a mental anchor to keep from being swept away by the flood, but found nothing. Great racking sobs overcame her, and she wrapped her arms around her body and rocked back and forth, feeling as if she were drowning in the deluge.

Then Mason pulled her across his lap, strong arms holding her close. She didn't know when he'd sat down, but she found her anchor and clung to it.

"It's all right," he murmured, rubbing circulation back into her arms and hands, and kneading the knotted muscles in her neck. "This is a delayed reaction. Hours ago, your mind decided it couldn't afford to let go. Now everything is over, and the bill came due. Let it out."

"This is so stupid," she gasped between unstoppable tremors.

Without a word, he shifted his hold and let her finish crying it out. She didn't know how long she cried, much less what time the storm finished, but she knew she should get off his lap. As drugged as she felt, though, she couldn't move.

"Your bath is probably cold," he said, lifting her off his legs and setting her down. "I'll warm it up."

"No, really. All I want is sleep. Please, go home—"

His instant glower strangled off the rest of her protest. "You need to eat, and you're in no condition to fix anything." He turned on his heel and strode into the bathroom.

"But...." She cut herself off, seeing no point in continuing. Even if he could hear, he wouldn't listen. Then, of course, he might be right. What an ugly thought.

"It's ready," he pronounced, once again reaching for her hand.

Self-protection made her want to sink into the couch cushions and turn invisible. "I don't want you to see me naked."

"Neither one of us has anything the other hasn't already seen."

"Not pregnant, you haven't," she protested.

He shrugged, his hand steady. It didn't go anywhere, and she finally took it. Her head had cleared some, and the sensation of his warm palm against hers filled some of the emptiness.

With crisp efficiency, he helped her out of her dress and the maternity support panty hose she wore to keep from getting leg cramps. The garments were not pretty, but they worked. Right now, they made her feel even more self-conscious. "I look like a deformed cow."

His gaze scanned her body as if he were unable to help himself. "I've never seen anything so beautiful in my life." She heard anger, true, but the undercurrent of awe riveted her attention. He meant it.

"In you go."

He'd filled the tub, leaving just enough room for the mountain of vanilla-scented bubbles. Holding his arm for support, she stepped in. As the warm water enveloped her skin, a groan rolled from the depth of her soul. It felt better than the milk had tasted. She sank down into the decadent luxury and closed her eyes. She almost forgot that she had an audience.

"I saw a boneless chicken filet in the refrigerator. Do you want me to cook that for you?"

She heard the words, but answering required too much energy, and she moaned instead.

"I'll take that as a yes."

Before she could pry her eyes back open, he disappeared. Within an hour, he had her dried, fed and tucked in bed.

"Get some sleep," he whispered as she drifted off. She didn't know for certain, but she thought he added that he'd be back tomorrow.

Mason returned to the furniture store, where the police were still collecting evidence. They made him wait around for another hour, but they finally allowed him to retrieve Jill's coat and purse. While he waited, he stewed.

Jill had gotten pregnant and hadn't seen any reason to tell him. Every time he thought about it, he wanted to explode. Part of him couldn't accept it. Part of him really wanted to believe he was having a nightmare. But then he'd seen her naked body, her belly swollen with his child, and he'd melted. As much willpower as it had taken for him not to rage at her, not turning into a doddering fool had taken more.

His *child!* All the years he'd wanted a family—and now it had caught him unaware. He'd have to pull out a calendar to figure out exactly how much longer he'd have to wait, but the little person had to be close to making his or her appearance in the world. Waves of love and tenderness swelled through him.

Then the complications set in. What on earth was he going to do about Jill? His divorce still felt as if it had happened yesterday. The idea of dating again sounded obscene. How could he face anything more serious—like a second marriage? That night, he lay in bed and stared at the ceiling until nearly dawn. From the moment Jill's pregnancy registered in his brain, there seemed to be no alternative courses of action. But how could he make the rest of his body go along with it?

Throughout his divorce, Jill had told him to survive it one day at a time. It was good advice then, and it was the best advice now.

Chapter 6

"It's eight o'clock in the morning, Bradshaw," she sputtered. "What are you doing here?"

From the iron set to his shoulders, Mason was a man with a mission, and it would take all her powers of persuasion to slow him down until she could think of a way to stop him altogether. He held out a white paper bag with a fast-food logo emblazoned across the front. "Breakfast. May I come in?"

"If I say no?" The really bad part was she didn't want to send him away. She wanted his arms around her. She wanted him to be her other half.

Mason drew in a long considering breath. "Then I guess I become a permanent feature on your porch."

"You wouldn't," she gasped.

"Try me." Then he held out her purse and coat. "I picked up these for you last night as soon as the police would let me into the building."

Jill groaned. "You make it very hard to be rude, Bradshaw."

"I hope so." His eyes glittered. "May I come in now?"

Their gazes locked in a contest of wills. The battle she'd feared most had begun, and she doubted there'd be any winners.

Logic told her to thank him for her coat and purse, then firmly close the door. It really shouldn't be hard. Her hand rested on the knob. So how come she couldn't make her arm move? With a sigh, she stepped back. "Welcome to your own funeral, Bradshaw."

His eyebrows lowered in a dark glower, but he stepped inside with the definitive air of a man who'd won. Without comment, he strode to her dinette table against the far wall and set down the bag. "Let's eat."

Jill didn't move, afraid if she closed the door, it would make this new wrinkle to the mess more final. As long as the door stayed open, she could pretend she had an avenue of escape.

"You're letting in all the cold air," he observed, pulling out paper-wrapped, ham-and-cheese muffins. "Do you like hash browns?"

She closed the door. "Would it matter?"

He looked at her then, the invincible set of his shoulders never wavered. "*You* matter a great deal to me, Jill. We have plans to make."

"In other words, we can do it easy, or we can do it hard. My choice?" She'd put her best Hollywood rogue cop drawl on it, and it earned her another heated glare.

"We're getting married. Now sit down and eat. That baby needs food. So do you."

Inside, Jill died a little more, but at least the worst had been laid out, the words spoken. "As proposals go that wasn't the most romantic I've heard of, Bradshaw."

He seemed to consider that. "Would you have said yes the other way?"

"No." She gravitated toward the table, unable to stop herself from being closer to him.

"Then I'll save the romance for a day I don't want to wring your neck."

That hurt. He had the right to be upset. Even so, she still would have liked to hear words of caring and affection, even if he'd had to invent something. "Would you propose if I weren't pregnant?"

She didn't like putting him on the spot like that, but they couldn't afford the luxury of illusions between them. The strain on his face deepened. Then his expression hardened into commitment to the ethics he lived by. "You are, and I'm not interested in playing what-if games."

"Mason, I love to dance. Did you know that? Would you take me dancing?"

Helpless, male confusion radiated from him at what must have appeared to be an idle subject hop. "I'll take you to China if you agree to marry me." His eyes narrowed with resolve. The intensity unnerved her. "Jill, today's Friday. I'm not sure what the Washington marriage license laws are. I haven't lived here all that long. But if we can't get everything arranged within a week, we can fly to—"

"You're missing the point, Bradshaw." She found a box of tissues and blew her nose. Her eyes were still swollen from the crying binges the night before, which had come at irregular intervals for hours. The memory of having a gun to her head for half a day would probably always remain vivid in her mind, but she'd come through it unharmed and she believed that she'd handle whatever healing process she had yet to go through.

His face tightened with exasperation. "All right, we'll dance every weekend if that's what you want."

"You're still missing the point. How about mountain bikes? Would you ride in the hills with me?"

Mason rubbed his hands violently over his face. When he spoke, though, it reflected a quiet, overwhelmed frustration that sliced open her already bleeding heart. "I'm talking about the future of my child—our child—and you want to talk about hobbies."

Compassion flooded the wounds. "Not hobbies, Bradshaw. Interests. Companionship. The things that make a marriage last a lifetime. I've been through one bad marriage. So have you. I can't go through another one."

"And, of course, that explains why you *deliberately* kept this from me."

With a groan, Jill sank down onto the couch. "Actually, it does. What makes you think I'd marry a man whose interest in me doesn't extend beyond the occupant of my body?"

"You're distorting things."

"Really? Right after I found out I was pregnant, I asked you out to dinner and a movie, remember? I needed to see if you had any genuine interest in me at all. You said, no. That's an answer that's hard to distort."

"You're not being fair, Jill. I didn't know about the baby. I also needed to give us both some breathing room until I washed Karen out of my system." His eyes swam with remorse and frustration. "The timing was wrong."

"There's more to it than that."

"Like what?" Frustration had definitely gained the upper hand, if the way he dragged his hands through his hair indicated anything. He must really be climbing the walls.

"Bradshaw, I don't know you well enough to answer for certain. Something about me bothers you. Always has."

"That's ridiculous. I told you last night, I think you're beautiful."

She frowned. "So it really does have something to do with my appearance?"

He froze, and Jill realized she'd hit the nail on the head. But how could he find her unattractive on one hand and beautiful on the other? It didn't make sense. Or did it? "Bradshaw, some men find the sight of a pregnant tummy a turn on. Do you?"

He blinked, seeming to think about that a minute. Then he waved her away. "Let's get back to the subject."

"I didn't think we'd ever left it."

"We're getting married."

"Right," she scoffed. "You'll marry me out of decency and obligation because that's the kind of man you are, not because you want me to share your life. I told you about Donald. Another one-sided marriage is not on my agenda."

"That doesn't justify you not telling me about the baby." Agitation simmered behind his hazel eyes as he weighed her words, and she sensed the moment he finally understood. Sinking beside her on the worn couch, he braced his elbows on his knees, his dark head sagging between his shoulders. "Did you plan to ever tell me?"

Jill nodded. "Yes, as soon as she was born and I wasn't so emotional all the time. I could have picked the time and place, and wouldn't be so susceptible to you talking me into doing something I sincerely believe will hurt us worse in the long run."

Mason's face was an easy one to read, and she fought back a sad laugh as he mentally regrouped. "We're getting married."

"Why?"

His eyes widened momentarily in shock. Then he got to his feet. "You're carrying my child. That's reason enough."

"Maybe thirty years ago, but not anymore."

He stared at her unblinking, obviously out of his depth, the conversation clearly not having gone the direction he expected.

Leaning back, Jill closed her eyes. She didn't really want to watch his expression when she made her position unmistakably clear. "I will *not* marry you. Not next week, not ever."

Silence slammed down like a heavy curtain that swallowed all sound. It didn't take much effort to sense his hurt.

Then, typical of Mason, he launched his attack. "Mountain biking won't be a problem. I run a couple of miles every morning."

"Didn't you hear me?" She snapped open her eyes and glared at him.

His expression stayed bland, determined. No argument would penetrate. "Bikes aren't that much different." He cocked his head. "What kind of dancing were you talking about? Ballroom?"

Jill remembered the classical music he favored and stared at him in challenge. "Line dancing, Bradshaw."

His entire body tensed in abject revulsion, his composure shattered. "That's country-and-western, right?"

She nodded silently, loving him with every heartbeat and hating the sacrifices he'd willingly make. Mason Bradshaw would do whatever it took because it was the decent thing to do, no matter how miserable marriage to a woman he didn't love would make him.

Swallowing hard, he asked, "Does it require…cowboy boots?"

"You can wear sneakers if you want to," she sighed, "but you'd probably feel a little out of place, especially at the club I go to."

Mason took a fortifying breath. "Okay, I can handle boots. How hard can the rest be?"

Tenderness welled up in her. How would she convince him that just because they'd made one mistake, they didn't need to make another? Covering his hand with her own sent warm shooting sparks up her arm. From the grim way he stared at her fingers, he didn't share the sensation. Through the pain, she self-indulgently studied his beloved face. *My dearest love, has anyone ever told you how sexy the gold streaks in your eyes are? Do you have any idea how badly I hate your ex-wife for what she did to you?* "Bradshaw, you're filet mignon and champagne. I'm barbecue and iced tea."

"So? We'll meet in the middle. Learn to appreciate each other's tastes." He stood up to glower down at her. "So what's it going to be? A church with a minister, or a justice of the peace at the courthouse?"

Groaning, Jill got to her feet. "Bradshaw, you're a real pitbull when you want to be." Unable to help herself, she lovingly smoothed back his rumpled hair, secretly reveling in its wavy softness. Love for him overwhelmed her. "Meeting in the middle is something couples do before they shell out money for a license. Afterward is a recipe for disaster."

He opened and closed his mouth several times, but no sound came out. Jill settled back into the cushions and watched him slowly get to his feet and pace the confines of the small room.

"Jill, what's wrong with wanting a traditional family?" His expression became tortured.

Inwardly, she wept for both of them. "Nothing," she whispered. "It's what I've always wanted. But people don't create a baby first, then get married, then get to know each other. Our problems are bad enough. Please don't make them worse."

"There must be some way I can convince you." Clawing determination gave his baritone a raspy quality that only emphasized their mutual pain.

Time to end this before they wound up more shredded than they already were. "How do you feel about your ex-wife?"

Defensive irritation flashed in his eyes. Then his brows furrowed. "What does Karen have to do with—?"

"Plenty if you still love her."

Every muscle in his body knotted. "I don't."

Jill gave him a hard stare. "Can you look me in the eyes and say one day you could love again—that it could be me?"

He turned away from her. "You can't have this baby alone."

You'll give me mountain bikes and line dancing, but your mangled heart isn't on the negotiating table. "Women do it all the time. Sure, it's not real pleasant, but so what? It's been a long time since anyone lived in the Garden of Eden.''

Mason paced some more, coming to a stop at the dinette table and scowling at her half of the breakfast that she hadn't been able to choke down. Slowly, he turned to her. Never before had she seen such purpose on a man's face. His eyes glowed with it.

"Jill, do you have any of that line dance music? After you eat your muffin, you can give me my first lesson. Then tonight, we're going out for a barbecue dinner.''

"Oh, Mason," she moaned. "I'm not up to this right now. Besides, I have to be at work in an hour—someplace you should be, too, by the way.''

Compassion softened the determined set to his face. "I'm sorry. I don't like rushing you, particularly after yesterday, but—'' He gave her stomach a wary glance. "—I want this settled before the baby's born. There's not much time.''

He'd bend, but only so far. The last three months had been lonely but peaceful, and she'd enjoyed her pregnancy. Now she would have to carry the burden of continually telling the man she loved "no" exactly as she'd feared. "You plan to be in my face every day, making my life the proverbial hell on earth, don't you?''

"If that's what it takes," he whispered.

"Doesn't it bother you that I love you and you don't love me in return?''

His skin flushed with embarrassed discomfort. That gave her all the answer she really needed, but she pushed for more anyway. "I've got to get it through your head that you'd be setting us up for an outrageous amount of misery.''

"That's my baby, and I intend to be a father to it.''

"You can do that without marriage.'' Even before she finished her sentence he began shaking his head. She doubted he even saw her at this point. Hunching her shoulders in resignation, she said, "Bradshaw, it's going to be a long day.'' With every cell in her body, she knew it was only the first of many.

Jill pulled into her usual parking spot at Casey's, about the only thing normal so far that morning. Her heart of hearts wanted nothing more than to be with Mason, but loving him in absentia these past three months had been far less painful than the constant ''look but don't touch'' she'd endured at the paper.

Then, after politely but firmly kicking him out of her apartment, she had to face going back into the same building, the same office, where she'd been robbed and taken hostage the day before. The skin along her arms crawled as she pulled open the door. That made her mad. ''No two-bit, brain-dead, lazy jerk who can't work for his money like everybody else is going to ruin a perfectly nice job!''

She stormed inside. The furniture displays hadn't changed since Wednesday. The room groupings hadn't become havens for ghosts and panic attacks. Muttering under her breath, she made her way to the break room for her daily half cup of decaf that the doctor allowed. Two of the salesmen and the warehouse manager were huddled over real coffee. Jill inhaled deeply. Her tastebuds whimpered.

''Is everyone okay?'' she asked.

They looked up, expressions grim. ''From the calls coming in on the back line, we may be the only ones showing up today.''

''You're kidding.''

''No, and did you hear about Mr. C.?''

Jill shook her head.

''He had a mild heart attack last night. Mrs. C. is staying at the hospital with him until he's released. Supposed to be today.''

''Then he'll be all right?'' Jill liked the new people she worked with. The Caseys were sort of like working for adopted grandparents. Rather than get upset that she hadn't told them up front that she had a baby on the way, they assured her that her job would be waiting for her when she returned. Then they offered to sell her their top-of-the-line baby furniture collection at cost.

Frank shrugged. "I have a bad feeling about all of this."

"Why?"

"Not sure. This place *feels* different this morning. Like it's never going to be the same again."

Jill had enough on her mind without borrowing trouble. "You've just got the creepy crawlies, Frank. For myself, I only woke up in a cold sweat once last night. Personally, I'm taking that as a good sign." Then she eyed the plate of sweet rolls on the table and sat down. "Oooh, cinnamon raisin. I've been very good, and what my obstetrician doesn't know won't get me fussed at."

Her tastebuds accepted the peace offering with joyful abandon, and she relished each morsel.

By noon, half the employees had either quit or were taking unpaid leaves of absence. Customers stayed away in droves. The only thing the store had in large numbers were curiosity seekers. Armed robberies weren't supposed to happen in small towns like Stafford, Washington. Hadn't someone discovered a law of physics to that effect?

With Jill at his side still looking skeptical, Mason opened The North Forty Club's door to the driving beat of something that sounded like a cross between rock and country. Even on the best of days, neither did much for him. His gaze swept the western-garbed, Saturday night crowd. Red-and-white gingham tablecloths covered rough-hewn tables. Cocktail waitresses balanced huge trays of beer as they squeezed past standing patrons. Good Lord, they'd even marked off the dance floor with split rail fencing and *real* bales of hay!

Jill fit right in with her blue, western-style dress, its flared skirt swirling around the tops of tan boots. Mason's dove-gray suit and striped silk tie couldn't have made him more conspicuous if someone had funded a study. The sideways looks flashed in his direction by the other denizens of this distasteful place only confirmed it. But the rapturous contentment in Jill's eyes gave him the incentive he needed to keep from grimacing.

Against a far wall, he noticed a group of seven or eight people crowded around a table meant for half that number. One man noticed him. With sinking realization, Mason recognized Bobby Creamer.

Bobby's eyes widened fractionally, and he bent to the other *Stafford Review-Journal* reporters and their assorted spouses. They all turned to get their own eyeful. Speculation spread openly on their faces. He assumed they knew about Jill's pregnancy from the story Bobby did, as well as from TV coverage of her rescue. But her being with Mason tonight fueled questions he'd just as soon not address until he had the situation more under control. Jill smiled and waved at them.

Mason squared his shoulders. This wasn't how he'd have preferred to make the announcement.

"Get used to it, Bradshaw."

"What do you mean?"

She turned and gave him an acid smile. "If you marry me, that means we'll be seen together a lot."

That made no sense to him at all. "Why wouldn't we?"

"Come on, Bradshaw. You can't tell me you're not squirming in your immaculately tailored suit at being here with little ol' plebeian me."

He didn't appreciate the deliberate goad. "Don't tell me what I do or don't want, Jill."

"Then let's go say hello."

Before he had the chance to protest, she headed toward the group. With a deep sigh, Mason tagged along behind.

"Hi, guys," she chirped.

Everyone smiled, casting glances at Mason then Jill. No one made a pretext of trying to hide their curiosity.

"How are you feeling?" Helen asked her. "I don't know

that I would have handled that robbery with the poise you did.''

Jill shrugged. Mason wondered if anyone other than himself had noticed how strained the gesture looked. ''I'm fine. Had a few nightmares the past couple of nights, but I understand that's normal. I'm dealing with them one mare at a time. The real test came Thursday when I had to walk back into that place. Supposedly, that's the worst part, and I passed with flying colors.''

''You didn't tell me you had nightmares,'' Mason interjected.

''Sorry,'' she tossed over her shoulder. ''I didn't think to tell you.'' Then she turned back to the group. ''Bradshaw was there for the big rescue. He's been my Lord High Protector ever since.''

The way she handled his presence surprised him. She could have exposed their personal problems to his employees and embarrassed the hell out of him. Why had she downplayed his involvement in her life?

''That's good...that you have someone,'' Bobby ventured. Questions gleamed in his eyes, but basic manners kept them unasked.

''I didn't know you had a baby on the way,'' his wife said. Mason could have sworn that the other seven people's ears grew as they waited for her reply.

''Yep.'' Jill grinned. ''Things are going great. I hated to leave the paper, but I make enough at Casey's to pay for child care.''

This whole conversation made him squirm. His and Jill's baby and their private lives were none of anyone else's business. He sat on the urge to grab Jill by the arm and steer her to the one free table, which just happened to be on the far side of the room.

''Boy, is that important!'' laughed Bobby's wife. ''Are you...okay?''

Mason was sure she really meant ''married.'' Discreetly, he clenched his jaw. Then he took Jill's arm. ''I'm sorry, but she's been on her feet all day—'' teaching me to line dance ''— and I think she needs to sit down for a while.''

Jill shot an amused look at him. She knew exactly how badly he wanted to get away from these people. "Sounds like a plan."

"See you all on Monday." He turned Jill around and guided her through the tightly packed crowd. "Why were you covering for me?"

Batting her eyes at him in feigned southern charm, she asked, "Now, sir, whatever do you mean?"

"Knock it off, and answer the question."

She slid into her seat and sighed. "Bradshaw, as agitated as you've been the past three days, if I'd spread out our personal business for public consumption, you would've had a coronary. I'm pregnant, not insensitive."

That should have made him feel better, but it made him irrationally angry instead. Anything he said at this point would only give her more ammunition, so he flagged down the waitress. "The lady will have a fruit juice, and I'll have a beer since it seems to be the drink of choice around here."

Jill snorted. "What are you doing? You hate beer."

He blinked. "How do you know that?"

"Ben tried to hand you one at the picnic last summer. When you declined, you covered your shudder of distaste pretty well, but I still noticed. Your rare indulgences are confined to wine—preferably ones you've had the fun of aging yourself—and the occasional bourbon."

"How do you…. *Why* do you remember all that?" The waitress chuckled at the byplay, and he wanted to snap at her.

"Women in love remember all sorts of trivia. It's what we're good at." She and the waitress shared a grin. "I'll have my orange juice on the rocks, and Mr. Fastidious here will have your house wine."

The woman looked at him for confirmation, pencil poised. He nodded. With a smile, she moved to the next table, leaving them alone. Learning that Jill knew that much about him made him feel extraordinarily exposed. Again deciding silence might be the better part of valor, he listened to the words of the song blasting through the speakers. Another mistake.

He bent to her ear. "Jill, are they really saying 'boot scootin' boogie'?" He sounded aghast.

"Yep. It's been one of my favorite songs for years. My CD bit the dust or you'd have heard it this afternoon." Her expression turned challenging. "Just remember, Bradshaw. No one forced you to be here."

Swallowing his exasperation and annoyance took an inordinate amount of willpower. Jill tucked a blond curl behind her ear, then let herself move to the rhythm. His attention riveted on the complex moves being executed by the dancers. Two dozen booted heels suddenly connected hard with the wooden floor. The room vibrated from the impact.

"You like this?" he asked, managing to sound enthralled and repelled at the same time.

"What's the matter, Bradshaw?" she teased, leaning close so he could hear above the canned music. "Forget the wolfbane?"

"What do you mean?" he asked suspiciously.

"From the look on your face, you'd feel more comfortable if you'd brought a couple of wooden crosses or silver bullets to ward off evil." Her eyes sparkled as she attempted to stifle more laughter. Shaking her head again, she slipped onto the dance floor and stepped into the flawless kick-turns and twists that line dancing made famous. Pregnant, her steps lacked the precision of some of the other dancers, but she looked good. Actually, with her generous bulge in front, she looked incredibly sexy.

He'd never known he found pregnant women a turn on, at least not until Jill had baldly pointed out the possibility. Maybe it was just her. Maybe he was just nuts.

The song ended, immediately followed by another with

an entirely different rhythm. The razor-straight lines broke up. Couples formed and whirled around the room. Jill sat down beside him, breathless, eyes glowing.

"See? It's a lot more fun with a bunch of people."

He tried to smile convincingly, but to his aggravation, she chortled at him. Anger flared, and he clenched his jaw. He would play this out one day at a time for now, but one thing he knew: no amount of hideous music would keep him from being a full-time father to his child.

Just the thought of the life growing safely beneath Jill's heart brought a lump to his throat. He'd lay down his life for that baby. He wanted to wake up Saturday mornings to a little body jumping on the bed and falling into his arms. He wanted to rub his beard-stubbled chin into a warm neck just to listen to a happy squeal. He wanted Little League games and dance recitals. In short, he wanted to be a dad.

His own parents had tolerated his presence only if they couldn't avoid it. He'd enrolled in college before he realized their lack of interest had nothing to do with him. Self-absorption and coldness had simply been their way. No child of his would ever go through that kind of emotional neglect.

With unwavering determination, he turned his attention back to the dancers. "What do you call what they're doing now?"

"The Texas Two-step." She smiled enviously at the couples.

"There really is such a thing? I thought that was a joke."

She smiled. "Like I said, Bradshaw. No one forced you to be here."

"If you'll put as much energy into our marriage plans as you do putting me off, our future will be a lot less complicated."

A slower romantic ballad began, and the couples settled into more of a freestyle dance. The steel guitar's whine still offended his ears, but at least he could handle this particular melody. Ignoring Jill's unconvinced smirk, he led her onto the floor. With the guilt he'd been carrying around over sleeping with her, he'd forgotten how perfect she felt in his arms. But unlike the night she'd spent in his bed, her stomach now pressed low against his belly.

Mine. The whole concept of fathering a child—and all its sexual implications—slammed with stunning force into some dark, primitive corner of his brain. Without warning, his body reacted. Only with effort did he shake off the wild, erotic thoughts.

The rest of the situation's various truths hit Mason equally hard. He was in a bar that played music he hated, dancing with a woman he didn't really know, and—as bizarre as it seemed, he desperately needed to convince her to marry him.

Marriage. The thought repelled him almost as much as the music—and that took some doing. Jill had always intrigued him, but he couldn't tell whether his reservations were because of her resemblance to Karen and the reminders it carried, or whether he just wanted nothing to do with *anyone.* And that completely unnerved him.

Then again, there was the baby. Before emotions and personal preferences got the better of him, he crushed the debate under the iron resolve to shoulder his responsibilities.

Two hours later, the evening mercifully ended, and he drove Jill home.

"You know, Bradshaw, we could always live together," she announced suddenly as he parked the car.

He gripped the wheel a little too tightly. "We could jump off a cliff too, but I'd rather not."

"Why?"

The barely disguised challenge in her voice made him suspect she had thrown out the idea as a point of argument, not because she regarded it as an option. Either way, it thoroughly annoyed him. "Why? Because I'm a dinosaur, one of those throwbacks who believes in hearth and home and—"

"Divorce and child support."

"Having parents with the same last name gives a child a stronger sense of identity and—"

"Right, Bradshaw. She gets to be the product of a broken home."

"The stability of a live-in relationship is an illusion, Jill. People who live together often subconsciously work harder to compensate for an inherent weakness, but it doesn't stop them from breaking up. In the long run, it often causes more misery, especially when children are involved."

"Oooh, psychology. I'm impressed."

He scowled at her. "Stop it."

Jill leaned back in the seat and closed her eyes, apparently weighed down by mental and emotional fatigue. A new guilt pricked him. He'd been so focused on his own perspective that he hadn't given much thought to hers. Still, he couldn't let her relegate him to the status of outsider.

"I know you're serious, Mason," she sighed. "That's what scares me."

He ground his teeth. "Our baby didn't ask to be conceived, but it deserves the right to have two, loving, full-time parents."

Her breath eased out in a heavy sigh. "Bradshaw, I have no doubts you'll make a great dad. I just don't believe you want me as your partner in life."

"That's not true," he lied. Inwardly, he knew he didn't have any more chance of convincing himself than he did her, but he had to find a way to do both.

Settling back, Jill stared at the sunroof. "You never answered when I asked if you could love again."

Brutally, Mason wondered if fate had condemned him to be one of those fools who loved only once, even when it had been the worst mistake of his life. Or, as the old saying went, would time heal? God, he wished he knew.

He yanked the car keys from the ignition. Attempting to analyze emotions he'd never really been comfortable with while proposing marriage was rough on a man's sense of order. He liked Jill, liked her quick wit and envied her openness. And he had to admit, her body—particularly pregnant—made him ache. In fact, he found her attractive on many levels. All but his in his heart, he acknowledged sadly, and not for the first time. "Karen's in my past."

Sad, disbelieving laughter rippled from Jill's throat. "Bradshaw, what am I going to do with you?"

"Marry me. Give our child a proper home."

Her expression softened, and she gently kissed his cheek. "Her home will be much more stable if she never loses something she never has to begin with."

"I'm going to be a big part of her life, Jill." Then he picked up on something. "Her?"

She nodded. "Ultrasound."

A decidedly silly-feeling grin crept onto his face. "A daughter," he sighed, mentally adjusting to the sure knowledge of his baby's gender. *Definitely dance recitals. Or maybe Little League, too.* The possibilities were infinite. Then he realized how neatly he'd been sidetracked. "Jill, we can build a good relationship. What we'd be starting off with can be more important than love. Respect. We can build from there."

She winced. "Thanks, but no thanks. I'm allergic to situations where I'm likely to get creamed. Don't worry about my feelings, Bradshaw. I'm an old hand at loving people who don't love me back. It stinks, but I'm used to it." She unlocked her age-scarred front door and stepped inside. "Good night, Bradshaw. It's been memorable." The door shut with a soft click.

Mason stared at the tarnished knocker. Her words over the course of the day played through his mind. Then it hit him. Jill had loved him the night after his divorce had gone to court. She hadn't arrived at his apartment just to commiserate with a fellow divorce veteran. Whether she'd realized it or not, she'd come to comfort the man she loved.

Disgust at himself filled up what little space anger didn't already occupy. If he hadn't been so self-absorbed back then, he'd have seen it, and he'd never have wound up in bed with her. They wouldn't be going through all this.

Then again, he wouldn't have a daughter about to be born, either. "Be careful what you wish for," he murmured, heading back to his car. "Getting it can be murder."

Chapter 7

"You have tickets for the what?"

Apparently, it was Jill's turn to look as if she'd forgotten the wolfbane. The small victory made Mason feel better. "The symphony. No steel guitars, no cowboy hats, no boots."

"I know what one is," she snapped. "The question is 'why'?"

Patience in emotional situations wasn't one of his strong points, but he'd had lots of practice lately. "Why do you think?"

"Common interests?" she asked, her huge brown eyes taking on the air of a condemned prisoner.

He crossed his arms and smiled. "During the last two weeks, I've listened to more country music than I ever knew existed. You've dragged me to every hoedown, shindig and—"

"I have not. Those were my normal activities. It's not my fault you're into masochism. Which reminds me. My idea of a fun evening is not sitting in a dark theater listening to funeral music.''

''Funeral music?'' He blinked.

''That's what that stuff sounds like to me.''

Delighted laughter bubbled up from deep in his chest. ''Only you would come up with an analogy like that.''

She gave him a mock scowl. ''I'm so glad you're amused.''

''The concert is tomorrow night at the college. I'll pick you up at six, and we'll have dinner first.''

Her face fell, and she fidgeted. ''Bradshaw, I'm sorry, but I really don't want to go.''

''I know, but you will.''

''Why is that?''

''I've learned a lot about you lately. Tonight, you'll gripe and complain like a spoiled teenager, but your inherent sense of fair play will ensure you're ready when I pick you up. Then you'll do everything you can to make sure it's an enjoyable evening for both of us—even if it kills you.''

Her mouth sagged open. Mason felt guiltily pleased. He rather enjoyed having someone other than himself opened up for public view.

She squared her shoulders. ''Bradshaw, I know exactly how much you draw for a salary. You can't afford to wine and dine me like this. So why don't you get a refund on those tickets and leave me alone tomorrow night?''

He didn't know where the idea to take her hands and kiss her cheek came from, but it tempted him. Maybe it had to do with missing her whirlwind, take-life-by-the-horns attitude. He leaned to her and brushed his lips across her cheek. She'd lightly perfumed her skin with something reminiscent of vanilla, and her distended belly pressed low against his midsection. The sensations they evoked combined into a heady mix.

What bothered him was that he felt so detached from it, as if he were watching it happen to someone else. Could she be right? Was he one of those who would never be able to put the past behind him? Would he be able to fall in love again? If so, could she be the one? Maybe if he didn't see Karen every time he looked at her, the whole disaster might not be so complicated.

He kissed her again, on the lips this time. She held absolutely still. He doubted she even breathed. Drawing her close, he kissed her properly and found the same fire he'd experienced their night together. All these months, he'd believed it had been emotions of the moment running out of control. Now, he no longer knew.

"Bradshaw, I think you'd better go," she said, trembling.

The full impact of where his thoughts had roamed slammed into him. "I think you're right."

Jill still owed about a thousand dollars on her charge card from her cruise last summer. In the overall scheme of things, the black satin gown she bought on her lunch hour didn't do too much serious damage to her long-term budget. But buying an expensive dress that she'd probably only wear once grated against her principles. Then again, she wanted to look nice for Mason—another complaint her common sense filed against her.

She hadn't been to a symphony since a high school field trip. In her opinion, classical music had been invented by the same sadist who'd come up with decaf coffee.

Suffering through one this time would be different, though. Mason loved classical music, and he wanted to share it with her. After she dressed, she sank down onto the edge of the bed. "You are setting yourself up for so much hurt." She buried her head in her hands. "Why can't your 'no' mean 'no?' Why can't you tell him to take a hike, then send him a birth announcement when the time comes?"

As always when she heard Mason's knock at the door, her heart leapt into her throat and beat with a slow, heavy thud. She loved him. Nothing would change that. He didn't feel the same. Nothing would change that either. "Jill, ol' girl, that man's not the only one with masochistic tendencies." With a groan of acceptance and a snappy retort poised on her lips, she opened the door.

Mason stood on her porch in a tuxedo, complete with starched white shirt and shoes with a shine so bright he could have shaved in the reflection.

"You look beautiful, Jill."

"I feel like a kid playing dress up," she said, nevertheless warmed by his compliment.

He snorted, then brushed past her into her apartment. She couldn't stop staring. She'd always suspected he'd come from money by the way he carried himself. The tux emphasized the possibility and how different their backgrounds were.

"Is that yours, Bradshaw?" she observed, only half aware that she'd spoken out loud. "That's too perfect a fit for a rental place."

He made a nonverbal noise of affirmation in his throat. "Does that bother you?"

"I've never known anyone who owned his own tuxedo before."

"That I can believe."

"What did you mean by that crack?" she snapped, bristling.

His expression tightened as if he'd just realized what he'd said could be taken two ways. "Your friends and hangouts show off denim like a badge of honor. I'm not used to jeans anymore than you're used to symphonies and black tie dinners."

"Which is why we're doing this thing tonight. Right?"

"Very good." His lips pursed. "Are you willing to admit defeat and marry me now?"

"No."

His shoulders rose and fell in a compressed sigh. "We've been at this for weeks. The baby is due in one month. I want this settled and both of us in a comfortable routine before she's born. Afterward, when she's awake half the night—as I understand most newborns are—it could be a more stressful time to try and build a marriage."

"Bradshaw, this isn't a financial merger with a timetable. We're talking about our lives here."

Some of his aggressive determination drained away. "I know, Jill. Please, meet me halfway. We might just make it."

She took in his tuxedo again, seeing represented there a lifetime of experiences that she knew nothing about. Maybe if she didn't love him so much, she could push him away and make it stick. "Lead on, Bradshaw. Maybe I'll do something tonight that will so repulse you that you'll be glad I refused your proposal."

"I doubt that," he said, helping her with her coat.

From the corner of his vision, Mason had watched Jill's face. At first, she actually seemed to be enjoying herself. The visiting orchestra had played an exceptional rendition of Rimsky-Korsakov's *Scheherazade*. The program explained the stories represented in the emotionally charged symphony, and he caught her smiling more than once.

The small step forward had given him cause for hope. If they could build a stable foundation of common interests and open communication, maybe they had a chance. He realized how many times he'd said those words to himself and how badly he needed to believe them.

But now he looked at Jill, who'd fallen asleep after the last intermission. Without waking her, he'd pulled her against his shoulder where she'd slept peacefully for the rest of the performance. In all fairness, a woman eight months pregnant and who'd put in a full day at work had a right to be exhausted. Even knowing that, he still found it a little discouraging.

Their constant confrontations had long since become an unbearable weight, and she had to be tired of them too, but as long as their child needed him, he'd never give up.

"Wake up, Jill," he whispered as the last note echoed into silence. "It's time to go."

The lights came up, and she forced her eyes open. A mortified blush stained her cheeks. "I didn't. Did I?"

He chuckled. People around them noticed her sleepy face, and the exaggerated way she blinked.

"How sweet," observed one elderly woman, smiling at Jill's belly. Then she looked at Mason. "When is your wife due?"

Jill straightened up with frozen humiliation, her jaw quivering as if suppressing a yawn.

"One month."

"Won't be long now," chimed in another lady. "Is this your first?"

"Yes, thank you," Jill said, tense. Embarrassment slipped into anger, and Mason helped her to her feet.

"They're just trying to be polite," he whispered in her ear.

"I know that," she snapped.

The friendly smiles became fixed. Jill scanned the group from beneath her lashes. "Sorry. I've been awfully irritable and moody lately."

Expressions turned understanding, but no one lingered.

On the way to the car, she apologized again. "I didn't mean to create a scene."

"It was my fault, really." He unlocked her door. "I should have waited to take you to one of these on a week-end when you wouldn't be so tired."

Inside, she seethed. "Do you know how aggravating you are? Ever since you found out about the baby, you've turned into this good-natured juggernaut who's determined to drag me to the altar. I am sick of it. I want a knock-down, let it all hang out, screaming fight."

He glanced at her stomach. In the last few weeks, she had gone from large to huge. To his untrained eye, she looked like she'd have that baby in the parking lot. "Marry me. Then you can scream at me about anything you want. If it makes you happy, I'll argue back."

For a moment, she thought she might go for his throat. Instead, she plopped into the passenger seat of his Buick, and he shut the door.

The next morning, Jill had her regularly scheduled obstetrics appointment. Mason always called her at lunch to find out what the doctor said, but a co-worker said she took the afternoon off—very unlike her. When he called her apartment, he got her machine. He left a message, then tried again in fifteen minutes. That turned into a routine that lasted three hours.

At four o'clock, he pulled on his coat and headed out through the reception area. "Vicki, I'm out for the rest of the day. If Jill calls, tell her I'm on my way to her place."

"You sound upset." Vicki got to her feet. "Is she all right?"

"That's what I'm trying to find out. The only thing I can think of is that she went shopping, but she still wouldn't be gone this long. Nor would she have taken time off from work."

"The baby's not due yet." The pinched worry on Vicki's face matched the knot in his gut.

"I know." He separated his car key from the others on his ring. "If she's having our daughter alone, I'll strangle her."

"Tell her I gave you permission," she fired back as the door closed behind him.

Jill's canary-yellow Volkswagen sat in its usual space in the parking lot in front of her apartment. When she didn't answer at Mason's second knock, he tried to convince himself she might be in the shower, but his instincts didn't buy it.

He tried the knob; it wasn't locked.

"Jill?" He stuck his head inside and found her sitting at the table in what passed for the dining room, her back to him, elbows propped and forehead resting in her hands. Even when he shut the door behind him, she didn't turn around. "Jill, are you all right?"

"No. I'm pregnant. I feel like a hippo with a thyroid condition, and I'm not very good company." The defiance didn't completely mask the tremor in her voice. "I'll call you later."

"Knowing you, I'll wait a long time before you ever pick up a phone." His frustration came through unmistakably clear in the harsh edge to his voice. "You've been crying." He took long strides across the room.

"No kidding, Sherlock," she muttered, her back still to him. "Go home."

"Are you in labor?"

Rounding the table to see her face, he found what he expected, tearstained cheeks and swollen eyes. Something deep inside turned over, and he pulled her into his arms. He didn't think about it first—he just did it. Maybe he felt more for her than he'd realized. Given the worry that had eaten at him on the drive over here, he found the possibility promising.

She glanced up at him through moisture-spiked lashes. "Why would you think I'm in labor?"

"Never mind." He waved her off. "What happened? Why are you in tears?"

"It's nothing."

Anger ignited in the pit of his stomach, and he gripped her arms, pushing her away from him just far enough to glare down into her reddened eyes. She wanted a fight. Fine. He'd give her one. "Do all women play this game? When something's obviously wrong, they say there's nothing. Yet they expect the poor unsuspecting male to be a mind reader. If he doesn't figure things out, he's in trouble forever." With monumental effort, Mason sat on his temper. "I don't know many men who handle that real well, Jill."

Defensive amusement lit her face and tugged a smile from her puffy lips. "Did you know you're kinda cute when you go ballistic?"

"Hurray," he muttered drily. "Tell me what's wrong, or we'll be at this a very long time."

Her brief foray into humor faded, and a trembling sigh shuddered from the depths of her soul. "Thanks, but the only thing wrong with me is a monumental case of humiliation."

"Over what?" He knew his mouth gaped open, but he couldn't do anything to stop it.

"I fell asleep on you last night. After my comment about doing something to repulse you, I'm having a hard time with it." She wouldn't look at him.

"You must be kidding."

She stepped away and poured a glass of water. Her hand shook.

"Jill, you needed to rest last night, not traipse around a college campus."

She shrugged and finished her drink.

Then it hit him. "You're telling the truth. Just not all of it."

Even through the generous cut to her maternity smock, he saw the muscles across her back tense. He turned her around and tilted her chin up. Keeping her eyes lowered, she jerked away.

"I'd like a little privacy, Bradshaw. Having you living in my back pocket for the last month hasn't exactly been a piece of cake. Go home."

"I'll be happy to," he conceded, "just as soon as you tell me what upset you this badly."

"I'm pregnant!" she snapped. "I have crying binges. Is that so hard to believe?"

"No, but—"

"I hate it, but it's one of the joys of life in the fat lane."

He tried to read in her face some clue as to what was going on here, but she wouldn't look at him. "Jill, carrying a baby isn't the same as being fat."

After taking a moment to apparently absorb what he'd said, she muttered, "You've got strange fetishes, Bradshaw."

He saw no point in arguing with her, so he watched her pace around her apartment. She opened the refrigerator, studied the contents, slammed the door, then wandered to the living room. Her movements were jerky and agitated, not at all like a woman having a simple crying binge. Worse, whatever bothered her seemed to have taken over completely. He wondered if she remembered she wasn't alone.

"Are you ready to tell me the rest of it?" he asked, sitting down.

Startled, her attention snapped to him. "Go home, Bradshaw. This is something I have to figure out on my own."

Well, that confirmed his suspicions. Controlling his anger suddenly became a lot harder. "Damn it, Jill. You won't even try to depend on me. Not even a little. This is my baby, too. It's not fair that you're calling all the shots."

"You're not the one whose body is occupied for the duration!"

Mason crossed his arms. "If I could take it from here, I would. Unfortunately, God didn't set things up that way."

She stared at him, her eyes huge. "You'd take over? Why?"

His emotionally charged outburst had come so unexpectedly that he hadn't had a chance to think about the words before they tumbled from his lips. A flush of embarrassment crept up his neck, and he shrugged. "Fathers are sort of on the outside looking in at this stage. I don't know exactly what you're going through. I wish I did."

Her expression turned wondering and infinitely tender, the look of a woman passionately in love.

Despite himself, Mason stiffened. Not only had he embarrassed himself, he'd inadvertently set himself up to look better in her eyes. He didn't want her—or anyone else—to love him, at least not now—not until he'd finished healing and could figure out what he might be able to feel in the future. Why couldn't they be on equal footing!

What a mess. He nearly groaned aloud under the weight of it. Deliberately, he leaned forward and projected a body language that said he wasn't going anywhere.

"Bradshaw, you never give up, do you?"

"When our daughter's grown, I'll think about it." He dragged in a long, slow breath. "Now, for the last time, what's wrong?"

Defeated, Jill's head slumped, and she looked down at him through impossibly long lashes. Then she slid into the other chair. "Just remember, I solve my own problems."

His instinctive reply wouldn't be one she'd accept, so he glared at her in silence.

"The Caseys are closing down the store. Mr. C. has to retire because of his heart. Mrs. C. has tried to come back to work, but she can't make herself get past the sidewalk." Jill looked at him, then. "*I'm* the one who had a gun pointed at her head. *I'm* the one with a right to be a basket case."

"Not everyone is as strong as you are," he said gently. "The Caseys are also almost eighty. Maybe the robbery was the last straw."

"And of course that explains why half the employees have quit or taken time off."

"That's not all that's bothering you."

She stared at him. "You don't get it, do you?"

"Apparently not."

"They are shutting the store down *now*. Their kids are flying in to take over the books and oversee the disposition of the inventory. Everyone except Frank, the warehouse manager, is out of a job on Monday." She stood up and turned sideways, giving him a perfect view of her stomach.

"Care to explain how I'll find a new job when I look like this?"

More truths settled on him. "How about unemployment benefits?"

She dropped her head in her hands. "I already checked. It'll barely cover rent. What about food? Or the hospital bill and clothes for the baby? I can't even finish paying for the crib now. And nobody will hire a woman with a new-born."

Mason's patience snapped. This nonsense had gone on long enough. Playing hardball wasn't any more his style than were one-night stands, but with Jill's and their baby's security at stake, personal ethics became irrelevant. The only remaining question was whether he could maneuver her into a very tight corner without her catching on.

"Well, if you'd marry me, we wouldn't have a problem, but—"

She opened her mouth to protest, and he held out a hand in a bear-with-me gesture.

"Unfortunately, you won't. Too bad, because I have a two-bedroom apartment. Lots of room." He took a deep breath. "So the next best thing I can do is take out a loan to cover your living expenses until—"

Her head whipped up. "Bradshaw, are you nuts? A mouse couldn't live on what you call a salary! You've thrown every scroungeable dime into that newspaper. There can't be anything left over to make loan payments."

"All the hard work is beginning to pay off," he countered. "Subscriptions are coming up."

Jill snorted. "Slowly."

"Eventually, I'll make a good living with the *Journal*."

"Not for several years yet. Certainly not soon enough to pay the bills on two separate households."

He allowed himself to be persuaded. "True."

A tight, I-knew-it expression settled over her features.

"Jill, how else are we going to survive this?" He scratched his head in a calculatingly thoughtful gesture.

PLAY "LUCKY 7" AND GET
THREE FREE GIFTS!

HOW TO PLAY:

1. With a coin, carefully scratch off the silver box at the right. Then check the claim chart to see what we have for you — **FREE BOOKS** and a gift — **ALL YOURS! ALL FREE!**

2. Send back this card and you'll receive brand-new Silhouette Intimate Moments® novels. These books have a cover price of $4.25 each, but they are yours to keep absolutely free.

3. There's no catch. You're under no obligation to buy anything. We charge nothing —  ZERO — for your first shipment. And you don't have to make any minimum number of purchases — not even one!

4. The fact is thousands of readers enjoy receiving books by mail from the Silhouette Reader Service™ months before they're available in stores. They like the convenience of home delivery and they love our discount prices!

5. We hope that after receiving your free books you'll want to remain a subscriber. But the choice is yours — to continue or cancel, any time at all! So why not take us up on our invitation, with no risk of any kind. You'll be glad you did!

YOURS FREE!

PLAY LUCKY 7 FOR THIS EXCITING FREE GIFT!

THIS SURPRISE MYSTERY GIFT COULD BE YOURS FREE WHEN YOU PLAY

LUCKY 7!

NO COST! NO OBLIGATION TO BUY!
NO PURCHASE NECESSARY!

PLAY THE

LUCKY 7 SLOT MACHINE GAME!

Just scratch off the silver box with a coin. Then check below to see the gifts you get!

YES!

I have scratched off the silver box. Please send me all the gifts for which I qualify. I understand I am under no obligation to purchase any books, as explained on the back and on the opposite page.

245 SDL CH5M
(U-SIL-IM-07/98)

Name
_____
PLEASE PRINT CLEARLY

Address _____ Apt.# _____

City _____ State _____ Zip _____

WORTH TWO FREE BOOKS
PLUS A BONUS MYSTERY GIFT!

WORTH TWO FREE BOOKS!

WORTH ONE FREE BOOK!

TRY AGAIN!

The Silhouette Reader Service™ — Here's how it works

Accepting free books places you under no obligation to buy anything. You may keep the books and gift and return the shipping statement marked "cancel." If you do not cancel, about a month later we'll send you 6 additional novels, and bill you just $3.57 each, plus 25¢ delivery per book and applicable sales tax, if any.*
That's the complete price — and compared to cover prices of $4.25 each — quite a bargain! You may cancel at any time, but if you choose to continue, every month we'll send you 6 more books, which you may either purchase at the discount price...or return to us and cancel your subscription.

*Terms and prices subject to change without notice. Sales tax applicable in N.Y.

"You're fine, Bradshaw. I'm the one with the cash flow problem."

He frowned at her. "Have you checked into Aid For Dependent Children?" he asked smoothly. Her horrified gasp gave him no pleasure. Her big brown eyes took on the bewildered terror of a trapped deer. "Maybe they have some kind of special handout." Even as a ploy, suggesting that welfare support any child of his revolted him.

Her breathing became alarmingly labored and irregular. "Mason, what am I going to do? I can't handle being on the public trough."

"It doesn't have to be a life sentence. Besides, that's what it's there for." He crossed his arms. "Since it may take a while to process the paperwork, I'd better take you to the county offices on Monday. No sense risking any delays."

She launched out of her chair and started pacing.

"Also," he continued blandly, "while we're there, we can establish up front that I'm the father, and they can begin steps to sue me for child support—or however they handle that sort of thing."

Jill whirled on him and took a step backward as if repelled by the entire notion. "You can't afford child support."

Another minute and he'd have her where he wanted her—he hoped. "I'm open to suggestions. You can't pay your own rent, and I can't pay it for you."

Inner turmoil tightened as she apparently ran through the well-worn paths of unworkable options. Defeated eyes looked up at him. "Did you say your apartment has two bedrooms?"

"What about it?"

"I hate to ask, but what about me camping out in your extra room? Not permanently—just until I can go back to work. That cuts out one rent."

Bingo. However reluctantly, she'd finally looked to him for help. Not exactly the course he'd hoped she'd take, but close enough. What was it about her that drove her to such independence? Probably the same as him: a lifetime of ingrained necessity. Slowly, he rose to his feet, deliberately towering above her, then dropped his hands onto his hips.

"Jill, you're the mother of my child. I will support you, care for you, see to all your needs." When she closed her eyes in abject relief and swallowed, his resolve to drop the bomb faltered. Glancing at her burgeoning stomach, he pushed onward. "But only if you're my wife."

Her eyes snapped open, her expression one of betrayed accusation. "How many times must I say this? I won't marry you!"

"Marriage or the public trough. Take your pick."

She sucked in her breath and blistered him with a glare. "Why does it have to be your way or nothing?"

"I told you," he said softly. "I'm a dinosaur. Living together is against who I am."

"Well, a farce marriage doesn't cut it either, Bradshaw."

"I'm sorry you feel that way."

"Not sorry enough to bend."

"True." He gave her a stony look. "By the way, it won't be a farce."

She returned the look.

"Jill, the only decision you need to make is whether we get married the same day we get the license or the first weekend afterward."

"Neither."

"Okay, I'll have Vicki clear my schedule for Monday morning, and we'll talk to the welfare people. How does nine o'clock sound?"

The defeated slump to her shoulders didn't make him feel particularly proud of himself, but he tried not to think about it. Only the end result mattered.

"You're despicable, Bradshaw."

Mason held motionless, allowing none of his own turmoil to show.

"Are you really going to stand up in a church and promise to love, honor and cherish?" she demanded.

"That's what I said, isn't it?"

"You're gonna lie to a minister?"

He took Jill's hand. Her fingers were ice cold, but he hardened himself to her pain. Knuckling under now would do neither of them any good, not to mention the impact it would have on their daughter's life. "Shouldn't your first concern be the baby?"

Instead of firing off a frosty comeback as he expected, she stared blankly into the distance, her expression trapped and very alone. Silence spun out, and Mason's blood tingled in fearful anticipation. His child's well-being lay in her hands, and there wasn't one thing he could do to change it.

Finally, Jill drew in a ragged breath. "If I'm going to marry you, at least I won't have to buy a new dress." Even her voice sounded limp.

With the future looking satisfyingly under control—if emotionally grim—Mason savored the bitter victory as best he could. "What do you mean?"

"That thing I wore the other night is brand new. I'll wear that."

He felt his eyes widen. "You mean the black gown from the night of the symphony?"

She nodded.

"Absolutely not."

"What's wrong with it?" she demanded. "Hippo or not, I looked pretty good. You said as much at the time."

Mason drew in a calming breath. "Jill, you will not marry me while wearing black."

"What difference does it make? It's paid for. Sort of."

"This isn't a funeral, no matter how much you seem to view it as one."

"Look, Bradshaw. We're not having a grand production complete with rented limo and a catered dinner for half of Stafford."

"Agreed, but this is the last time I plan on getting married, and I'd like it to be pleasant—no undertones."

She tilted her head, mocking him. "No regrets, either? How about misgivings?"

"Stop it, Jill," he growled.

"How about no hits, no runs and no errors?" Her voice broke on the last, and he pulled her into his arms.

"It's okay to be scared," he murmured.

She didn't answer, and Mason held her as she trembled in silence. The tension across her back and in her arms told him how desperately she was trying to regroup. If he had to guess, one of the cruelest things anyone could do to Jill would be to make her feel helpless—and he'd done an award-winning job just now. After a moment's reflection, he kissed her hair in wordless apology.

She pulled away. "So, what do you expect me to get married in? My best maternity jeans? Wouldn't *that* look good with your tux!"

"Don't be ridiculous." He shook his head. "I want you to wear something bright and cheerful. How about something you bought on your cruise last summer?" He hated being the villain in this scenario, but he had to take care of her and she'd left him no other avenue.

"Oh, a bikini with a maternity panel in it. You have a sick imagination, Bradshaw."

He smiled. If she could crack jokes, then maybe she was pulling herself together a little. Then again, maybe not. "Just call it part of my fetish."

Her lips parted in a return smile, but the effort fell flat. "We can't afford another dress I'll only wear once. I just did that."

"You'll have your dress if we have to eat beans every day for the next six months."

A reluctant chuckle rolled softly from her throat. Then she interlaced her fingers with his. Tenderly, deliberately, Mason drew Jill into his arms again.

The wounds of his first marriage reared their heads in

the defensive wall that went up around his heart. He cared for Jill, cared deeply, in fact. He made no effort to deny to himself he also found her sexually appealing. But love?

The mental image of Karen crawling all over her lover seemed particularly vivid at the moment, and the concept of ever trusting another person so completely repelled him to the depths of his soul.

Chapter 8

"Shopping for a wedding gown at a maternity shop has given me a whole new standard to define depression," Jill muttered to Vicki, sliding another rejected dress down the rod. "Even so, I have to admit that the store's new selection of formal wear has turned out to be a pleasant surprise."

The gown that kept catching her eye was a floor-length, lavender satin with a lace overlay. With her creamy skin tones, she knew she'd look like a million. It would even go well with Mason's tuxedo. Unfortunately, the dress cost two weeks' salary— provided she still had one.

"You're right. There's some nice stuff here," Vicki said. "By the way, how are you and Mason doing these days?"

"He's still camped in my back pocket. I would have thought since he won, he'd give me some breathing room now, but he hasn't."

Vicki laughed. "You sound as if you lost a war and the enemy is lining you up as a prisoner for execution."

Jill mulled that over. "Couldn't have put it better myself." Then her acid humor took over. "I know! Rather than carrying a bouquet, maybe I ought to wear manacles made from concertina wire.''

"That's really sick.''

"Or how about this?'' she asked, a farcical lilt to her voice. "Instead of a flower girl tossing rose petals as she walks down the aisle, we can have her toss those little fortune cookie papers. On the backs will be the Articles of the Geneva Convention.''

Vicki closed her eyes and groaned. "You've been on your feet too long.''

Ignoring her, Jill raised her hand and swept it in a slow arc as if making a banner in the air. "The newspaper headline can read Masochistic Woman Marries Man Who Doesn't Love Her—The Sequel.''

The baby moved. Suddenly even her defensive humor stopped being funny. Tears formed in her eyes.

"Girl, I'm taking you home. You're punch drunk.''

Jill picked through the rest of the dresses in her size. "Nothing here I like. Let's go.''

"No, you don't.'' Vicki reached past her and checked the price tag on the lavender one that Jill had been silently drooling over.

She wasn't sure, but she thought her friend smothered a gag before lifting the hanger from the rod and handing her the dress.

"You've gone back to this one three times. Try it on.''

"My charge card will collapse from the weight.''

"It's *supposed* to when you put a wedding dress on it. Now get your lily-white behind into that dressing room.''

In spite of herself, Jill laughed. "Vicki, you don't understand. I just spent almost this much on a one-wear-only dress. My nervous system can't do that twice in one month.''

Scowling, Vicki inspected the lace overlay. "Wilson would love to hear me worry about how much I spend on clothes, but that man knows better.'' Vicki didn't dress extravagantly, but she did dress well. The bills couldn't be cheap.

"So, in other words, to put Mason off I should have gone through money like water since the day I met him?"

"No, that would be giving him ulcers about now, but I doubt it would have changed anything." She glanced at Jill's protruding abdomen. "Men don't think beyond the immediate when they're turned on."

"I thought you were my friend."

"I am." Vicki shoved the dress at her, forcing Jill to take a step backward to keep from touching it.

"Then why are you on Mason's side?"

"I'm not." A defiant grin split her face. "I'm just not taking sides now. I'm not keeping any more secrets, either."

"That's not the same as aiding and abetting the enemy—which you ought to be tarred and feathered for."

Vicki's expression hardened. The phrase "tough love" came to mind. "Girl, you can either try on this dress and see if it fits, or I'll tell Mason about it. He can come down here and pick it up without you. If it doesn't fit, too bad."

The two stared at each other in an affectionate battle of wills. Then Jill snatched the hanger from Vicki's fingers. "If he and I end up eating beans forever to pay for this thing, I'm going to remind you daily," she tossed over her shoulder.

"Fine with me," Vicki laughed.

A moment later, with a quick look in the dressing room mirror, Jill groaned. The lavender gave her skin a radiant glow, and the silver threads in the lace twinkled with feminine splendor. Glancing at the tag again, she grabbed the zipper. "That's got to be an inventory code. Price tags don't have that many numbers."

"I want to see it," came Vicki's muffled but firm voice through the closed door.

"Why?" she asked suspiciously.

"Because if you say it looks horrible, I'll know you're not making excuses."

Accepting the inevitable, she opened the door and stepped out.

"Ooooh," Vicki chirped. A smile of appreciation lit her face. "That ought to make him sit up and take notice."

Jill looked away. "That's part of the problem. He doesn't notice on his own. Watching him try to feel something for me hurts worse than you can imagine." Clenching her jaw and blinking hard, she fought back another round of threatening tears.

"It's going to be okay." Vicki gave her a warm hug.

"I wish I could believe that." Succumbing to the pregnancy maudlins embarrassed her, so Jill stiffened her spine and gave Vicki a fierce look. "I know! I'll run away and join the circus! I'm a natural to play the fat lady."

"I'll tell Mason," Vicki singsonged back.

"Spoilsport."

Two days later on a Friday afternoon, Jill and Mason stood in the county courthouse, along with two other couples waiting for a marriage license. She'd spent the last forty-eight hours mulling over Vicki's wisecrack in the maternity shop. The situation between her and Mason *had* been a war—one Jill knew she'd lost badly. Defeat weighed heavily on her. How could Mason expect a marriage like this to work?

The amused looks they received from people openly staring at her stomach set her temper on edge. How dare they assume this was some sort of shotgun wedding!

Then she glanced into Mason's woodenly stoic face, an unwanted reminder of the full truth. *Okay, it is. But it's not just the groom who'd rather be somewhere else today.*

Misgivings and memories of her first marriage's heartaches closed around her. One-sided love—again. Life in emotional hell—again. Her self-respect balked, and she stepped away from him. "To thine own self be true, Brad-shaw."

Smoothly, Mason slipped his arm around her. The casual observer would never notice the iron in his grip. "It's your choice, Jill," he whispered into her hair. "As my wife, what little I have is yours. The alternative is a too-small welfare check." Then, he added, "I wonder how well you'll handle people glaring at you in grocery checkout lines when you whip out your food stamps."

Bitter reality choked her. Both her financial survival and Mason's depended on the success of a marriage neither wanted. Tears fell so quickly that her eyes hadn't burned a warning first. "Just don't gloat," she gritted out between her teeth.

"Wouldn't dream of it." He shifted his hold, tucking her head beneath his chin and tenderly rubbing her back. She swiped at her eyes, loving him so much she hurt from it, and not believing for one minute that she'd ever hold his heart.

The baby kicked, and Mason jumped, awe claiming his face. "Was that her?" he whispered.

The poignant wonder made her swallow hard. Only then did she realize he'd never felt their child moving within her. What right did she have to deny him this? Gamely, she smiled at him. "Sure was, Dad."

He seemed to stop breathing as he gazed at her belly with melting affection.

Why can't he look at me like that? Jill turned her back to him, leaned against his chest and guided his hands around her tummy as casually as if it were an everyday occurrence. The baby kicked again, this time clipping the inside of her ribs—hard. She winced. Mason chuckled, pre-sumably unaware of how badly it hurt to have one's body kicked apart from the inside. For the next few minutes, their daughter performed *in utero* gymnastics worthy of an Olympic athlete, and Mason softly kissed Jill's hair. She wanted to cry.

By the time they'd paid the fee and signed on the dotted line, she had her emotions more under control. But not even the momentary closeness they'd shared eased her fears that she'd just signed up for a repeat performance of the same misery she'd known the first time around.

"I'm not Donald," he whispered as they left.

She blushed, furious that he'd so accurately read her mind. *No, Bradshaw, in many ways you're worse.* "Never doubted it for a minute," she fired back, forcing an ornery grin. "Your tush is much cuter."

A strangled cough spasmed from his throat. He took her arm and turned her to face him. His hands burned through her sleeves like liquid fire.

"Can I trust you to show up tomorrow?" he demanded. "Or are you planning more stall tactics?"

She knew what her answer would be, but that didn't make her in that big of a hurry to answer. She took a moment to study him. The lines of his face were a bit too harsh for the classic ideal. The current strain didn't help any. But his deep-set hazel eyes were flawless. Then again, maybe not. Shadows from lack of sleep made them look too miserable, too—

"Are you listening to me?"

That pulled her back to his original question. "Yes, I'll be there. The circumstances haven't offered any alternatives."

"Good. Our rings are supposed to be ready this afternoon. Let's go pick them up, then go out to dinner."

At the jeweler's, Mason placed the engagement ring on Jill's finger and dutifully—it seemed to her—kissed her cheek.

At seven the next night, Vicki helped her into the lavender dress. Vicki and Wilson had graciously opened their home to the wedding. They'd built the ranch-style house themselves and had indulged in a massive stone fireplace that made the living room a perfect setting for celebrations.

Jill stood in front of the full-length mirror in the master bedroom and touched up her hair. For once, she had pulled her blond curls up into a stylized French knot at the crown of her head. It didn't look bad, she decided.

Vicki wove in tiny rosebuds and baby's breath as a finishing touch.

"I still think a lily in my navel is more appropriate."

Vicki sighed heavily. "Girlfriend, you're scared to death and saying anything that pops into your head that might give you some space."

Jill blushed. "Am I being that bad?"

"No, but it could get away from you if you're not careful." Then her best friend pulled out the set of diamond earrings Wilson had bought her the previous Christmas. They were gorgeous. "Here's your 'something borrowed.'"

"I can't wear these," Jill gasped.

"Sure you can. They're good luck. Wilson and I never squabble when I have them on."

"Well, in that case...." Jill shyly put them in place. She'd never even tried on jewels like these. Between them and the gown, she felt a little like Cinderella.

After Vicki finished primping her to bridal perfection, Jill checked her reflection again. The lavender-and-lace gown swirled around her ankles with a soft rustle each time she moved. Her hair and the diamond earrings added an aura of elegance that she never dreamed she could pull off. Saying "thank you" seemed so trite, so inadequate. She hugged Vicki instead. "You're a good friend."

The other woman smiled, and the two held each other for a moment, strengthening the bonds between them.

Then Jill stole another peek in the mirror. "Think he'll like it?" she ventured with uncharacteristic timidity.

"Unless he's gone blind," Vicki muttered, "he'll be groveling at your feet."

Jill snorted. ''I'll settle for some genuine affection, if you don't mind.''

Vicki didn't comment but the compassionate glint in her eyes told Jill she'd heard it and understood.

In the living room, nerves ate Mason alive, but he put on a calm facade as he milled with guests. Most of them were employees. The rest were people he'd met in Stafford during the ten months he'd lived here. Wilson poured him a glass of an excellent chardonnay. Unfortunately, like everything else he'd consumed during the last twenty-four hours, it tasted like cardboard.

To give himself something to do, he took another sip. Then he heard a door open down the hall. Everyone—him included— turned toward the sound. Jill stepped into the room, chewing the lipstick off her lower lip.

My God, she looks just like Karen! He swallowed wrong, and then choked. He could have sworn the entire swallow went down his windpipe. Wilson slapped him on the back. It only made things worse. The wine burned like fire. Even as he fought for air, a distant thought acknowledged the abominable timing. All wedding guests want to see two things, their first glimpse of the bride and the groom's face when he sees her. So what does he do? Choke to death.

''I'll be right back,'' he wheezed between rounds of gasping for breath. As he turned toward the kitchen, someone handed him a glass of water. He gratefully swallowed it, but that didn't help, either. Before the next round of spasms overtook him, he actually inhaled half a breath. Then his throat locked up on him again, and the thought occurred to him that he might be in serious trouble.

''I don't believe I've ever had that effect on a man before,'' Jill quipped. The assembly laughed, but as he left the room, he wondered if anyone but him heard the pain beneath it.

Jill watched him all but run to the kitchen. Somewhere deep down, she'd hoped to see his eyes light up as he saw her. *Everyone has their little fantasies,* she supposed. But having him choke on his wine hadn't been part of it.

Nor had the glimpse of shocked horror just before he swallowed wrong. She remembered remarking to Vicki when Mason first bought the paper that he'd looked at her as if he'd expected one thing and gotten the Bride of Frankenstein, instead. Maybe he still thought so. She passionately wished she knew why.

The frequency and intensity of Mason's coughing slowed after another minute or two. Sympathetic murmuring filled the air as Jill stood, bouquet in hand, waiting for her groom to recover.

When he returned to the living room, his face was flushed. "I'm so sorry, Jill."

"Don't worry about it, Bradshaw," she said. "It's not every bride who waits for the *groom's* grand entrance."

Normally, he at least smiled at her jokes, no matter how dark the humor. This time, his eyebrows lowered in speculation. Had he begun to see through her defensive armor? She hoped not. Then she remembered Vicki's observation about her verbal barbs, and she tried to feel a little more hopeful. She and Mason were two reasonably intelligent human beings. If both of them worked hard enough, maybe they had a chance.

Whatever Mason had been thinking, he shifted gears, smiled warmly and reached to her. She glanced at his outstretched hand. As was to be expected, every eye in the place was on them. Jill stiffened her spine and laid her palm across his. He drew her to him and chastely kissed her on the lips. Their guests sighed in contentment at the romantic gesture.

Jill's feet seemed to have more common sense than the rest of her and kept wanting to carry her out to the car. She would see this through, though, no matter how painful it became.

The minister took his prearranged place by the cheery fire, and Mason and Jill stepped before him. With the exception of holding her hand, Mason stood at rigid military attention. She wondered if he'd faint if someone yelled "boo." She was half tempted to try—anything to ease the impossible tension.

Before long, they'd recited their vows, Mason's baritone as clear and stiff as his backbone. Hazarding a guess, Jill figured she sounded pitiful. When he slipped the ring onto her finger, she morosely thought it ought to feel heavy— like a link in an iron chain—but it didn't. Then Vicki handed her Mason's ring. The prisoner image returned to mind. She felt as though she were chaining the man she loved to a dungeon wall.

"You're thinking too much," he whispered, a warning glint in his eyes.

The minister looked confused, but Jill blushed in understanding. "*Semper Fi,* Bradshaw." As she slid the ring into place, a yearning blossomed deep inside that the symbol would someday have substance.

The ceremony came to a close, and Mason tilted her chin up for the traditional kiss. His lips brushed across hers, light and undemanding, holding a hint of experimentation and far too much of what she interpreted to be male relief over a task completed. Jill ached from wanting the kiss to be a real one, offered in passion, but she settled for quietly savoring the taste of him on her lips.

Politely, they accepted the minister's congratulations and their guests' applause while the photographer did his thing. Frankly, she'd have preferred to do without a photographic record. As condemned as she felt, she assumed she looked the part.

With all the life of automatons, they went through the ritual cake-cutting and champagne toasts—except her glass was filled with sparkling apple cider.

"You two are doing fine," Vicki murmured over their

shoulders as guests broke up into various knots of conversation.

"The incarcerated usually do." The comment slipped out before she could stop it.

Mason bristled. "Excuse us a minute, Vicki." Then he took Jill by the upper arm and steered her into the kitchen. "I've never seen you like this," he whispered furiously. "Has everything become a sick joke?"

"Actually, it has." It could have been another flippant remark, but this one she meant.

He seemed to sense the subtle difference, and the anger leached away, easing the implacable set to his shoulders. "You're making me feel like an ax murderer."

She almost told him that it beat feeling like the Bride of Frankenstein, but she kept that one to herself. "Sorry. I'll try to do better." Self-indulgently, she studied his beloved face. This wonderful, honorable man belonged to her, though his heart did not. But maybe now they were married, he wouldn't be feeling so much pressure, and they could see where they stood. Maybe.... *Dream on, Jill,* she chided herself.

"Shall we go out there, face the crowd and smile until our face muscles cramp?" she asked.

He frowned at her.

Oops. "Sorry."

He cradled her face in his hands. "We're going to make it, Jill."

He sounded so positive. Maybe hope wasn't so far-fetched after all. "If you're sure." She swallowed. "What do we do now?"

Sighing, he gestured toward the door. "Smile until our face muscles cramp."

She laughed, and he led her to the family room where Vicki had set up the buffet.

"What's your favorite food?" he asked.

"Chili dogs. Why?" She sat down and checked her

watch. Only eight-thirty. Hours to go yet, but she'd made it through the hardest part.

Mason glowered at her. "I don't think those are on the caterer's menu. Even if they were, I'm not bringing my bride a plate full of junk food."

Jill managed to bite back the snappy retort that came to mind, but another one tumbled out anyway. "Whatever. I'm yours to feed. Then again, isn't that the whole point of—"

"Knock it off," he mouthed so no one could hear. "You gave your word."

She looked up at him, only now realizing he still held her hand. "Sorry. Momentary lapse. I guess the scared spitless aren't very trustworthy."

He muttered something reassuring under his breath and filled her plate with a little of everything.

Later at his apartment, the exhausted slump to Mason's shoulders didn't escape Jill's notice as he unlocked and shoved open the door. He lived in a better part of town than she did, but the rental complex still wasn't anything to brag about. So much for the image of the wealthy publisher.

Swallowing hard, she forced herself to step inside. Somehow, coming "home" felt more final than the ceremony. Sort of like the difference between a criminal being sentenced in court and actually being locked into the cell.

"Not so fast." Mason caught hold of her arm and gently turned her around.

Jill had only *thought* being his unwanted, unloved wife would kill her. Experiencing his gentle touch and knowing he only acted out the expected motions really *would*. She raised her eyes to his. Big mistake. In the sharply defined lines of his lean face, she saw the strained tenderness of a man every bit as miserable as she was.

"Isn't it a little late for second thoughts?" she asked in tired resignation.

Clearly irritated, he lowered his dark eyebrows. "I'm a dinosaur, remember? We don't have second thoughts. Not about things like this." Before she had the chance to respond, he swept her into his arms.

"Bradshaw, are you out of your mind?" she shrieked, latching onto his neck.

"I'm carrying my bride over the threshold." His entire face smiled except his eyes, but he was giving his best. The least she could do was meet him halfway.

Through the heartache, she doubled her efforts to smile back. "What's the plan now, oh tyrannosaur mine?"

His grim determination took on a softer cast. It made her glad she'd attempted the regular humor. If left to her, Mason's every smile would be real. Her hold on his neck loosened to something less than a panicked death grip, and she savored the warmth of his skin in the cool, April air. Desire shivered through her body. *Not very bright,* she chastised herself silently.

"What's my plan?" Mason repeated. Brushing a kiss on her lips, he strode inside. "We work our way through this one day at a time."

Afraid to trust her voice, Jill nodded in simple agreement and concentrated on the next step—whatever that might be. They had slept together exactly once. That night, passion had overcome them so quickly she didn't remember taking her clothes off. But the raging need of eight months ago was a far cry from cold-bloodedly setting up housekeeping with a man who felt only obligation toward her. The traditional wedding night held all the appeal of delivering her baby on the freeway during a snowstorm.

She squirmed in a subtle request to be set down. When he complied, she marched down the short hallway. "What's in your spare bedroom?"

"Why?"

Emotions rose too close to the surface for her to dare answer. The first door on the left was the extra bedroom—

and future nursery. Inside, she found a couch that looked suspiciously like a sleeper. "Does that thing unfold?"

"Again I ask, why?" came the wary masculine voice from behind her. "What are you up to?"

She whirled around. "I think I'll crash here until we get the terms of our marriage straightened out. Tomorrow we'll start cleaning out my apartment. Wilson's brother has a pickup truck we can borrow."

His hazel eyes darkened. "This is going to be a real marriage, Jill."

"Fine. I just don't think it's necessary to add sex to our problems."

Slowly, pointedly, he crossed his arms and glowered at her stomach.

Jill blushed to her toes. "You know what I mean, Bradshaw."

"No, I don't, *Mrs.* Bradshaw," he growled, his throat working to swallow his anger. "Care to explain?"

"Not particularly." By her estimation, Mason had aged ten years during the past six hours. It half destroyed her to know she was the cause. Granted, she hadn't gotten pregnant by herself, but that didn't change the basic situation.

"Separate beds doesn't get us off to a good start."

"I'm eight months' pregnant. Sex isn't a good idea."

"All I'm asking from you is to share a mattress. Since you mentioned it, though, I've read up on pregnancy."

"You would."

He ignored the jibe. "Sex won't hurt you or the baby. So stop the excuses and tell me the real reason."

The anger that had flared moments ago once again blasted its way to the surface. She planted her hands on her hips. "Okay, how's this? I've had all the loveless sex I intend to. Is that real enough for you?"

"I told you. I'm not your ex-husband." Each syllable was enunciated with brittle precision. He opened his mouth to say more, but she cut him off.

"You're worse. You've got enough integrity to fill Car-

negie Hall. You'll fake caring until you've conned yourself
into believing it's real.''

Deepening displeasure glittered in his eyes, triggering
warning alarms in her head.

"Jill," he ground out slowly, "we're exhausted,
stressed, and we've both had one helluva day. I won't force
you to share my bed, but if you don't, you're jeopardizing
our chances of making this marriage work.''

"Hormones got the better of us once. I assume that once
I'm not pregnant anymore, it'll happen again," she said.
"How do you expect me to make love with you when all
I'll be is an available body?''

Pride warred with fury for control of his face. Pride won;
resolve followed quickly. "I wouldn't do that to you, Jill.''

All the starch drained from her. "We'll talk about sleeping arrangements and/or sex when I know it's *me* you
want.''

The wall between them thickened. They couldn't have
made it more impenetrable with actual mortar and brick.
With crisp efficiency, Mason tossed the couch cushions into
a neat stack in the corner and flipped open the bed.

"If you'll excuse me, Jill, your room is down the hall.
I'd like to put the sheets on this thing.''

"Wait a minute, Bradshaw. You're not giving me your
room!''

The muscles worked in his jaw as he wordlessly brushed
past her to grab sheets and blankets from the linen closet.

"I won't take your bed.''

"So you said," he snarled tightly. "But I won't be there.
Remember? All I'm doing is giving you the better mattress.''

She wanted to strangle him. "Would you stop being so
damnably gallant?''

The look he gave her seemed to question her sanity.
Then he took a long-controlled breath. "Jill, it's almost one
o'clock. If you want to fight, let me get some sleep first.
I'll make a better opponent in the morning." With a flick

of his wrist, the sheet billowed out across the thin, lumpy bed.

Hysteria flooded her, and she fled to the master bedroom before erupting into tears again. The emotional storm worsened when she stood beside the masculine, dark-walnut bed with its familiar mahogany-colored comforter. Eight months ago, their child had been conceived here. Her hands involuntarily came to rest over her grossly distended abdomen. Disturbed, the baby kicked beneath her fingers, and Jill closed her eyes. It wasn't fair that one night in the arms of the man she loved had turned both their lives into such a nightmare.

Taking a deep breath, she dropped her purse onto one of the matching bedside tables and draped her coat across a wingback chair, the only other piece of furniture in the room. Mason set her duffel bag just inside the doorway. Her heart constricted, and she waited for him to break the silence, hoping he would—but he didn't. They shared a long, indecipherable look.

"Good night, Jill." He turned off the hall light and closed himself in the spare bedroom.

She found herself in total darkness except for a faint strip of light glowing from beneath his door. With a heavy heart, she changed into a nightgown and slipped between the cold sheets. For nearly a year, she'd fantasized about being married to Mason, sharing his bed, his life. Spending their wedding night alone hadn't been part of the picture. The choice had been hers. Only time would judge whether she'd made a mistake.

From the other room she heard a crash followed by a muffled and irritated "ow."

"Good night to you, too, my love," she whispered. "Maybe we'll do better tomorrow." She rolled onto her side, hugged his spare pillow to her chest and tried to sleep.

Jill slept in fits and starts. Mostly, she lay thinking about how bad it could have gotten if they tossed and turned beside each other all night, both miserably aware of each other's proximity. As dawn finally showed up, she decided waking up in Mason's apartment alone in his bed was only marginally better than sharing it with him all night would have been.

She listened for any sound in the apartment to tell her if Mason had gotten up for the day, too. After several minutes of silence, the only thing she heard was the furnace kicking on. Could he be in his room listening for her? *Yeah, right.* "The romantic stupidities never give up, do they?"

She really needed to make a trip to the bathroom, but wasn't anxious to run into him until she had herself together for the day. Her comfy, knee-length, sleep shirt wasn't even remotely attractive. Given the circumstances, the faded rabbit on the front with the slogan You're No Bunny Till Somebunny Loves You made her self-conscious. Maybe she'd change first.

Her body's demands became more strident. "I guess that eliminates that option." With a moan of resignation, she folded back the rumpled blankets and put her feet on the floor. "If I'm lucky, seeing each other for the first time will be like having a tooth pulled. Over in a minute." She looked down at the rabbit. "No, it'll probably be more like a root canal. Long, drawn out and hideous."

Padding down the hall, she saw that his bedroom door was still closed. She nearly cheered. When she finished in the bathroom, she had almost made it back when she heard his door open behind her.

"Good morning, Jill."

Her heart leapt at Mason's pleasantly raspy morning voice. "How did you sleep?"

She plastered a confident smile on her lips and turned to face him. He'd smoothed down his hair with his fingers if the furrows through it were any indication. "Shouldn't I be asking *you* that? You're the one who slept on a sofa bed."

He shrugged, yawned, then caught sight of the rabbit. His pupils contracted, and he winced. Dark beard stubble made the effect more pronounced. She pretended not to notice.

"So, how'd you sleep?" she asked.

"Fine." The too insistent overtone failed to mask the lie. "Quite comfortable."

Seeing no point in pursuing it, she said, "We need to congratulate ourselves, Bradshaw. We survived our first night as husband and wife. Now what?"

His shoulders rose then fell on a sharp sigh. "Have breakfast. Then we'll see if Wilson's brother will part with his pickup truck for the day and start moving your things."

Relief flooded her. They had a plan. No casting around all day for something to say to each other. On the other hand, a day of quiet conversation might have been nice. The potential pitfalls made her shudder, though. "Moving is good."

"Are you cold?"

"Nope. Hauling all my worldly possessions from one home to another isn't my favorite contact sport." She headed into her room. "The bathroom is yours. How do you like your eggs?"

"I'll do them," he said.

"No, you won't," she called back. "The least I can do is fix your breakfast."

"I have an omelet every morning, Jill. Slicing, chopping and dicing helps clear my head for the day."

She didn't miss the defensive edge to the explanation. Mentally, she backed off. Apparently, the kitchen was his exclusive domain at that hour, and the better part of valor dictated that she leave it alone. "Ahhh, the old philosophy that if you're awake, you won't slice your fingers off?"

"Something like that."

Later, when they met in the living room, he wore sweats and sneakers. She'd forgotten that he ran every morning. They watched each other for long moments, both struggling for a conversation opener. The tension became almost palpable. No normal newlywed couple should have trouble coming up with small talk the day after their wedding.

Jill couldn't stand it anymore. "Give me a minute to change, Bradshaw," she deadpanned. "I'll go with you."

"What!" His jaw sagged in horror. "You're not having the baby at the corner of Fourth and Maple!"

She winked at him and watched the stiffness ease from his body.

"Okay," he murmured. "I know when I've been had." After a bare hesitation, he leaned over, kissed her cheek and headed out the door. "I'm only running two miles today instead of five like I usually do on the weekends. Be back soon."

Jill touched her face, the afterglow of his lips warm and tingly against her skin. The affectionate gesture hadn't seemed to give him any problems. In fact, she got the impression that he hadn't thought much about it first.

Don't read too much into it. Just strive for normalcy. Still, she tucked the memory away and savored it.

As Jill's due date came and went, her blood pressure skyrocketed. Dr. Gray allowed her on her feet long enough to shop for groceries and to cook—but not on the same day. Then it was back to the couch or bed.

Mason left for the paper at four-thirty every morning, leaving her with no one to talk to until he returned about six at night. Today was Sunday, and he normally stayed home, but a problem at the paper had taken him down there just after breakfast.

Alone and bored out of her skull, she succumbed to the nesting instinct and fudged a little on Dr. Gray's orders. The arrival of her belongings meant Mason's apartment held two households. The larger things like her furniture went into storage. At first she'd hoped Mason could use her bed, but it wouldn't fit in the small second bedroom and he was stuck on the sofa bed. Boxes and bags were stacked everywhere. What should have been a comfortable living space for two felt more like a rat maze. With his work schedule and her restrictions, neither could do much about it. Not being able to settle in had created one more aggravation that they didn't need.

Mentally, she'd long since developed a plan of attack. Today would be the day, starting with cleaning out the boxes from the closet shelves to condense some of Mason's belongings. She and the baby needed space, and Jill had to find some. One large box had assorted journalism awards and half a dozen school yearbooks. All were covered with archeological layers of dust. Absently, she decided it might be fun to go through them one day. No time now, though.

Mason might have an old, beat-up stereo for his office, but the unit in his home was enough to make any music nut salivate with envy. After programming in a station she doubted the equipment had ever deigned to consider, she cranked up the volume. Diamond Rio blasted into the room, and she got to work.

Three hours later, she noticed the flashing light on the answering machine in the dining room. "Well, when one plays it loud, one misses things, I guess." Curious, she punched the button.

"Hi, Mason," came a tentative but far-too-seductive female voice. "It's me." After an uncomfortable pause, Jill thought she heard the woman swallow.

"You know how I hate leaving messages on your machine, but I need to talk to you. Call me back as soon as you can, sweetheart. We need to discuss some things."

Karen! The competition had a voice. Jill gasped as overpowering jealousy wrapped itself around her like a snake.

"This is going to be great. I promise. Love you. Bye."

Jill's hackles came up, and she glared at the machine. The moment the tape finished, she hit rewind and listened to it again. Hearing the words the second time wasn't any easier. Nor was it the third or the fourth. With each replay, she studied the nuances, dissected the overt sexuality.

"I'm going to lose him." She went back to the kitchen, snatched the celery out of the crisper and tore off a couple of stalks. "You never had him to begin with, you idiot, and now you're talking to yourself. Way to go!"

Fresh waves of helpless heartache assailed her. Marriage to Donald had been bad enough. But he hadn't cared about any of the women he'd slept with. They were just conquests.

Mason was different. He'd loved Karen. Denials aside, did he still?

Jill slammed the celery onto the cutting board and chopped the daylights out of it.

Chapter 9

By the time Mason walked into the apartment, the rich aroma of fried chicken and marinated vegetables filled the air. He dropped an overfilled leather satchel and his briefcase on the dining room table and inhaled appreciatively. Then he frowned. "How long have you been out of bed?"

"All afternoon." Deliberately, she avoided looking at him. Her mind's eye held a perfect picture of the answering machine.

"Dr. Gray said no more than two hours." For a moment he appeared to debate whether or not to give her a hug, but his natural reserve won out and she remained hugless. "Jill, why don't I finish dinner?"

"I'm fine." Glancing up at him, she saw stress lines carved into the corners of his sensual mouth and across his brow. "Bradshaw, instead of cooking, why don't you go for a run and unwind? From the looks of you, today was a real witch."

Mason often did serious road work if a workday had been particularly ugly. Then he came home and ate everything in sight. It amazed her the little things one learned about a person in a couple of weeks of living under the same roof.

Mason's tension seemed to ease. "You're right. I went in to figure out a cash flow problem and found a worse mess than I imagined." He wandered into the dining room and saw the blinking light on the machine.

A knot lodged itself painfully in Jill's throat. Like a masochistic moth drawn to the flame, she moved to where she could watch his face. Involuntarily, her fingers came to rest over their child.

Karen's seductive voice filled the air once more, and Jill felt the already insurmountable gulf between her and Mason widen. Mason dropped one hand low on his hip. Every muscle in his body knotted up. When the message ended, he made no attempt to save it. Instead, he stared at the machine, strong but unidentifiable emotion in his eyes. Was it longing? Regret? Anger? Passionately, she wished she knew him well enough to tell.

Afraid of what he might read in her own expression, Jill turned back to the stove and flipped a piece of chicken. In the process, she splattered a drop of hot oil onto her arm. She shrieked more from surprise than pain, then turned on the cold water and stuck her wrist under it.

"How badly are you burned?" he demanded, suddenly hovering behind her.

"Chill, Bradshaw. It's just a wimpy little kitchen owie."

His worried gaze zeroed in on the dime-sized red mark, but she'd have preferred to know his reaction to the phone call.

"I'll get the salve and a bandage." Within moments, he returned with the first-aid kit. "It was pretty obvious who the message was from. Do you want to talk about it?"

"Do we need to?" she snapped. "I thought she was part of your past." Snatching an ice cube from the freezer for the burn, Jill turned her back on him. She wanted to apologize for coming across like a first-class bitch, but couldn't bring herself to be that vulnerable. A lot of time had passed since Mason's divorce. Had he come to a place where he could forgive his ex-wife? Would he be with her now if there were no baby? Did he feel trapped, only his integrity keeping him from the woman he loved?

"Karen's calls aren't new, Jill. She craves attention and whatever is just out of reach. After I divorced her, I became the thing she can't have. That made me very attractive. If I ignore her long enough, she'll eventually lose interest and leave me alone. It's working. This is the first call in months."

The pragmatic response should have pleased her, but it didn't. Hating to think she was so petty as to blame him for a phone call he had no control over, she forced herself to calm down. "You could call her back and tell her you're married. That ought to make her quit."

He shook his head. "Our lives are none of her business, and I have nothing to say to her."

Our lives. The sound of that warmed her, tempting her to snuggle into his embrace, but he didn't seem inclined to offer one. She turned back to the chicken and put the golden brown pieces on a plate. "What's in the satchel?"

"Payroll, if you're interested. I figured you could work on it stretched out on the bed. Might beat daytime TV."

The knot in her stomach uncurled a little. "You brought me something to do?"

He nodded, then looked sheepish. "Actually, I really need your help. After what I found today, I'm firing the new bookkeeper. I brought hard-copy printouts of everything she's done since you left."

Jill smiled at him. "So we're back in the saddle?" With her doing the books, they had familiar ground to stand on. "I'll need the computer to—"

"It's in the trunk."

He needed her! She'd have preferred it to be personal, but she could live with business for starters.

* * *

As it turned out, he'd even thought to buy a keyboard extension cable so she could work from the bed. Having a constructive project to do eased some of the depression and gave her mind something productive to chew on. She actually caught herself humming along to the stereo as she untangled the disaster her replacement had created.

The sleeping arrangements didn't change, and Jill had begun to wonder if she'd made a mistake. Mason never again indicated an interest in sharing a bed with her, and she had too much pride to ask. She was afraid that if she did, he'd oblige just to be agreeable, not because that's where he wanted to be. With each passing day, fewer of his clothes hung in the master bedroom closet.

A week and a half overdue, her joke about running two miles with him in the morning sounded more and more attractive. Each day, Mason called home mid-morning and mid-afternoon to check on her. Vicki often arrived with a brown bag and ate lunch with her, helping to keep her mind off her myriad physical discomforts.

"That baby is sure happy where she is," Vicki observed. "Has Dr. Gray mentioned when he's going to induce labor?"

"He told me this morning that he'll boot her out day after tomorrow." Jill took a bite of her sandwich. For some reason she just didn't want food today. "In the meantime, I'm going back to my regular activities. Maybe it'll hurry things along."

Vicki laughed. "Your feet will swell up like footballs."

"Tough. Give me laundry, or give me labor, but this little fat girl is getting off the couch."

Two hours later, she had five boxes unpacked and the living room floor covered with piles of dirty clothes. The doorbell rang. "Of course," she muttered. "Company never shows up when a place is clean."

The bell rang again as she reached for the knob. The moment Jill pulled it open, she forgot about her housekeeping. Her jaw hung slack, and she couldn't believe what her brain said her eyes were seeing.

A woman who looked like she'd just stepped from the pages of a fashion magazine stood on the porch. Her hair was only a shade darker than Jill's own tawny curls, but the dramatic, fluffy mane hung well below her shoulders and was glorious enough to give Reba McEntire fits. Unnerved, Jill felt like she stood face to face with a long-lost sister, a beauty queen from a family of frogs. She'd always considered herself passably attractive, her short curls sassy and distinctive. Now, she just felt plain—plain and decidedly fat.

Whoever the woman was, she stared back at Jill with equal shock. "Pardon me," she said. "I'm looking for Mason Bradshaw."

It took a minute for Jill to find her voice. "He's not here."

The other woman seemed to be experiencing the same trouble. "Then I do have the right apartment?"

Jill nodded. "Who are you?"

"Karen." She delicately cleared her throat. "Karen Bradshaw."

Feeling faint, Jill leaned on the doorjamb for support.

"Who are *you?*" Karen asked.

"His wife."

Karen actually recoiled, her lips moving around a wordless denial. If Jill had slugged her with a baseball bat, the effect couldn't have been more dramatic.

Suddenly Jill understood Mason's shocked expression his first day at the paper, and all the startled ones later when she'd come upon him unexpectedly. Her observations about the Bride of Frankenstein hadn't been that far off the mark.

She swallowed hard as another truth settled into the pit of her stomach. The night he'd made love to her, he hadn't found consolation in another woman's arms; he'd found a substitute. No, she decided, there was more to it than that.

He'd found as close to a duplicate as was humanly possible. She trembled as anger blasted through her.

I knew he didn't love me, but I always believed it was me he made love to that night. Not even Donald at his worst had made her feel so insignificant or unloved.

Holding her head up, she carefully pulled her tattered pieces together into a semblance of normalcy. She couldn't afford to fall apart, not now. "Karen, I thought you lived in Los Angeles."

"I did."

Jill would have preferred the woman to answer the unspoken question. *What are you doing in Stafford, Washington?*

The silence crackled with confusion and tension.

Karen cocked her head, her incredible hair swinging heavily over one shoulder. "Tell me again. You're Mason's what?"

Jill lifted her chin. "His *wife*."

"My God," she breathed. Her gaze wandered to Jill's belly. "He can't have...." She lifted her eyes again, a slight frown creasing her perfect brow. "You can't be."

Saying anything would have been like giving information to the enemy, so Jill kept her mouth shut.

"When?"

Jill felt an old-fashioned blush stain her face. What was she going to do? Tell the ex-wife of the man she adored that he'd found himself the star in a shotgun wedding less than a month ago? "Maybe you need to take that up with Mason. Now, if you'll excuse me." She moved to shut the door.

An increased attentiveness in Karen's expression told her the woman wanted to say something else, but Jill didn't want to hear it—not until she'd had the chance to absorb the latest disaster.

In shock, she closed the door, then dropped onto the couch next to a pile of Mason's socks. What had she walked into the night she'd come here nine months ago?

Even then, it wasn't me he wanted. She wrapped her arms around her stomach, silent tears streaming down her face. In the distance, she heard an engine start, then a car back away from the building. Karen was leaving.

"Mason is a good man," she whispered into the silence. "Give him a chance to explain."

But how do you know he's a good man? taunted insidious whispers in her head. *What kind of man marries a woman who looks like the unattractive fraternal twin of his elegant ex-wife?* Jill shuddered.

With the baby's birth imminent, she needed answers to questions she'd tried not to think about. What *exactly* did he feel for her? What about his family? Did he have one? Did he have brothers and sisters? Were his parents still living? He hadn't mentioned wanting to let anyone outside Stafford know he'd remarried, so she had assumed not. Then again, this new twist had never occurred to her, either.

How could she find out? Could she believe anything he said? Jill shook her head. "Stop," she told herself. You're borrowing trouble as fast as you can grab it. When he gets home, talk to him. See what he says." She rose to her feet, her legs not as sturdy as she would have liked. "Above all, stop being a wuss."

More than an hour passed as Jill puttered through the apartment, trying to clean. But all she accomplished was to wander from place to place, watching her feet swell. Endless questions swirled through her mind.

The doorbell rang again. A feeling of dread came over her as she answered it. Even suspecting who she might find didn't lessen the impact of Karen's presence. The woman's eyes glistened with purpose. Apparently, she'd been able to recover from the shock better than Jill had. Then again, Karen didn't have raging pregnancy hormones and a case of marital insecurity big enough to register on the Richter scale.

"Yes?" Jill tried to match the woman's self-assured

poise. She noticed the red, designer suit Karen wore, the matching heels. *Just your everyday power suit.*

"May I come in?"

"You must be kidding."

Karen's gaze dipped, giving the impression that perhaps what looked unshakable was only a facade. "No, I'd truly like to talk to you. I need to know what's going on."

The strain of being on her feet too long, plus the stress, had begun to exact a heavy toll on Jill. She wanted nothing more than to put her feet up and rest. She didn't feel right. No, more than that. She felt indefinably strange. She wished passionately she hadn't opened the door.

"Is Mason home yet?" Karen asked when Jill didn't immediately ask her in.

"No, and I don't know when to expect him."

"Oh." She chewed on the edge of her lip, giving the impression of a little lamb lost. "May I *please* come in? I promise not to bother you long. I'm just so confused."

"I can understand that," Jill said drily. Detached, she watched herself open the door wider in invitation.

Karen smiled in relief and swept inside. "He remarried?" Her big brown eyes glistened with moisture. "I don't understand this at all. Are you sure he's not home?"

Jill made an irritated noise low in her throat. "If he was, believe me, I'd have dragged him into the living room the first time you were here."

"Oh. Yes, of course." Karen couldn't seem to take her eyes off Jill's abdomen. "When are you due?"

For once, Jill's wit deserted her. The answer held more potential for conflict than she could handle. Worse, she didn't want to get into anything that smacked of fighting over a man. "I'm as overdue as doctors allow these days."

"That means...."

Jill watched thoughts play behind Karen's eyes as the woman backtracked through the calendar.

"That bastard," Karen whispered, breathless. When she looked up again, the fire and hate in her eyes made Jill brace for attack. But Karen seemed to conquer it and the moment passed. "What did you two do—have a quicky wedding the second he was free?"

"Not exactly."

Evidence of more thoughts rippled across Karen's expressive face. "The last time I spoke with him, he didn't say anything."

"When was that?" Jill asked.

A probing glint sharpened her rival's expression. "Not long ago." She seemed to be analyzing the conversation, weighing her response against whatever conclusion she'd drawn. "I think I've been played for a fool."

"Oh?"

She nodded, deliberately flinging her hair behind her shoulders. "About three months ago, he finally began listening to reason. Or so I thought. I offered to quit my job and move to Stafford so we could work through our differences."

Three months ago. Before he found out about the baby.

"What I don't understand is, why didn't he say anything about having remarried?" Karen cocked her head expectantly.

"He hadn't—I mean *we* hadn't—yet."

The woman pounced on that tidbit like a cat on a mouse. "So he's been stringing us both along?"

That didn't sound like Mason at all. On the other hand, why would a woman uproot herself completely and move hundreds of miles without concrete encouragement? "Are you sure he didn't tell you he'd changed his mind?"

The probing quality to Karen's gaze intensified. "He said he had a complication that would take a few months to resolve. I was to come on up. He promised to explain after I settled in." She looked at Jill's stomach again. "He said there were things he needed to tell me face to face. Now I see why."

Jill exploded inside. Mason had practically waxed poetic about hearth and home and how family stability was important to raising children. Beneath it all, had that been part of a secret agenda? Had he married her only to divorce her after the baby was born? For what purpose? To try to better his bid for custody later?

Despite the way things appeared, she'd never seen a hint of deceitfulness in Mason's character. Then again, her track record with selecting men didn't bear close examination.

Jill hated being an emotional wreck. Maybe once the pregnancy crazies were over, she could trust her judgment again. She wouldn't be so terrified of getting hurt again or be such a world-class pessimist. That day couldn't come fast enough to suit her, but future sanity didn't help her right now. She could hardly choke out the words to her next question. "So you moved to Washington under the impression you two would be reconciling soon?"

"Mmm, hmm." With a toss of her head, Karen dragged her long, red, manicured nails through her hair. The blatant sensuality in the gesture tore Jill's already bleeding heart into open shreds. "I can't believe that Simon and Madeline didn't warn me. We're so close."

"Who?"

Karen blinked in bafflement. "His parents."

"I've never met them."

The woman's jaw dropped. "Mason has some serious explaining to do." She cocked her head. "Do they even know about you?"

Jill felt like a bug in a science lab. "Do they know about your reconciliation?" she countered hotly. This conversation had all the potential of deteriorating into a catfight.

Karen took her time in answering. "The specifics, no. They're in Europe again. Mason and I intended to surprise them when they returned."

"Europe? Again?"

A slow smile crossed Karen's lips. "He's told you nothing?"

Holding absolutely still, Jill just stared at the woman. She'd already given away far too much.

"Not even who they are?"

Again, Jill stayed silent.

"What kind of games is Mason playing these days?" Karen shook her head. "No matter. You have a right to know. Simon Bradshaw is the industrialist who regularly turns the stock market on its ear. Madeline Bradshaw just retired from the California State Supreme Court. They just bought sizeable interest in a cruise ship line and sailed to the Caribbean to celebrate. Then they flew on to Spain."

Mason was the son of *those* Bradshaws? Jill's knees wobbled, and the room tilted. She'd always suspected that Mason had come from money, but she couldn't begin to relate to the privileged life his family had known.

A cruise ship line. Last summer she'd been euphoric just to be *on* one. His parents were part-owners of several.

"I think I need to call them and find out what this is all about," Karen drawled.

Jill shook herself. "I'd like you to leave now. If you give me your phone number, I'll have him call you, and the three of us can straighten this out."

"I'd like that." Karen pulled out a note pad from her purse. "My business cards won't be printed until next week, but here's all the information you'll need to find me." She scribbled on a sheet of paper, then handed it to Jill. On it was the name of a local business and its address and number. "I've been hired as human resources director of a new telecommunications company in Stafford. The bottom number is my home phone."

Jill got the message. The woman held a prestigious position with a big company, and she was here to stay. But not in this apartment, and not today. Jill showed her the door.

Alone again, Jill trembled with anger and shock. None of what Karen said fit the Mason she knew—or thought she knew. If he really was the son of Madeline and Simon Bradshaw, why was he a struggling, small-town newspaper

editor? Why hadn't his parents set him up financially? Why
didn't he run around in the elite circles of the rich and
famous?

From what Mason had implied about Karen, she thrived
on deceit and betrayal. Had that whole conversation been
designed as the cold-blooded revenge of a woman scorned?
Or did it have some truth to it? Could it be a combination
of both? If so, where was the line between fact and fiction?

The questions swirled endlessly through Jill's head until
her skull began to throb. She needed answers, and Mason
wasn't home to ask. Then she remembered something she'd
found when cleaning. It wasn't much, but it was all she
had. Going into the master bedroom, she pulled down the
box into which she'd put his old yearbooks and awards,
plus assorted income tax returns. She hadn't dusted anything, and her fingerprints indicated no one else had
touched them in a long time.

With a combination of curiosity and dread, she curled up
on the bed and dug through the record of Mason's life. She
knew so little about him. That made the treasures in the
box even more precious. In no particular order, she perused
the yearbooks first. The school turned out to be a prestigious college preparatory school for boys. He'd received
his bachelor's degree from an Ivy League university back
east. His tax returns only went back five years, far enough
to see that he and Karen had made a respectable living.
Even so, it wasn't what she would have expected from a
wealthy industrialist's son. She compared them with the
minuscule salary he drew from the *Journal* and the simple
apartment in which he lived. Nothing fit.

Jill came from lower-middle-class parents and had only
one year of business college to her credit. She was fiercely
proud of her accomplishments, considering she'd had no
one but herself to rely on. Could Mason be ashamed of
her? Was he hiding her from his family?

Condemning him without trial was unfair, and she returned everything to the box. If she wanted the truth, she

need only ask, then weigh his honesty for herself. Would he lie outright or just soft-pedal everything to keep from hurting her? Either way, at least the issues would be out in the open.

"Maybe on a less-pregnant day when I'm thinking with my head and not my hormones," she said aloud. She put the box back on the shelf. "Right now, I can do nothing. I have enough on my plate, thank you very much—Karen and his parents can wait for another meal."

Moving like a zombie, she returned to the laundry project and tried to think positively. The idea was great in theory, but she hadn't counted on an unutterable fatalism wrapping itself around her. She'd never been helplessly dependent on anyone before, not even her parents—especially not her parents. The word "divorce" dropped into the emotional stew. Once the baby was past the newborn stage, she'd find a job away from the *Journal.* She'd done it once. She could do it again. Complete dependence on another human being was intolerable. Even if Mason didn't have any dark and evil secrets, what chance did a marriage have that was built on obligation?

"Then again, when I'm no longer pregnant, things might look a little brighter." Grabbing the corners of a bath towel, she tried not to think about anything.

Mason called. "On top of everything else that has gone wrong today, the roof leaked. I've got the insurance company and a contractor out here now. Apparently, the insulation has been soaking up water for a long time."

"What did it do?" she asked. "Hit its capacity, then flood the world?" Civility took every shred of willpower. She wanted to rant and rave. *Why can't you love me? Why couldn't I have lived the rest of my life without ever knowing you existed?*

"According to the contractor, that's exactly what happened. I don't know when I'll be home."

"If you're going to be late, why don't you grab a bite

there? Letting your blood sugar go to pot won't accomplish much.''

He chuckled, and her throat clogged with tears.

''Bobby is out picking up Chinese.''

''Good,'' she answered, struggling to sound normal.

There was a long pause before he spoke again. ''Are you okay?''

She swallowed, then discreetly cleared her throat. ''Sure, why?''

''You sound…odd. You're not in labor are you?''

''No, unfortunately. Just do your thing, and I'll see you when you get here.'' She knew her voice didn't square with the flippant comments, but it was the best she could do. Once he got home and she could see his face, then they'd talk.

After she hung up, pain rippled across her lower abdomen. ''Probably more Braxton-Hicks,'' she muttered. ''Life wouldn't be rude enough to do the real thing today.''

By the time Mason cleared the door, the contractions were a respectable fifteen minutes apart and sharp enough to grab her attention—and *keep* it.

''Are you still awake?'' he asked, stifling a yawn. Mud in varying degrees of drying had taken up residence on his gray suit.

''It's only ten o'clock,'' she said, drinking in the sight of him. She needed to confront him, needed to learn the truth, but fear of what he might say held her words back. What she and Mason had shared so far wasn't great, but it beat some of the alternatives. Without thinking first, she met him halfway across the living room, the same spot where Karen had stood. She put her arms around him.

From the sudden stiffness in his body, her actions had startled him, but she ignored it, silently pleading for him to hold her in return. When he pulled her close, only then did she realize she'd wanted it so much she'd been holding her breath.

"What's wrong?" he asked, worry thick in his voice.

"Just a rotten day, and I need a little TLC."

"I wondered about that when I called," he said, caressing her back. "What happened?"

Jill felt the explosion in her brain a scant heartbeat before the vicious salvo erupted from her lips. "Did you make love to me that night because you were looking for a substitute for Karen?"

The tension in his body tripled. She looked into his eyes for an explanation. The shock she found there made her wonder if he'd turned to stone.

"Where did that question come from?" he demanded faintly.

Jill pulled out of his embrace and put some distance between them. The next contraction hit, and she took great care not to react. "If this were Hollywood, I could stand in as a stunt double for her."

He gaped.

"That's me. Jill Mathesin Bradshaw, stand-in for the beauty queen."

For the first time ever, she heard him truly swear, the expletive sharp and uncharacteristically crass. He dragged in several long, slow breaths, obviously fighting to regain enough self-control to speak civilly. "When did you meet her?"

Jill had hoped he'd deny she looked anything at all like his ex-wife. She wouldn't have believed him, of course, but a loving fiction might have been nice to hear.

"I asked when you met her." The anger hardened his expression. "Is she in Stafford?"

"As if you didn't know. How long did you think I'd keep from finding out?" Inside her head, a neon warning sign flashed Bitchy Pregnant Woman Here.

He gave her a blank, uncomprehending stare.

She crossed her arms. "Are you going to answer *my* question?" She'd wanted to sound defiant, but her voice cracked on the last syllable and ruined the effect.

Mason stared at her a long time before answering. "What is it you think I know, Jill?"

"That Karen moved to Stafford—per your request. That as soon as you get your current complications straightened out—" she spread her arms to indicate herself "—the two of you are going to put the pieces back together. I assume good ol' Simon and Madeline will throw a tasteful and very highbrow reception in your honor."

Shadows whipped behind his eyes as he analyzed what she'd said. Every muscle in his body looked as if it had been carved from marble. "Jill, I'm going to ask one more time," he ground out. "When and how did you meet Karen?"

"This afternoon. Right where you're standing."

"*Here?* In my house?"

"It's an apartment, Bradshaw," Jill fired back. "The house, you lived in with *her*."

His breathing came unnaturally deep and rapid. His fingers curled and uncurled into white-knuckled fists. "What did she tell you? *Verbatim!*"

Jill realized at that moment that she'd only thought she'd seen Mason angry before. Murderous fury billowed from him like a blast furnace. Having no reason to keep anything secret, she related both conversations as close to word for word as best she could remember.

With each word she spoke, his rage heated a few more degrees.

"Who are you mad at, Bradshaw?" she demanded. "Me for finding out? Yourself for having your secrets exposed? Or her for lying?"

He made an abortive attempt at raking his fingers through his hair, but his rage had thrown him far beyond his usual mannerisms. "How can you even ask!" he yelled. Then he became deathly still. "Where is she?"

"Home, I suppose."

"What is that supposed to mean?"

"Where she sleeps. Where she waits for you with bated breath."

Mason turned away, she assumed to calm himself. He still hadn't answered any of what she wanted to know. Then again, Jill couldn't remember what—if anything—she'd asked.

"Do you have the address?" he asked low, through gritted teeth.

That surprised her. "You mean you don't have it?"

He glowered at her over his shoulder. "If I did, I wouldn't have asked for it."

Jill considered that. As enraged as he was, she doubted he'd be thinking in terms of subterfuge. Maybe he really didn't know. Fragile hope latched onto the idea. In labor with his child, she needed something to cling to—even a chimera would do.

The contraction ended, and she retrieved the piece of paper from where she'd set it on the counter.

He scanned the information, then shoved the paper into his pocket. "I'll be back later."

Don't leave me! her heart cried. "Whatever, Bradshaw." Watching him storm out the door mangled her, but she'd be damned before she'd beg him to stay.

Mason stuffed his driver's license and the speeding ticket into his wallet.

"I don't know where the fire is, Mr. Bradshaw," the cop said, his expression as bland as his voice. "But I think it'll still be there if you do thirty-five on this street. Okay?"

"Thank you." Mason meant it. If he hadn't gotten pulled over two blocks from Karen's house, he might have murdered her. How dare she do that to Jill!

The motorcycle cop gave him a strange look. Few people probably thanked him for handing out a ticket for a moving violation. The few minutes being cited gave Mason the time to regain a little control. He'd never known such blinding rage. Pulling back into traffic, he maintained a saner speed and frame of mind.

The red convertible in the driveway told him he had the right address long before he saw the house numbers. A Realtor's sign on the lawn had a Sold tag covering one corner. It threatened to ignite his temper again, a self-indulgence he couldn't afford.

Mason saw the bell, but pounding on the door with his fist gave him more satisfaction. He had no fear of waking her up. The porch light was on; she expected him. True to form, though, she took a fashionably long time to answer.

"Mason," she breathed, a practiced smile on her lips. She had dressed the part of seductress for her charade, a short silk nightshirt with a gauzy robe. "I asked your…wife…to have you call me at your convenience. I never intended for you to—"

"Save it for someone who doesn't know you, Karen."

She blinked and recoiled. "What are you talking about?"

"That little production number you played out for Jill."

"I don't know what you mean. Why don't you come in and—"

"You have nothing I want, so stop the theatrics."

"Mason, I really don't know—"

"I came here for one reason, and one reason only. You may take it as a threat or a warning—your choice. If you *ever* contact me or my wife again, I'll take out a restraining order against you. If you violate it, I won't hesitate to press charges."

"Sweetheart, I don't know what she told you I said, but—"

"I will *enjoy* watching them arrest you." He turned his back and stepped off the porch. "Count on it."

"You're serious." The incredulity in her voice stopped him.

"I'm not as gullible as I used to be," he said. "My eyesight has improved, too."

"I don't understand this," she said, wounded. "You

come to my house late at night, yell at me about who knows what, then threaten me.''

''It's not working, Karen.'' He headed across the lawn.

''Mason, you still love me, and nothing on earth will convince me otherwise. Once you realize that, you know where I'll be. My door will always be open to you.''

He didn't answer. What would be the point?

''Don't you see?'' She followed him. ''You were looking for me when you settled for her. She's just a poor imitation.''

That got him. Mason turned back around but didn't close the distance between them. ''Poor imitation?'' He shook his head in wonder. ''Karen, you bury yourself inside a makeup bag for an hour every morning to look half as good as she does before she has the sleep from her eyes.''

It was a cheap shot, but her outraged gasp made it worth it. He pivoted on his heel, aware that she'd recovered and was fluttering along behind him.

''What lies did she tell about me? Mason, be fair. Give me a chance to defend myself.'' She darted around to the driver's side and hung onto the door. ''What did that little bitch say?''

''Give it up, Karen.'' He flashed his wedding ring at her. ''This stays where it is. Get used to it. Then go back to L.A. where you belong.'' He slammed the door and hit the ignition.

As he pulled from the curb, she stood in the street, her planned seduction in ruins—though he doubted that her ego permitted her to see why.

With that done, he turned his thoughts to Jill. How could he undo the damage? She had every reason to be hurt. No woman wanted to believe she was a substitute. But given the strain they were both under, how could he convince her otherwise?

Chapter 10

Jill tried to imagine floating down a peaceful river as the pains came and went. Mason hadn't been gone long, but the contractions were a steady ten minutes apart now, and she needed the breathing techniques she'd learned in childbirth classes. Alone and worried sick over what was going on across town, anything resembling relaxation seemed like a concept from another planet. That made riding out labor a little rough.

"Well, you planned on having this baby alone anyway, so what's the big deal?" she said to herself.

A quiet inner voice sobbed that it was a very big deal.

She rubbed her stomach and breathed through the next pain. Vicki had offered to be her backup labor coach if needed, and twice Jill reached for the phone, but changed her mind.

Then she heard Mason's car pull up. How could that be? He'd been gone less than an hour.

"Congratulate me," he snapped, storming inside and

slamming the door. "I didn't kill her. Do I get any game points for that?"

Between his muddied suit, the rat's nest he'd made of his hair and serious beard stubble, Mason looked horrible. Then again, he was the most beautiful sight she could imagine.

"What are you blithering about?" she asked warily.

"Homemade games. Like the one we played the night we made a baby. Remember?" There was a wild quality to the way he looked around their apartment. "I need to decontaminate something."

"You what?"

"Nothing."

She gave him a sidelong glance. "Back to the games, is that what we're doing tonight? Playing our version of Who's On First?"

He blinked at her, and his eyes focused. "I'm not making any sense, am I?"

"Nothing in my life has made sense since I came back from that cruise and you walked into my office."

He rolled his head back and closed his eyes. "I had myself together a couple of times on the way home, but I can't seem to hang onto it for long."

"I can relate to that." Another contraction began. Before it hit full force, she walked casually into the bathroom and shut the door. If he couldn't see her, maybe she could keep this a secret another few minutes. If she had to wait until after the baby was born to find out what had happened with Karen, she'd go stark raving mad. "So, do I get an explanation, or do I have to fill in the blanks myself?" she called back through the door.

"I truly believed that if I ignored her, she'd lose interest and go away." He sounded so distracted, she suspected that if a bomb went off, he probably wouldn't notice.

"Then you aren't planning to divorce me for her someday?"

Footsteps approached the door and stopped. "Does that

sound like something I'd do?'' The raw indignation in Mason's voice made a stronger denial than the words.

White-hot agony tore across her belly, and she bit her lip to keep from crying out. *Get it together, or this will be an ugly delivery,* she yelled silently at herself. She started her breathing, but it was too late to catch the rhythm. Leaning over the sink, she tried to think of peaceful rivers.

No rivers.

''Jill?''

She couldn't answer.

He knocked. ''Jill? Are you all right?''

Drawing a deep breath, she said, ''Just cut to the chase and tell me where she stands with you.'' Her voice quavered.

Mason burst in. He took one look at her white-knuckled grip on the faucet handles, and his eyes became piercing. ''I knew it. When did this start?''

''So much for personal preferences,'' she muttered breathlessly as the contraction ebbed away.

He blinked. ''What are you talking about?''

''Nothing.'' She straightened her smock and pushed past him.

Gently, he caught her arm. ''How long have you been in labor?''

Throwing a look over her shoulder, she pulled free and kept walking. ''How long have you been seeing your ex-wife?''

The answering string of expletives was even more succinct than the previous one. ''I'm not! She called here about a month before I learned you were pregnant. Before I could hang up, she told me about her planned move to Stafford. I made the mistake of telling her 'no.' I should have just hung up. That was the last time I spoke to her until today. For the last time, Jill, how long have you been in labor?''

''About six hours. It's getting nasty, okay? My turn for questions. Do I mean anything to you other than Karen's look-alike and your daughter's mother?''

This time when he caught up to her, he took both her arms. She saw no point in trying to get away.

"Jill, you are *not* second string backup to my ex-wife. The resemblance has unnerved me from the beginning. It's a bizarre coincidence that I'm still not completely comfortable with, but the two of you are nothing alike. That suits me just fine."

She hadn't realized she'd developed a knot in her throat until it eased a little. "Then why did you make love to me?"

His breath eased out in poignant defeat. "I've been attracted to you from the first day—your personality, not your face." His eyes widened in horror. "That came out wrong."

Despite herself, she found that funny, and laughed. He crimsoned.

"Want to try again?" she asked.

His expression became guarded, as if he didn't trust his mouth. Not that she blamed him.

"I don't think I'd better." He stared at her a moment, then wrapped his arms around her, pulling her close.

Jill had no delusions about what the hug meant. Mason Bradshaw was decent and kind and would always go through all the right motions. "So you're not having second thoughts about having divorced her?"

"If she bothers either one of us again, she'll find herself in more legal hot water than she can swim in." He tilted Jill's face up to make sure she was looking at his eyes. "I promise. You're my wife now, and nothing Karen says or does changes that."

The worst lies are the ones we tell ourselves, she accused silently. In her mind's eye she kept seeing Karen, the perfect skin, the magnificent hair. By comparison, Jill Mathesin Bradshaw came up short in all departments. "No one should have that much hair, Bradshaw. No one."

Mason's eyes sparkled. "We can always hope she comes down with mange."

The comment sounded more like something she'd say. Maybe she'd begun to rub off on him. Jill smiled again.

"Does that take care of everything?" he asked tenderly.

She nodded. It really didn't, but she'd had enough for one day.

"Okay," he said. "Let's get this baby born."

"Push, sweetheart," Mason urged, his face inches from Jill's. "Just once more."

"That's what you said the last time," she wailed as the agony blasted through her body into her brain. Labor had been long and ugly, and Jill wondered how much more she could stand. "I'm tired of this."

Someone chuckled, and she latched onto the rush of anger as the only strength she had left, then bore down. Without warning, a strange slithery sensation between her legs left her feeling oddly vacant.

A war-whoop of delight erupted from Mason's throat. "We did it!" Through the surgical mask, he planted a hard kiss on her mouth, then reached toward the mewling infant her obstetrician laid across her belly.

With a flood of maternal devotion, Jill closed her arms around the warm, wet baby girl. Mason touched and stroked the dark, little head, a mirror image of Jill's own love and euphoria in his eyes. They counted fingers and toes, and cooed to the tiny person they'd created. Even now, the infant quieted as a nurse laid a blanket over her and rubbed her dry. Afterward, Jill and Mason tucked a fresh blanket snugly in all the right places. Jill had wanted a baby of her own for so long. Now that the moment arrived, the joy surpassed her greatest fantasies. Overflowing with love, she looked up at Mason.

"We did good, Bradshaw," she whispered, breathless.

Beyond speech, he nodded, and she reached up to wipe away the single tear that spilled over his lower lashes. His eyes were luminous, the gold flecks more pronounced than usual. Even his features seemed softer.

He'd been a rock as the hours dragged by. For the first time, she seemed to connect with him. Jill supposed childbirth did that to a couple. It didn't fix the problems, just provided a glorious, temporary reprieve. On the tip of her tongue rested the words to let him know how much she loved him, but she bit down on the foolishness. What right did she have to damage the moment for either of them?

Within minutes, the medical team had Claire Antoinette Bradshaw cleaned, checked over, wrapped and back in her mother's arms. The nurse helped put the baby to her breast. The little one latched on like a half-starved pit bull.

"Is this normal?" Instinctively, Jill looked to Mason, not that he had any more idea than she did.

Dr. Gray smiled in reassurance. "Just what we want to see."

Jill lay in a miserably rock-hard bed in the maternity ward, counting the hours until she and the baby could go home. Hospitals had always given her the crawlies, and she figured she could just as well be sore at home. At least *there* she'd have a comfortable mattress.

Convincing Mason to go home to get some sleep had taken an hour all by itself. He hadn't left her side since he'd exploded over Karen. He needed sleep as badly as she did. To pass the time between contractions, he'd given her a gratifying number of details about the confrontation. By the time they needed to go to the hospital, the only thing missing had been his undying declaration of love.

"Oh, well," she murmured, smiling at the baby. Little Claire—all seven pounds, fifteen ounces of her—snoozed in her bassinet. "Just because I want it all, doesn't mean I don't appreciate what I've got."

Dr. Gray came by right after a breakfast that tasted like recycled plastic. "Mrs. Bradshaw, what kind of help do you have at home?"

Jill cocked her head at him. "Maybe I'm a little dense, but help with what?"

"Cooking and infant care. You must take it easy for a few days. Do you have a mother or sister who can stay with you?"

Family. Most of the time she ignored the lack. It beat dwelling on something she'd had no control over. Reminders like this shone a spotlight on it, and made it hurt. "My husband is the only family I have."

Gray's face smoothed in surprise, but he recovered quickly. "Well, then you can't go home tonight."

"You mean I'm stuck here?" she squeaked.

Mason came in, a bouquet of roses in one hand. Her heart turned over. He frowned from her to the doctor. "What's the matter?"

"He's holding me and the baby hostage because I don't have a bunch of relatives to impose themselves on our hospitality."

Gray laughed. "Mrs. Bradshaw, you're a first-time mom. You can't do as much as you think you can. You need help around the house. Here in the hospital, the nursing staff can make sure the baby's taken care of while you regain some of your strength."

"I'm taking a week off from work," Mason said. "I'll handle everything."

"You're what?" Jill sputtered. "Bradshaw, I've never known you to go an entire weekend without trotting down to the paper for a few hours. You'll never last seven whole days. You're a work addict."

"Maybe." He looked sheepish. "But would you have a little confidence in me, please?"

The request had an edge to it she wasn't sure she imagined or not.

Gray still smiled. "Well, if that's all settled and there aren't any problems when I check on you tonight, you'll be out of here right after dinner." He didn't waste any more of his time or theirs, and left.

Once they were alone, an unexpected shyness came over

Jill. "I take it those are for me?" she asked, looking at the roses still in Mason's hand.

He bent and kissed her cheek. The warmth of his breath on her skin made her want to ask him to sit beside her so she could curl up in his arms. She needed them to bond as a family. It wasn't the same as having bonded as a couple first, but she'd settle for door number two. All she needed was to find a way to pull it off. Placing the roses on the bedside table, she glanced at the baby. "You know, Bradshaw, if you hand her to me, we could count her fingers and toes again.

He sucked in a breath. "You want me to pick her up?"

"Is that a problem?"

"Well, no." His expression held a wild-eyed apprehension that he valiantly tried to suppress. "I know the basics. She won't break."

The pep talk he gave himself surprised her, too. He always seemed to be so together that it was nice to see the other side. He bent over the bassinet and smiled down at the sleeping infant. The tenderness and love on his face brought tears to Jill's eyes.

"Hi, sweetheart," he murmured, running his fingertip along one cheek.

"You'll be a good dad, Bradshaw."

He gave her a doubtful look over his shoulder.

"But you do have to pick her up first."

"Right." He took a fortifying breath and cautiously cradled the baby in his hands. Claire arched her back, bunched her legs and frowned. Mason looked stricken.

"You're doing fine. You just disturbed her nap. She'll settle down in a minute."

"Where did you learn all this?" he asked, crossing the short distance to the bed and handing the newborn to Jill.

"Truthfully? Vicki showed me quite a bit when her boys were little. I didn't babysit as a kid, so I was pretty inept the first few times I tried helping her out." She cuddled Claire close, love flooding her. "Sit down."

Mason considered the space beside her, his expression closed. For a moment she thought he might pull a chair to the bed. If he did, she doubted she could handle the pain. "Please?"

He eased down, the mattress sinking under his weight. Jill savored the contentment. Gritting her teeth against sore muscles, she raised her knees and laid the baby on her thighs. Mason leaned close enough to touch, but she made no outward reaction. No sense making him feel threatened. He might get off the bed.

Claire stretched again, and drifted back into her doze. They watched the baby sleep, checking each other's features and comparing them to hers. The head full of black brown hair definitely belonged to Mason, but time would tell if it would stay that color.

Jill treasured each moment. She and Mason had known such little closeness. Each detail needed to be committed to memory.

By the time Claire was four days old, Mason thought he might collapse. Between the baby and overseeing roof repairs, he operated on adrenaline and willpower alone. Jill wasn't in much better shape. The baby woke up every hour or two around the clock, squeaking loudly to be fed. The newborn's cry didn't sound like anything he'd ever heard.

"You don't have to get up with her, Bradshaw," Jill muttered.

"If I don't, how are you going to get fresh blankets and diaper wipes and so forth?" he snarled. "There always seems to be something just out of your reach that I can get for you." He meant it to come across as supportive. Unfortunately, his tone ruined it. They were both so exhausted, they'd taken to snapping at each other over everything.

"Just go back to bed. I'm fine."

Mason glanced at the graying dawn sky and checked his watch. "Why don't I make coffee instead?"

"Won't matter to me. I'm still stuck with decaf." Jill

curled up on the couch. Murmuring softly, she lifted the baby to her breast.

With amazing speed, Mason grew hard. The first time it happened after they'd brought Claire home, his reaction startled him. Worse, it had intensified each time he saw her feeding their child. That worried him. *What are you doing? Becoming a pervert?*

He turned away and tried to think pure thoughts. Nothing came to mind. His wife nourished their child with the fruit of her body. God, what an erotic image.

"Are you coming down with something, Bradshaw?" she asked.

"No, why?" He kept one foot moving in front of the other until he had rounded the corner into the kitchen.

"You coughed."

Had he? This was not a subject he wanted to pursue. "Would you like cran-apple juice or the tropical mix?"

He heard her voice, but didn't catch the reply. Finding out what she'd said entailed walking back into the living room. His body throbbed, and he didn't really want another blast of visual heaven—or hell, depending on one's point of view. He poured her the cran-apple.

What else was I supposed to do? He gritted his teeth. *Oh, yeah. Make coffee.*

When he steeled himself to face the living room again, he had his body under control—but it wasn't happy. Neither was the rest of him. The idea that his attraction to Jill had grown horrified him. How could he even consider opening himself up for that kind of hurt again? Her physical resemblance to Karen seemed particularly pronounced today. "Here's your juice."

Her eyebrows lowered at the sight of the red liquid, and he figured he'd guessed wrong on the flavor.

"Bradshaw, are you upset with me over something?"

That stopped him. "No, why?"

"You look at me like you resent the space I occupy."

"You're imagining things."

"I don't think so." She tipped Claire onto her shoulder to burp her.

Mason reached for the baby. "I can do that. Drink your juice." His heart melted as it always did when he held his tiny daughter to his chest. He tucked her warm body beneath his chin and patted her back. Jill's gaze on him made him uncomfortable. He wanted her. He tried to ignore it, but it wouldn't go away.

Minutes later, she had downed her juice, and Mason had Claire dry and back in bed. Jill set her glass on the kitchen counter, turned to him and crossed her arms.

"Okay, Bradshaw, spill it. What are you mad at me about?"

"I'm not. Do you want an omelet this morning?"

"No, I want to know why you look disgusted every time you catch me nursing the baby. If you find it repulsive, then we need to talk. If it's something else, we need to talk about that, too."

Repulsive? How could he explain to her how beautiful he found the sight? He couldn't, at least not without embarrassing himself and probably offending her.

"Okay," she said. "Since you won't answer, let me ask another question. Does this have to do with Karen?"

Oh, good. She'd handed him an excuse to get angry. "I'm not interested in her, Jill."

She shrugged. "Well, something's eating at you other than fatigue. Unless you 'fess up, I can only assume. And you know where assuming gets people."

Fatigue, guilt and sexual frustration lit a very short fuse. "You're right," he snapped. "I assumed you knew me."

"What do you mean by that crack?"

"How could you believe I wanted to marry you just so I could divorce you later? What did you think I had planned? To set you up so I could take the baby in the divorce?"

Her gaze skittered away. "It crossed my mind."

That floored him. True or not, he'd expected a vehement denial. "How could you think so little of me?"

"You're committed to Claire, not me, Bradshaw. Karen's tale fell into the realm of possibility." She crossed her arms beneath full breasts.

The sensuality of the gesture slammed into him. "You were wrong."

She shrugged. "It's not the first time."

Watching her lift one shoulder shoved Mason over the edge. He was kissing her hard before his brain noticed that he'd pulled her into his arms. Her firm breasts pressed against him, burning his skin through his shirt. Her lips became a fire that seared him to the core. *She had a baby four days ago. Four! Back off.* She hung limp in his arms as if paralyzed.

"I'm sorry," he murmured. With a groan, he set her from him.

"What was that for?" she asked, her eyes glazed over from shock. Or was it revulsion?

"Good question." He brushed past her. "I'm going for a run."

They spoke little for the next week and a half. Jill couldn't get his kiss from her mind. What on earth had possessed him to do that? There'd been no warning, no explanation and no reoccurrence. She tried asking him about it a couple of times, but he downplayed the incident and changed the subject.

He took her to Dr. Gray's office for her postpartum check-up. When she finished, she returned to the waiting room where Mason gently rocked their sleeping infant. Claire's tiny head tucked securely under his chin had become a familiar sight. His eyes were closed, his long legs stretched out before him, one ankle crossed casually over the other. The deep shadows beneath Mason's eyes testified to his continued insistence that he share the parental load.

To the world, she and Mason presented a flawless picture

of the traditional, nuclear family. Jill wished she could be content. She had so much—everything but his love. With the exception of seeing to the baby's needs, they were further apart than before. Loving Mason hurt so much worse than had loving Donald. Her ex had treated her with disdain so much of the time that the lack of affection had remained the one constant. But Mason tried so hard.

Silently, she caressed him with her eyes, reveling in the moment. For once, she didn't have to worry about him seeing the love on her face or her seeing his guilt reflected back. Claire squirmed in her sleep, and Mason adjusted his hold without waking. Jill knew she should say something to let him know she was there. Instead, she brushed loving fingers along the arm he had wrapped around Claire's back. It made as good an excuse as any to touch him. Unfocused, bloodshot hazel eyes flew open.

His attention quickly settled on her face. "All finished?"

So much love filled Jill that breathing caused excruciating pain in her chest. She could have sworn a boulder had taken up residence between her heart and lungs. Unable to speak, she nodded.

He drew in his long legs and stood. Belatedly, he remembered to smile at her. Jill looked away. She wondered what it would be like if he meant it.

"How about I chauffeur you home?" she offered. "You look like the only thing you're capable of right now is sliding into bed."

She took the baby from him, and he nodded an exhausted agreement, scrubbing at his face with his hands. "What did Dr. Gray tell you?"

"To take it easy for another week or two. Other than that, I can do whatever I want." Her mouth twisted into a mocking smile. "He didn't sound real thrilled when I asked if that included going back to work."

Mason stiffened. "You're doing most of it at home now. I've—we've—only had to pay for part-time help."

His innocent slip cut clear to the bone. He might go out

of his way to profess that the *Review-Journal* was *theirs* now, but in his unguarded moments he still viewed himself as single, and the paper as his alone. Moreover, after the kiss the morning they'd fought, he'd returned to keeping the world—and her—at arm's length.

"Tell the temp I'll be back on Monday," she said as they headed to the car. "What I can't get done in the mornings, I'll take home. It'll mean we'll need to take separate cars, but I think it can work. Do you have any objections if I bring the baby with me?"

He looked a little stunned. "To a newspaper office?"

"Sure. Your office is fairly quiet. She's young enough to get used to the noise. I'll put a mini-crib between the file cabinet and the window."

Once in the car, Jill concentrated on adjusting the driver's seat to accommodate her shorter legs, while Mason strapped Claire into her car seat. The mundane activity beat looking at his expressive face, the one that said he felt like a failure.

"Cut yourself some slack, Bradshaw," she muttered, pulling from the parking lot.

"The baby's barely two weeks old," he snapped. "You shouldn't have to return to work this soon."

"Temps are expensive. The extra strain of paying her makes meeting payroll an interesting exercise in juggling funds," she countered. "So put your macho on hold."

He looked like she'd stabbed him. Then a hardened resolve crossed his face. "It won't always be like this, Jill. I swear."

Her gaze cut sharply to his. His voice had carried an undertone she didn't know how to read. "Are you talking about our finances or our marriage?"

He gave her a long look. "The baby's only two weeks old," he repeated, sounding as if he were reminding himself of something.

"So?"

"Vicki said the first three months are the roughest on parents."

She'd never seen him this rattled. Nor had she ever known him to be evasive. "That's not what you were talking about."

He glared out the windshield. "Just drive."

Chapter 11

"You ready for lunch, girlfriend?" Vicki asked. She wandered into the office that had housed both Jill's and Mason's desks for the six weeks Jill had been back. The idea that the publisher should have his own office died under the financial necessity of bringing Claire to work.

Jill looked up, smiled and stretched her shoulders. Claire lay sound asleep in her mini-crib. "I wish she would sleep like this during the night."

Vicki chuckled softly. "She will. Give her a little more time."

Retrieving her brown-bag lunch from the bottom drawer, Jill followed Vicki to the break room.

"What's with the fern on your desk?" Vicki asked, the moment they were seated.

"Mason saw me drooling over it at the store yesterday."

Vicki pulled out her carton of yogurt. "Sounds like you two are doing better, if little gifts are any indication."

Jill's smile faltered. "He has an extra active thoughtful

gene in his chromosomes. It kicks in even at the worst of times. But that fern just made me feel funny.''

''Why? Doesn't it show he cares?''

''Oh, he cares all right. I'm Claire's mommy.''

Vicki gave her a dark look. ''Please, tell me you two stopped sleeping in separate beds. That baby's two months old now.''

Jill's appetite vanished. ''Looking back, I wish I'd swallowed my pride on our wedding night and accepted the sleeping arrangements he offered. Granted, sex would have been pushing it. But, Vicki, I'm no longer eight months pregnant. Even if he never made any advances, I could pretend I was asleep and accidentally-on-purpose snuggle up to him. Or maybe rest a thigh suggestively on his. Do anything sneaky I could think of to encourage nature to take its course.''

Looking thoughtful as she swallowed a bite of yogurt, Vicki asked, ''Any chance of renegotiating the terms?''

''Not really. I created quite a mess that night.''

''So? Plead temporary insanity. Do whatever it takes to get him in the right bedroom.''

Jill shook her head.

''Tell him he's *fine,* and that you want to get it on. There's not a man alive who can resist that one.''

She smiled weakly at the mental picture that created. ''Mason just isn't a man to change affections the way some people change shirts. He needed time to heal, time to let the memories of his bad marriage fade. But he got stuck with a pregnant woman, one he knew loved him. The whole situation was guaranteed to ruin any chance we might have had.'' She stared at her sandwich, trying to convince herself she wanted to eat it. ''I wish he'd never found out how I feel about him.''

''Level playing fields don't happen often in life.''

Jill looked up pleadingly. ''Can we talk about something pleasant? Like root canals?''

Vicki then regaled her with the latest round of nonsense

between her husband and his youngest brother, the latter being a professional race car driver.

Jill came in from work, laid the mail down on the dining room table and put the sleeping baby in bed. She tried not to spend more than four hours each day at the paper, but today had been horrible, and she hadn't had the chance to come home until late afternoon.

Alone in the silence, she replayed her conversation with Vicki, once more castigating herself for falling in love again, for arriving on Mason's doorstep the day his divorce had been final, for....

"That's old news," she muttered. "Vicki's right. If I don't take matters into my own hands, Mason and I will spend the next fifty years like this. Maybe if I torch one of the beds he'll have no choice. Now wouldn't *that* be subtle?"

Dinner was about finished when the phone rang. She propped the cordless on her shoulder. "Hello?"

"Is this the Mason Bradshaw residence?" asked a puzzled-sounding male voice.

"Yes, it is."

"Who is this?"

That lit a fire under one of her pet peeves. What was it with people who invaded someone else's privacy, then demanded names? Not only was that rude, but if this idiot was a crank caller, identifying herself could set her up for all sorts of grief. "You first, mister. You called me, remember?"

"I beg your pardon?"

"As soon as you recall your phone manners, we can start over. Either that or I hang up."

The pause on the other end of the line lasted so long, she considered doing just that. Granted, she'd been harsh, but two months of getting up four and five times a night had left her patience account badly overdrawn.

"Listen here," he snapped. "I'm not accustomed to being spoken to in that manner."

"And I'm not accustomed to talking with people who call me at home and refuse to identify themselves. Have a nice day." She was pulling the phone away from her ear when she heard him tell her to wait.

"I'm listening," she said.

"This is Simon Bradshaw," he ground out. "I'm looking for my son."

Mason's father. She needed to say something intelligent— anything—but her mind went blank. Stick with the basics. "I expect him home from work any time. I'm his wife. I'll tell him you called."

"Karen was right, then," he murmured so low that she wondered if he intended to be heard. Then louder, he asked, "He has remarried?"

The elder Bradshaw's unguarded surprise cut deep. Mason hadn't said a word to his family, not one. What possible excuse could he have for keeping her a secret? Karen's claim that Jill was nothing more than a temporary complication came to mind. That would make sense, sort of. She shook her head to clear it. As mad as Mason had been at his ex-wife, Jill had a hard time believing anything Karen had told her.

"Are you still there?" Simon asked.

She cleared her throat. "Yes."

"You're pregnant?"

"Our daughter was born eight weeks ago."

"So, it's here."

Jill bristled. "Yes, *she* is."

After another pause, he asked, "When did all of this happen? Why weren't we told?"

Claire chose that moment to wake up and demand to be fed.

"Mr. Bradshaw, I assume Mason has your phone number. I'll have him call you as soon as he gets in."

"Did he have you sign a prenuptial agreement?"

How dare he! Jill wanted to climb through the phone and hit him with it. "I suggest you take that up with Mason."

"That answers that," he snarled. "I wonder how much this one will cost him to get out of."

She bit her tongue to keep from answering in kind. The fact that the man would automatically assume Mason would want out added to her insecurities. "Goodbye, Mr. Bradshaw. Very pleasant talking with you."

The tears held until Jill had curled up in the rocking chair Mason bought her and she had the hungry baby nestled to her breast. What had hit her now? Why had Mason kept her from his family? Given his privileged background, did marriage to someone who'd put themself through business school embarrass him? But that didn't make sense, either. He hadn't done one thing to indicate he might be a snob. So what was the answer?

The baby stopped nursing long enough to roll her china-blue eyes up at her mother. Then she settled down to filling her tummy. Love and warmth flooded Jill. Claire was the one bright spot in an otherwise intolerable situation. She'd lost most of her newborn look and had perked up to a cherubic level of cuteness. Her mop of midnight brown hair had been replaced by a gorgeous peach fuzz but the color had remained the same. It pleased Jill that Claire would resemble her father.

"Think positive," she said, smiling at her daughter. "If I had stuck to my original plan and not married your daddy, you'd be spending most of your little life at day care." She shuddered at the thought. "If only I weren't so greedy and wanted it all."

A key sounded in the lock, and Jill looked up as Mason entered their apartment. He smiled a tired greeting. The long hours and lack of sleep showed in deep grooves in his lean face, making his features more sharply defined than nature intended.

His dark eyebrows lowered in consternation. "You've been crying."

The hop from confused pain to defensive anger was a short one. "That's right, Bradshaw. I've got a newborn who thinks two a.m. was made for playtime, a checkbook that's on the verge of bleeding red, and somewhere in cyberspace I lost the payment records for the Happy Mart ad campaign." She glared at him. "When I get overtired, overstressed or generally peeved, I cry." She sniffed for emphasis.

He didn't answer immediately, but thoughtfully scratched a beard-stubbled cheek. "Why don't you give Claire to me when she's finished, and you can take a nap until I have dinner ready."

That really made her furious. "Over my dead body, Bradshaw. It's bad enough that you put in twelve- to fifteen-hour days at the paper. You're not going to come home, take care of the baby, fix meals, then walk the floor half the night, too. I will at least carry my own weight."

He gaped at her as if she'd lost her mind. "You're upset with me because I'm trying to be considerate?"

"Yes!" Realizing she sounded like a complete idiot, Jill shrank into herself. "Only because it makes me feel like a liability rather than an asset."

Claire pushed away, and Jill put her to her shoulder and began patting the tiny back. Mason's gaze dipped to her exposed breast, and she saw a flicker of quickly suppressed desire. Just a flicker, but it ignited an answering flame low in her belly, the first one since the baby's birth. Flustered, she adjusted her clothing, got to her feet and handed Mason their daughter. As she pulled dinner from the stove, she saw him watching her from the corner of his eye.

He patted Claire's back, and the infant loosed a remarkable belch for someone her size. He kissed her on the top of her head but didn't take his attention from Jill. "The last time you acted like this was because of Karen. Has she been here again?"

"No. Can't I be irrational once in a while?"

"You're never irrational without cause."

She spun around. "Bradshaw, that didn't even make sense."

He said nothing, just continued to stare.

The pressure of the man's patience was more than she wanted to deal with. "When something happens," she said, "sometimes I need time to figure out how I feel about it. I need to sort through the facts, separate the truth from false conclusions. The last thing I want is a confrontation."

"So something *did* happen."

Jill groaned.

"If Karen called or came over, I'll take out a restraining order tomorrow." He adjusted his hold on the baby and leaned against the counter to face her, fire blazing from his deep-set eyes.

"Karen didn't call. But your father did." Hurt and anger made it hard to think straight, and shutting her mouth before she did any more damage took all her willpower.

"My what?" His generous lips thinned. "What did he say?"

"*Verbatim?* Or my interpretation?" Her voice broke on a sob. So much for willpower.

His expression darkened. "Yours."

"Your ex-wife has been filling them in on things about your life—our lives—that they should have heard from you." The hurt took some of the wind out of her anger. "Mason, why were you keeping me and Claire a secret?"

He blinked. "I planned to tell them soon. Frankly, I wasn't looking forward to it."

The gut-level honesty of his reply extinguished the faint hope she'd held that perhaps one day they could have a normal marriage. "Soon? What was wrong with *before?* At first when you didn't mention any family, I attributed it to your natural reserve. I even thought maybe you didn't *have* any family—like me." With a sinking heart, she watched his expression close. He walked into the living room and set Claire in her swing.

"No, they're very much alive."

"So why is it I'm such a chore to tell your family about?" Taking a long, slow breath, she faced the pain head-on. "Is my Ivy League husband ashamed of his lowly little bookkeeper wife?" She knew she sounded bitchy, but pain leaked from every pore on her body. She'd kept it bottled up for so long in the dark recesses of her mind; she hadn't realized just how badly things had festered.

Mason's face darkened ominously. "How in hell did you come to that conclusion?" The demand came in a low, offended growl.

"Can't imagine, Bradshaw. Do I occupy one side of your life and your family the other?"

Mason's chest expanded on a sharply indrawn breath. "So you decided that I think you're not good enough for me, that the pedigreed Bradshaws would be scandalized to find a mere commoner among their illustrious ranks."

The sarcasm hung so thick that she could practically see it in the air between them. "Something like that."

He took a controlled breath, and briefly closed his eyes. The thought crossed her mind that he might be trying to avoid strangling her.

"Jill, you and Claire *are* my family."

That rattled her so badly she couldn't move.

"Let me explain something about my parents," he growled. "During my childhood, my mother was too busy climbing the judicial ladder to give a damn about anyone, particularly her son. The same can be said of my father, except his career ladder was Wall Street and assorted places in Europe. If abortion had been legal thirty-eight years ago, I wouldn't be here."

Horrified shock cemented her in place.

"Last I heard, they weren't planning on returning from Spain for another month. They left on that trip the week before I learned about the baby."

Jill couldn't begin to relate to what had spilled from his lips. She found herself staring at him as if he were a complete stranger. The words echoed through her mind several times, but it didn't help make them any more tangible.

"As you've probably gathered, we're not close. Back in college, a friend talked me into becoming involved with the school paper. Within a week, it went from hobby to passion. I changed my major, and my parents were furious. They expected me to go into finance or law. They paid every dime of my education, then cut me off without a cent the day I graduated. They told me never come to them for anything again."

Jill swallowed hard, unable to tear her eyes away from him. Everything she'd ever known or suspected about him played through her mind. More pieces to the puzzle materialized and fell into place. This all explained so much— the air of aloneness she'd sensed they had both lived with all their lives, his inability to write off Karen as quickly as another man might have.

Mason had apparently experienced little love in his life. Had he been subconsciously afraid that if someone took away his meager portion he might not get another? If so, no wonder he found it hard to make himself vulnerable again.

"I'm sorry," she said, her voice a constricted whisper.

His damning glower shot pure venom. "I don't need your pity, Jill." He turned on his heel and headed for Claire, whose face had scrunched up, threatening tears.

"That's not entirely what I meant."

He stopped but didn't turn around.

"I didn't understand. I made assumptions based on stereotypes and my own battle scars. I was wrong, and I'm sorry."

He cast her a wary look over his shoulder. "Apology accepted." The words fell dead and lifeless in the room. "You're normally very up front about things, Jill. If not knowing about my family bothered you, why didn't you ask before it became a problem?"

She mulled over her answer, picking her words carefully.

"I think 'problem' is the operative word. We have too many of them to tackle more."

Curiosity mixed with caution, and he turned to face her.

"Mason, you're in a marriage you don't want. I'm in a marriage that's killing me by inches. In light of what we're living day to day, parents seemed sort of trivial for now."

Claire squalled, her face pleading with somebody—anybody—to pick her up. Mason scooped her out of her swing, and she grinned at him. The love that shone from his eyes as he kissed one chubby cheek made the gaping wounds in Jill's heart ache more sharply.

With a sigh, she said, "Since she has wrapped you around her finger, I'll serve dinner."

Jill woke gasping for air, wringing wet and clinging to the blankets for comfort. She bolted from the bed to the crib wedged in the corner of the master bedroom.

Claire slept peacefully, her tiny chest rising and falling with each breath, but that did little for Jill's racing pulse. The need to touch the soft, warm, tiny body overwhelmed her, and she laid her hand on the baby's back, knowing that she risked waking her.

Mason rushed into the room dressed only in his briefs. "What's wrong?"

Underwear. The man looks good even in underwear! Convinced that even in the deep shadows, he would be able to see the lust that must be written all over her face, she turned her back to him. "Just a stupid nightmare," she whispered, fighting to keep her voice normal.

Mason stepped into the hall and flipped on the overhead. A wedge of light spilled into the room, angling across the bed, missing the crib completely. *That's my Mason,* she observed with silent pain. *Thinks of everything.*

"Have you been having nightmares lately?" He stepped back into the room.

Jill needlessly fussed with the baby's blankets, acutely aware of his proximity to the bed where Claire had been conceived, a bed he showed no interest in sharing with her. Claire bunched into a ball, then frowned and squeaked in her sleep.

Mason's hands closed around Jill's shoulders. Liquid heat oozed from his fingers into her skin. Every muscle in her body rebelled from her brain's command to move out of reach.

Slowly, inexorably, he pulled her away from the crib and turned her around. Concern etched into taut lines of his face, his hazel eyes a warm invitation to share her burden. Sexual need ran hot. Held immobile by the power of his gaze alone, she stared into his face, drinking in every detail.

"Want to talk?" he whispered, his voice low and caring.

For a moment, she stared helplessly at him. "Yeah," she whispered back. "There ought to be a law against any man throwing off as many pheromones as you do."

He started, his eyes round. Then his dark eyebrows lowered in dawning illumination. Taking her arm, he steered her ahead of him out into the hall. "Humor," he muttered tightly. "Well, that tells me how badly that dream scared you."

"What do you mean?"

The arms she ached to have hold her crossed over his lean, naked chest. "I've learned a few things in the last two and a half months."

"About what?"

"You. Whenever you're feeling overwhelmed, your sense of humor comes out to play. I used to see it all the time at the paper, but I didn't know what it meant."

She stood gaping at him like a beached trout, feeling so thoroughly exposed that she was tempted to crawl into her room and bolt the door. Unfortunately, it would be a juvenile stunt to pull. Besides, the door didn't lock. "You're imagining things. I'm a smart aleck. That's all."

"Now it's *me* who's frightening you, not the nightmare."

If she had felt like a beached trout before, now she felt

like he'd just hauled her up for inspection. "Bradshaw, you're suffering from sleep deprivation. I'll talk to you in the morning."

Mason's eyebrows shot up. "Now you're really hiding," he said, somewhat amazed. "You have absolutely no qualms about invading my personal space, particularly if it keeps me on the defensive. But if I invade yours, it scares you to death."

"Don't be absurd." It gave her great satisfaction that her voice held steady, not an easy task in the face of humiliated exposure. Jill doubted he'd intended to embarrass her, but knowing that didn't lessen her discomfort one bit.

He made a scoffing sound low in his throat. "As you've told me more than once, 'spill it, Bradshaw.'"

Such a statement was so out of character and his mimicry of her voice so perfect that she wanted to wrap herself in an invisible cloak.

Telling him the details of the nightmare would just give him another handle on her she couldn't afford. Mason would never deliberately hurt her, but the fact remained that he held her heart in his hands and the best he could do was try not to mangle it. That made for the greatest pain of all.

"The dream, Jill," he urged, sounding more like himself. "Tell me about it. You're as pale as a corpse."

Jill's mind kept telling her the danger to Claire had only been a dream, a figment of her subconscious mind, but the terror it had spawned hadn't begun to abate. Groping for a rational thought, she waved him off dismissively. "Hormones, Bradshaw. Nothing more."

"You lost me," he said blankly.

"I dreamt she died of crib death. That's why I bailed out of bed to check her. My body chemistry is still out of whack. Hormones."

"Are you sure?" His brow furrowed.

So much concern was written on his face that if they had shared anything more than a baby and a last name, she'd have slid her arms around his ribs and burrowed into his embrace. A taunting voice told her to go ahead. Mason would never refuse her. She need only take one step forward. The yearning to be held became strangling in its intensity. Maybe another night, when she felt more in control. In mock camaraderie, she made a fist and lightly punched him on the chest. "And you thought the pregnant crazies were over, didn't you?"

"Stop it, Jill." The order zinged from his lips like the crack of a whip, shredding her last defense from the wrenching vulnerability she feared more than the loneliness.

"All right," she snapped, determined to go down with her chin held high. "The nightmare scared me out of my wits. I could use a little TLC, and you're standing here in your Fruit Of The Looms, flaunting the best set of buns I've ever seen." She hadn't intended to slip back into wisecracks.

Mason's spine straightened almost convulsively, and Jill was ashamed to admit how much better it made her feel to shove the vulnerability onto someone else's lap.

"Good night, Bradshaw." Pointedly ignoring him, she went back to bed. His speculative gaze never wavered, and she had the hideous feeling he stood there analyzing her as thoroughly as if she'd handed him a full set of X-rays.

"Hello, Dad, it's Mason." He'd procrastinated for two days before making this call.

"Mason? What the hell have you done now?" bellowed the familiar voice. His father was in his early seventies, but that hadn't dulled the authoritarian edge. "I got the damnedest call from Karen."

"So I hear."

"Well?"

"Well, what? You know everything. I married my bookkeeper. Her name's Jill, and we have a two-month-old daughter named Claire."

"Judas K. Priest, boy. What did you do, fall for the old

'oh, woe is me, I'm pregnant' routine? I'd have thought you'd know better than getting wrapped up with another social climber.''

Mason had a lifetime of experience dealing with his father. Even so, it never ceased to amaze him how someone with his education, resources and advantages had so little class. "When did you and Mom get back from Spain?"

"Don't change the subject."

"The one you chose is none of your business. My wife said you called. If you want to be civil, I'll talk to you. If not, I have other things to do."

The older man sputtered in outrage. This, too, was familiar ground. "We made you what you are, Mason."

"You're too used to buying and selling people, Dad. Check your inventory. I'm not on the list. Now if that's all you called about, I've got a paper to run. Tell Mom 'hello'."

He started to hang up, but his father yelled, "Wait a minute!"

"Yes?" A bad taste had settled in Mason's mouth, the usual result of talking with either of his parents.

"If you think it will help, you can tell her that you've been disinherited because we don't approve. I'll back you up."

Mason clenched his teeth and let his breath out slow. "That's quite generous of you. I'm sure she'll be devastated to learn I won't be coming into money she never knew existed." He almost fired off a Jill-type retort. It sure would set the old man back on his heels. Following through was tempting—very tempting. Oh, what the hell. "Live long and prosper, Dad. Bye."

A few minutes later, Vicki walked in with a bunch of letters for him to sign. "Mason, I have *never* seen you grin like that."

He chuckled. It felt great. "Jill's good for me, Vicki."

"I'm glad you're seeing the light." The satisfied smirk on his secretary's face made him defensive. He just wasn't accustomed to revealing his inner thoughts to other people. "I'm starting to see a lot of things."

"I still think white people can be damned slow sometimes." Her eyes twinkled.

Mason spread his hands in helpless resignation. "Just give me the letters."

After she left, he pondered how he'd handled his father. For the first time in years, the conversation hadn't deteriorated into a shouting match. Whether Jill realized it or not, she was largely responsible.

He just wished her humor wasn't her way of protecting herself. He didn't know when she'd laid out her soul before him like a blueprint, but she had. When he'd first met her he'd admired how she handled anything that came her way. Then again, he'd been mildly jealous of it, too. Learning that much of her strength was a facade shook him.

She deserved his best, and guilt blasted him that she wasn't getting it. Looking back, he'd welcomed the fight on their wedding night. He wouldn't have been averse to making love to her. Lord knew, he wanted her. But every time he thought about approaching her, he saw the love in her eyes—a love she desperately tried to hide. It made him feel like a louse. Sex would only make the guilt worse.

Perhaps he could find a way to use this new revelation as a pathway to building a marriage both of them could live with. Win or lose, he was sick and tired of that sofa bed.

The next morning, Mason walked back into his office after the production meeting and grimaced slightly at the country music blaring from his stereo. In all fairness, Jill had the volume at a reasonable level. But any of that stuff loud enough to actually hear was entirely too loud.

Jill sat with her back to him, working on invoices. From the tense set to her shoulders, she'd heard him come in and knew he watched her. Claire lay in the crib on her back, contentedly staring at the stuffed bears on the mobile suspended above her.

Feeling like he had lost all conscious will of his own,

Mason moved across the room to lift the infant into his arms. Her big blue eyes stared intently into his face, and he cuddled her against his throat. If only he could fall in love with her mother as easily.

"Why the long face, Bradshaw?" Jill looked up at him, her dark gaze penetrating. He found her desirable most times, but knowing that she'd given birth to his daughter added a startling dimension. Her resemblance to Karen no longer hit him every time he looked at her, he assumed because of the tremendous differences between the two women.

"Tough question?" she asked, flipping the radio station over to the classical one he preferred. Her question was a typical wisecrack, but this time he noticed a difference in the delivery. It lacked the usual spark. Her limited bag of tricks no longer worked. She hadn't had the time to find new ones, and she knew that he knew it. Guiltily, he admitted to himself that he liked it better this way. Being the only one on the hot seat all the time got old.

Claire began to fuss and squirm in obvious hunger, and Jill held out her arms. Mason braced himself for the usual. As she fed the baby, he grew hard, a miserably predictable reaction. He'd seen Jill nursing their child, cooing softly, countless times, and it never failed to turn him on. Now, in the light of his recent discoveries, it defied description. Possessive fire roared through him, its force nearly dropping him to his knees. Shocked, he sat down at his desk and rummaged through the stack of letters to the editor, pretending she wasn't there. The alternative was to keep staring and make a fool of himself.

He needed time to think.

For the rest of the day, Jill sensed a major change in Mason, but couldn't define it. Actually, he'd been watching her speculatively ever since the night she'd accidentally wakened him with her nightmare. When asked about it, he shrugged it off and walked away. But something was brewing, and Jill had the horrible feeling she was in the middle.

That night, Mason came home an hour earlier than he ever had before. Weird. Jill crossed her arms and cocked her head. "Either the *Journal* burned to the ground and there's no work left," she quipped, determined to let go of her insecurity, "or you're my publisher husband's long-lost, non-workaholic twin."

Normally such a comment would have warranted a smothered smile or a shake of his dark head. Instead, his eyebrows lowered, and he impaled her with a look that took her breath away.

"Spill it, Bradshaw." His flawless mimicry made her wince. "What's wrong?"

"Nothing," she lied. How had he figured her out?

He dropped his briefcase by the couch and crossed his own arms in perfect imitation of her stance. More unnerving, he said absolutely nothing else.

"Knock it off," she snapped. "There's nothing wrong." Turning on her heel, she marched into the kitchen, hoping she projected the image of insulted innocence.

He followed her, stopping in the doorway, feet spread, relaxed. His penetrating gaze held steady. He had all the time in the world, and knew it.

"Well, nothing wrong, exactly."

"Oh?"

She'd dreaded this moment most of the afternoon. "Your mother called today."

His spine snapped so straight that she thought she should have heard vertebrae pop. "How nasty was she?"

What an odd thing to ask. "The conversation started out a little tense, but we worked our way through it."

"And?"

Maybe her nerves hadn't been for nothing. "She indicated she wanted to meet me and the baby."

"And?" His single-word response had an edge.

"Your parents are coming up next week."

"Absolutely not!"

Jill recoiled. "Why?"

"I know them, Jill. They want to pass judgment, not get acquainted."

She thought about that. "In other words, you got your egalitarianism from someplace other than your genetic makeup?"

"I'm sorry, Jill." The tension on his face told her that he was sincere. "If I could change them, I would."

"So what do you want to do?"

"Like you said, there's too much unsettled between us. My parents are problems we don't need right now."

The "we" in that sentence sounded like they were on the same side of the fence—a nice change. "Then we'll cancel."

He blinked. "That may not be as easy as it sounds. They both have had a lifetime of manipulating people to suit themselves."

She felt a belligerent smile creep onto her face. Without a word, she went to the phone and dialed. "May I speak with Mr. or Mrs. Bradshaw, please?"

"Jill, you're setting yourself up." He reached to take the phone from her, but she turned away.

"This is Madeline Bradshaw," came the austere feminine voice. The lady was definitely not a warm, fuzzy person.

"Hi, Madeline. This is Jill."

There was a pause on the other line. "I'm sorry. I don't recognize the name."

"Bradshaw. Jill Bradshaw." It sounded like a poor imitation of James Bond, and she almost giggled. "Your son's wife?"

"Oh." The older woman cleared her throat. "It's...it's good to hear from you."

Sure it is, lady. "Mason and I talked it over, and next

week isn't good for us. We'll call you back another time and reschedule.''

"What do you mean?" Madeline gasped.

"Just that."

"But we've made our reservations."

"I'm sorry." She made a credible effort at sincerity. "As soon as we figure out a better time, we'll let you know." She kept an eye on her husband's astonished expression as he listened to her half of the conversation.

"We're coming up as planned."

"Fine. I hope you enjoy Stafford. It's a nice little town. As for us, we won't be available. Talk to you soon. Bye." Jill hung up.

Mason gave her an I-told-you-so look. "I didn't think she'd back down."

"Yes, she will, once she realizes she lost. The alternative is the equivalent of home-crashing, and I don't think that would settle well with either of them."

"You're right." Mason whistled low. "Maybe I misjudged your abilities. Maybe you *can* handle them."

"You were protecting me?" The concept made her want to gape at him.

"And myself," he added. "You're not intimidated by them at all?" He stared in amazement.

"Why should I be? Your mother may be a retired judge, but she still puts her panty hose on one leg at a time just like I do." A new thought came to her. "Mason, you're not one of those dysfunctional adult children who knuckles under to control-freak parents, are you?"

He almost laughed. "Not hardly." Cautious, he picked his next words. "The situation is just...unfortunate."

Seconds spun out as they evaluated the new information about each other.

Jill broke the silence first. "You may not like them very much, Bradshaw, but they're Claire's grandparents. At some point, we need to establish some normal contact, but with boundaries that we can live with."

"I agree." His eyes glowed as he gazed at her, and Jill would have given a great deal to know his thoughts.

"Mason?" she asked shyly, "are you really going to be a millionaire one day?"

He looked mildly uncomfortable. "Unless they disinherit me."

It would take time, and some serious discussion to absorb the full implications—but not today.

The phone rang once, then twice. The answering machine picked it up.

Vicki's confident voice boomed out. "How about me watching Claire tonight so you two can have an evening out? Parenthood isn't a business contract. What you need is a little romance." She chuckled. "The North Forty Club has a live band tonight. I checked. See ya."

He cocked his head. "Interested?"

"A date?"

"It's been a while."

A while? Try never. The only time they'd gone anywhere was while he was trying to manipulate her into marrying him. The confidence Jill had known moments ago fled. The extra fifteen pounds she hadn't shed since the pregnancy felt as conspicuous as a hundred. "Thanks, but no. It has been a rough day, and I'm bushed." *Liar. You're just not up to being vulnerable.* "Besides, Claire is asleep for the night."

"I understand."

It bothered her that he probably did. It bothered her even more when he didn't insist that they go anyway.

Chapter 12

From the other end of the apartment, Mason heard Jill turn on the shower. He knew his struggle to put the past behind him was costing her far more than she should have to pay. No wonder she'd turned him down tonight. His inability to commit himself to her completely was enough to make any woman feel insecure. He'd been trying, but she deserved much better.

Knowing that didn't solve the problem, though. Her love for him still made him feel tremendously threatened, but at least he no longer believed that he'd never risk loving again. What more could he want in a woman than what he'd found in Jill? With a smile, he looked at his briefcase. Perhaps the impromptu purchases he'd made after work had been providential.

Jill rinsed the soap from her eyes just as she heard Mason's footsteps on the bathroom tile floor.

"Look up, honey," came his tender voice on the other side of the shower curtain. She froze; other than when she'd been in labor, he'd never used an endearment before. What was going on now?

Involuntarily, she lifted her gaze above the rod. Between his fingertips, he held a single red rose. She reached for it, then pulled back. More than ever, she wanted to fling herself into his arms. "Where did that come from?"

He either didn't notice her ungracious tone or chose to ignore it. With Mason, it was hard to tell.

"I bought it for you on the way home."

Jill's throat locked up, and she couldn't answer. He jiggled the rose slightly to get her attention. *My attention is the last thing you need to worry about getting,* she cried inwardly.

He jiggled the flower again. Feeling possessed, she reached up and took it, careful to avoid touching his fingers. She was certain if she brushed her skin against his, she'd self-destruct. Water pounded her back unheeded as she inhaled the pungent scent of the perfect rose.

"Would you come out so we can talk?" he asked gently.

The idea of him seeing her completely undressed and wet from the shower intimidated her beyond words. "Talking isn't something we do very well, Bradshaw. Why don't I meet you in the living room?"

"To give you time to put up more walls between us?"

"You're a fine one to talk about walls." *Why, oh why, did you have to become so unnervingly perceptive? It just complicates our lives.*

"Jill, are you coming out?"

"Cut me some slack. I'm buck naked in here." After the wisecrack slipped out, she realized she'd meant to embarrass him into leaving. Then more normally, she added, "I don't think it's possible to build any more walls between us."

"I'll hand you a towel."

"You're a real pain when you've got something stuck in your head. I don't think I like that very much."

"Sorry." The apology would have worked better if he hadn't sounded a trifle smug.

Jill shut off the water. His presence focused so tightly on her that the tiny bathroom seemed hideously cramped. A towel appeared as if by magic between the curtain and wall. Never in her life had she felt so exposed and helpless. "May I *please* have some privacy?"

"Absolutely not," he murmured. "Our marriage has had far too much already."

What did he mean by that? she wondered. Jill clutched the rose, then covered herself as modestly as a bath towel allowed. With all the bravado she could muster, she whipped open the curtain, ready to do battle.

The tender disquiet on his face killed the snappy retort she'd intended to flay him with. Mason Bradshaw was so achingly beautiful that she couldn't breathe. She wondered if she'd ever tire of just looking at him, his chiseled features, his lean, well-kept body. *Just once, why can't love be nice to me?* she prayed. *Is that really too much to ask?*

"Would you like me to dry your back?"

Jill couldn't begin to divine his thoughts, but she doubted he had much concern over her wet body. "I can handle it."

"That's not the point," he said blandly. "Beginning our marriage is."

Blinding, jealous-green fury swept through her in an unstoppable wave. "If you think I'm going to crawl in bed with you while you grieve over the bitch your ex-wife turned out to be, think again."

Mason stared at her for long moments, his expression a blend of disappointment and irritation. When he spoke, his voice was only slightly tight. "I thought we had that worked out."

"Not by a long shot."

"You honestly believe I'd do that to you?"

"Not consciously," she fired back, clinging to the top edge of the towel. She held the rose so close to her face that she couldn't ignore the drugging fragrance or the knowledge that he'd bought it for her—only her. No, don't read too much into it, she thought. This is just more of him trying to convince himself he cares.

He stepped toward her, and she froze. He'd been much closer on countless occasions. But not since he'd learned she carried his child had she experienced the full brunt of his will. Mason's laid-back approach to most situations made it easy to forget his other side, the one that relentlessly pursued a goal. Despite herself, she shuddered.

"Jill, are you saying you want things to remain the way they have been between us?"

Her face crimsoned. "I love you. What do you think?"

To his credit he didn't flinch, but neither did he answer. "What is this, Bradshaw? Corner Jill Day?"

Without speaking, he pressed an aristocratic finger against her lips. The simple contact sent a shudder of need through her body with demonic force, and she nearly whimpered aloud from it. He took another step closer, standing so near that she could see the tiny lines around his mouth, the gold flecks in eyes that were trained on her like weapons.

"I have fewer monkeys riding me now. I want to see what we can build."

"Yeah, right." She brushed past him, but his hands closed over her shoulders. The heat from his fingers penetrated deep into muscle and bone. Fire danced up her spine, and her heart thundered in her chest. His breath caressed her ear and cheek, scorching her skin, and she kept her face turned away.

"I mean for *us*," he whispered. "Not Claire. Us."

"I'm not a charity case, Bradshaw." Jill wanted it to come across defiant, quelling. It didn't. Worse, an unmistakably plaintive note even she could hear emphasized the haunted loneliness.

"Charity case?" he repeated. "Is that what you think

this is all about? Or are you shooting in the dark because you're afraid?''

His probing question stripped her defenses bare. Defeat tasted bitter on her tongue, but she knew at that point that she'd do whatever he wanted. When it came to Mason, she had little fight left and no pride, not anymore. She was too tired.

''We live like strangers, Jill,'' he murmured.

''What did you expect?''

His whisper-soft breath tickled her cheek the moment before he slid his arms around her and pressed her body against his. Jill closed her eyes against the onslaught, trembling as his breath feathered her hair.

''Honey, when we're not busy with the paper, you're keeping me at arm's length.''

''I'm keeping *you* at arm's length?'' She tried to squirm from his grip.

''Oh, no, you don't.'' The warning in his quiet baritone surprised her almost as much as the sensual assault. He turned her around to face him, his gaze boring into hers with an undeniable intensity. ''I want you to listen to me, because I'm not going to say this again.''

She wouldn't look at him. It hurt too much. From the corner of her eye, she saw him press his lips together in a thin line of annoyance.

Cupping her chin in one hand, he tilted her face to meet his gaze. She thought of pulling back, but resistance had become a more ethereal concept with each passing moment.

''Jill, you're not second string backup for my ex-wife. I don't know whether Karen's finally convinced of that yet, but what she does or doesn't believe isn't my problem.''

With her entire soul, Jill wanted it to be true. ''She hasn't acted very convinced.''

''If she bothers us again, she can deal with the law. That should end it.''

Jill moistened lips gone dry. ''Maybe that particular

problem. What about all the rest? We have quite a mixed bag.''

"We'll take everything one day at a time."

Numb and defenseless, she could only stare at him in the hope that she wasn't about to get shredded.

"This marriage is about to get off the ground, *Mrs.* Bradshaw, and you have exactly one choice to make."

"What's that?" her voice rasped out.

"Which room we make love in."

Her ears rang with the echo of his words. Surely she hadn't heard right. Had she? "Oh, so we're going to start off with loveless sex?"

"Stop it." His undemanding hold turned possessive. His eyes glittered. "What we shared that night was good, Jill. Very good."

The muscles in his arms bunched as he pulled her hard against him. "I want you, honey. If we hold back until everything is perfect, we may sabotage the very thing we're fighting for." He didn't wait to hear whether her answer would be acceptance or protest, but lowered his head to meet her lips.

All worry over getting hurt vanished as the fire consumed conscious thought. Energized and drained at the same time, Jill no longer possessed the strength to stand under her own power. Nor could she find the coordination to hang onto the bath towel, the rose and Mason at the same time. Clinging to his shirtfront, the towel came loose. Fear slapped her like a blast of cold water, and she scrambled to cover herself.

"No, you don't," he said. "You've made the rules long enough. It's my turn."

That raised the temperature of her blood a few degrees, something she hadn't thought possible. Mason lowered them both to the floor, drawing her beneath him on the carpet in the narrow hallway.

"The last time hormones took over, we increased the

world population by *one*," she protested, still trying to wrap the towel around her overexposed skin.

He nuzzled the corner of her mouth, then sprinkled feathery kisses across her cheek and neck.

"Bradshaw, did you hear me?"

"I've got it handled, honey. That was the second stop I made on the way home."

Birth control. "How long have you been planning this?"

He stopped kissing her long enough to glare into her eyes. "Making love again was inevitable. You and I both know that."

Drugged with wanting him, she could hardly think. "I can't do this. I don't like being a target."

His expression softened, and he stroked her hair back from her face. "What's happening between us isn't steps on an agenda. Just hopefulness on my part."

Even if she'd had any fight left, she couldn't have resisted being wanted. She had no answer, and he once again claimed her lips for a kiss that stunned her overloaded senses. With methodical precision, he kissed and caressed her into a mindless mass of heated nerve endings. Mason shifted as if to leave, and she grabbed at the sides of his shirt to keep him close.

"Trust me, honey," he murmured in reassurance as he peeled off his clothing.

Breathless, Jill watched the play of muscles across his chest as he flung his shirt and pants out of the way. The full power of his masculinity cast an aura that blocked out the rest of the world. He wanted her. That much was obvious. Maybe later the reasons would matter, but not now. In the midst of the firestorm, she noticed she still held the rose.

Rolling to his side, Mason's hands blazed trails across her sensitized skin. "Let go of the towel, Jill," he whispered, each word a seduction of promised passion.

She had nothing left to fight with, no willpower to call up the strength to get up off that floor and walk away.

"Touch me, honey," he moaned. "I need you."

His lips covered her again, and she matched his fire with an inferno of her own. For the second time ever, her hands roamed the warm satin of his body at will, and she reveled in the pure drunken freedom of it. The towel fell away. He dragged his thumb across the fullness of her breast, then possessively closed his hand over her. She groaned, unable to move. With painstaking slowness, he kissed his way from her throat to her breast, taking a maddeningly slow journey.

Finally, the warm firmness of his mouth closed over the erect nipple and the drop of milk poised there. The primal groan that rumbled from his chest catapulted her over the edge, and waves of ecstasy pulsed through her body. She had no idea she'd been that close, but Mason held her tightly, fanning the flames as she writhed under the onslaught.

Time crawled by unheeded as the world regained some of its focus, and then he brought them together, taking them both to new heights. Once more he took her crashing over the edge of sensual insanity. Only then did he allow himself his own release. Finally they collapsed against each other in sated exhaustion.

It wasn't love. Jill accepted that. It was pure sex, driven by stresses and needs too overwhelming to keep at bay. They drove each other to the pinnacle and beyond an impossible number of times, or so it seemed to her. They didn't even stay in the same room. She'd never considered using a kitchen table in quite that manner before. Calling Mason an inventive lover was a major understatement.

"Convinced?" he murmured, breathless, his heart still pounding beneath her ear.

"Only that we're fools."

"Is that always bad?" he asked.

"Not necessarily." She burrowed more deeply into his embrace, only slightly surprised to discover that they'd found themselves back where they'd started—the hall carpet outside the bathroom. A sigh rippled from her throat that sounded embarrassingly like a purr. Mason's chest vibrated with unabashed male satisfaction.

Before they turned out the lights for the night, they closed up the sofa bed in the spare room and brought a few of his things back into the master bedroom where they belonged. She lay in his arms, physically sated but unable to sleep. Mason drifted off within minutes, but Jill's mind picked up a few disjointed thoughts—others adding their voices along the way—until she realized she didn't have any more chance of sleeping well than she'd had on their wedding night.

Being in his arms again was every bit as wonderful as she'd remembered from the night they'd conceived Claire. Then, she'd been so bound by heartaches of the past and the need to be loved that she'd grasped at the chance to feel complete, if only for a little while. Tonight was different and a thousand times worse. She needed more now.

Mason's body wanted her, but not the part that counted. She tried to tell herself it would have to do, but she couldn't. She prided herself on facing life head-on, but she didn't have the strength now. Where it concerned him, she wondered if she ever would again.

At ten weeks, Claire finally began sleeping through the night. Mason brought home a bottle of champagne to celebrate. If he was this thoughtful when he didn't love her, Jill couldn't begin to imagine what he'd be like as a man in love.

For the last two weeks, she had been an eager participant in the sexual escapades Mason initiated virtually every night. She couldn't bring herself to call it making love, not when the magic left her achingly hollow and alone. Putting on a brave front when Mason popped the cork and poured the champagne wasn't easy.

He raised his glass. "To one day at a time."

She dutifully touched her rim to his and took a sip. From

the looks of things, tonight would be one more nail in her heart's coffin.

"Tired?" he asked, pulling her closer beside him on the couch.

The loneliness had built up inside her to the point she couldn't contain it any longer. "I can't live like this, Mason. I can't."

He froze. "Meaning what?"

"Meaning, our lives were easier before. We never touched. The buffer zone and walls between us kept things from getting too close."

"You preferred that?" His eyebrows rose in incredulity.

"Actually, yes."

She saw no hurt in his eyes, just puzzled disagreement. Miserable, she looked away.

"Now the buffer zone is gone, and my face is smashed against the walls."

He blinked.

"Mason, you can't, don't or won't love me. I don't know which, but I can't give you my all when the best you can do is lie to yourself."

He pulled away, and something broke inside.

"So what are you suggesting?"

"I need some space."

His expression tightened with displeasure. "How much?"

"I don't know. But what's going on in the bedroom has to quit for a while. It's too much."

Mason didn't move a muscle, but she felt the distance between them expand until it seemed as though they stood on opposite sides of the Grand Canyon.

"If that's what you want." He set down his glass and left the room.

Mason didn't know who he was more angry with, himself or Jill. Blaming Jill meant he could avoid examining his own feelings. She'd been incredible in bed, and he'd focused on the pragmatic. They were married, They had needs, and that's all he'd chosen to think about. Now the whole truth landed back in his face where it belonged. *She loved him.* What had been sufficient for him had been agony for her. Somehow he'd found a way to ignore the love in her eyes whenever she looked at him.

When she'd asked for space, guilt slammed into him. She'd been right. He'd truly intended to play the role of loving, devoted husband until he one day believed it.

He found his briefcase and sat at the dining room table. Getting a jump on tomorrow might keep his mind off the fact that his marriage had returned to square one.

"Mason, are you angry with me?"

He didn't look up from his notes on the editorial column he wrote for the Sunday edition. "You haven't done anything wrong."

He sensed her gaze on him. When she didn't say anything, he glanced over his shoulder. Her big brown eyes were liquid with regret.

"You made the right decision for you, Jill. It's not as if this marriage hinges on an active sex life."

"For now, maybe."

Swiveling in his chair, he faced her. "What are you saying?"

Her shoulders drooped, and she rolled her head back in abject misery. "That every decision we make seems to be the wrong one."

"Don't, Jill." He stood. "Wanting sex again will help my libido but nothing else."

At first she didn't react. Then her face clouded in anger. "Why can't you be a louse?"

Startled, he felt his eyes widen. "Come again?"

"There's such a thing as too considerate, too nice, too Mr. Wonderful. Why can't you have flaws?"

This made no sense whatsoever. "Are you telling me that after all we've been through, you think I'm perfect?"

She blushed. "Oh, stuff it, Bradshaw. I'm going to bed."

Bewildered, he watched her leave. Did she love him to the point that she dismissed his shortcomings? The thought humbled him. No one had ever accepted him that completely before, and humility gave way to raw intimidation.

He dragged one project after another from his briefcase, unable to concentrate. Even so, he kept at it until he was certain Jill had fallen asleep.

When he climbed into bed, she lay on her side, facing away from him. The tension across her back told him she was no more asleep than he was. At a loss as to how to solve anything, he carried through the charade, carefully pulling back the sheets so as not to disturb her. Reaching out and pulling her into his arms tempted him, but hadn't that created part of the problem? Turning out the light, he watched her until a troubled doze claimed him.

Vicki and Wilson Haynes invited everyone at the paper over at least once a year for a party, and Jill decided this one couldn't have come at a better time. She and Mason needed to spend an evening around people other than just themselves. It had been a week since she'd asked for a little space. What she'd gotten was a marriage where neither spoke unless necessary.

Tonight, they made the drive in a silence broken only by Claire cooing in her car seat. Occasionally, Jill spared a glance at him to gauge his mood. His expressive face had closed, leaving her nothing to even guess at.

She thought about his upbringing and his first marriage. Neither had given him much by way of love. After being raised by self-serving parents, it was little wonder he'd married a self-serving woman. Scraps of affection had probably been thrown his way only if it suited someone's needs. She had no trouble imagining him pouncing on the flawed tidbits like a starving puppy. The walls he'd built around himself couldn't have been by choice, and she found it miraculous that he was capable of any tenderness at all.

As Mason knocked on Vicki and Wilson's door, Jill

came to another unpleasant realization—just how much she'd defeated herself since the day he'd found out about the baby. She'd been so convinced that her second marriage would turn out like the first that she'd unconsciously given up and, in her mind, become too close to the mousy door-mat that Donald had enjoyed tormenting. Granted, a lot of it had to do with pregnancy having made her weird, but even so the realization made her furious.

Quietly, she stood there, running it all through her mind. As clearly as if a spotlight had been thrown on her mistakes, she saw how the barriers she'd thrown up to protect herself had sabotaged the greater goal.

The Jill she liked to believe herself to be would never have retreated. She spared another glance at Mason's expressionless face. "I love you" were words he undoubtedly rarely heard. The whole picture finally came together. No matter how threatened the words made him feel, he needed to hear them—frequently.

Vicki pulled open the door, her face wreathed in smiles. She gave Jill an enthusiastic hug. "How are you?"

"Not bad for an idiot."

The other woman's eyes grew huge, and Mason's head snapped around.

Once Vicki recovered, she started to laugh. "Do I detect a note of awakening?"

"A loud one," Jill fired back, grimacing. With a sigh, she looked at Mason, wanting desperately to be alone with him so she could tell him.... No, right now she needed to finish thinking through the details. Their marriage couldn't afford any more trial and error. "Come on, Bradshaw. Let's get this show on the road."

He blinked warily at her, as if she'd suddenly sprouted two heads—or perhaps lost the one she'd had. He hesitated a fraction too long. Jill grabbed his hand and dragged him inside the ranch-style home where they'd been married.

The living room was decorated with expensive but family-friendly sofas and chairs in inviting blues. Wilson came from the kitchen carrying two glasses of white wine. He smiled broadly and, with a kiss, handed a glass to his wife. Then he shook Mason's hand.

"Welcome. You're the first ones here."

A war-whoop of delight blasted the air, and a three-year-old boy with a tobacco-brown, adult-size ball cap hanging down around his ears blitzed into the room from the hall. Hot on his heels strode a jeans-clad black man in his late twenties, maneuvering crutches, a full cast on his left leg, and a five-year-old clinging to his right crutch. Vicki squeaked in horror and lunged for the second boy.

"Get off Uncle Winston! You'll knock him over."

"Aw, Vicki," the man drawled, "cut the kid some slack. It's not like I'm some sissy teacher." He canted a mischievous grin at his older brother.

Wilson ignored him.

"I heard you tangled with a wall somewhere," Jill said, remembering how disgusted Vicki had been when she'd mentioned the injury over lunch one day. "How are you healing up?"

"Just fine." The grin widened. "I was third with five laps to go. Hit some debris on the track, blew a tire and spun out."

Mason looked blank. Wilson, his face tight with condemnation, enlightened his guest. "My fool brother is a professional race car driver."

"How interesting," Mason answered, his eyes avid. Jill watched his journalist's radar come out.

"When the boys get old enough to reach the pedals," Winston said, "I'm teaching them to drive. They'll love it."

Wilson's expression became a frozen parody of a smile. "Over my dead body."

Vicki rolled her eyes at him. "Baby, why do you fall for his nonsense every single time?"

Jill chuckled. Those two brothers heckled and harassed

each other mercilessly. Tonight was tame compared to some episodes.

"Well, hell, it beats them being something horrible like a high school principal. It's bad enough that your sons will have to admit to their friends what their daddy does for a living."

"I like what I do," Wilson muttered.

Winston shuddered and retrieved his hat. "Son of Principal Haynes. What a stigma to stick on a kid."

Something dark and unfamiliar clouded Mason's eyes, something Jill had never seen before. It took her a moment to identify it—envy. As a child, had he fantasized as much as she had about having brothers and sisters? The good-natured bickering grew louder, and Jill squeezed his hand. He shot her a sheepish look, as if she'd caught him during a particularly vulnerable moment—which she probably had.

Masking his emotions under an unconvincing smile, Mason pulled his hand away, then turned to their hosts. "I just made the connection," he said, conversationally. "You're *the* Winston Haynes. Some of your races have set records that experts expect to hold for years."

"In the flesh." He spread his arms wide, basking in the recognition.

"A little humility wouldn't kill you," Wilson shot back.

Mason stepped in, apparently unsure whether they'd draw blood or not. "Has the paper ever done a feature on you?" He set Claire on the floor on her blanket. Vicki's boys immediately surrounded her, thrilled to have someone smaller than themselves in their midst.

"You mean 'local kid does good' type of thing?" Winston asked. "Nobody ever asked."

Three other members of the *Journal* arrived. Assorted greetings interrupted the conversation, but Mason, true to his calling, returned to the subject at hand. He flagged Helen. "Let's set up an interview for next week. Get some pictures."

"Cool." Winston smirked at his brother.

Wilson groaned. "Mason, my friend, if you do that, he'll wallpaper my whole house with copies of it."

"It'll improve the decor," Winston chortled, his smug grin growing.

This time the envy on Mason's face looked like a raw and ragged wound. He caught Jill watching him and shook it off. Then he smoothly presented an idea for an angle on the story. The air of the professional surrounded him, outwardly calm and controlled, no inner turmoil showing.

Pride ignited and grew until Jill thought she might be consumed by it. This quiet man of strength belonged to her. Maybe not for all time, but for now.

"You look like a cat in the cream," Vicki observed, pulling her aside.

Jill curled up on the sofa and leaned back. "More like the cat who's had the cream all along and just realized she's starving because she's been dumping it on the floor."

"And when did this revelation descend upon your psyche?" Vicki sipped her wine and poured a glass for her friend.

"Your front porch." Jill took it, knowing she'd only have the one. More than that wouldn't be good for the baby. "Mason and I have both made so many mistakes. I don't know how or if we can fix them all, but I've got some ideas now."

"So things are looking up?"

"I hope so, Vicki. The alternative doesn't bear thinking about."

Vicki raised her glass. "Then here's to a woman with a plan."

After the party, as Jill and Mason got ready for bed, they said little to each other. They shut off the lights, slid under the covers, and she rolled over to face him. Now was as good a time as any.

"Listening to all that bickering and nonsense between the Haynes brothers was fun, wasn't it?"

In the dark, she couldn't see him, but she heard the pillow shift as he turned his head toward her. "It was...different."

"Hurt like crazy, too." She felt all his defense mechanisms slam into place. "They're lucky to have each other."

He didn't answer, and she let it hang.

"Bradshaw, when you and I were kids, we didn't have anyone like that," she added.

After a long pause, he asked, "Jill, where are you going with this?"

Then she drove her point home. "That we both envy them with every cell in our bodies."

He recoiled into himself.

"When I was a little girl, I used to fantasize about having a big sister who would let me steal her sweaters or yell at me for losing her best pair of earrings. How about you?"

He swallowed hard. "Why are we talking about this?"

"It's as good a subject as any." He didn't answer, but she hadn't expected him to. "Did you ever dream of siblings?"

After a long pause he said, "I spent a good portion of my childhood in boarding schools, Jill. There were a lot of kids."

"But none to call your own. No 'just us against the world.' Am I right?"

He cleared his throat. "Jill, this conversation bears a bad resemblance to the one on the night of my divorce. You had a purpose then, and I suspect you have one now."

"Journalists are such suspicious creatures."

"It tends to be justified." He flipped on the light and stared at her, his expression probing. "What are you up to?"

"Want to play another game?"

"You mean like the one we did that night?" he gasped, horrified.

She giggled. This had proved very promising. "Sure. This time the subject is our childhood."

"No." He turned the light out again and presented her with his back.

"Come on, Bradshaw. You're not getting away with this."

Jill flipped on her light. Mason groaned.

"I'm not spotting you any points this time because I think we're about even. Only our parents' bank accounts were different."

"What happened to wanting space?"

"Oooh, good. Attacking is always an effective defense ploy."

"Out with it, Jill."

"I think you were right the night you said our marriage had too many walls and barriers and space and whatever."

"Is this a long-winded way of saying you've changed your mind about making love?"

"Sort of."

He tensed.

"For a woman, no communication and no closeness equals no relationship. No relationship equals lonely sex. So here's the point where you and I start our marriage. You like me, right?"

The wariness in his expression as he rolled over made her want to smile, but she didn't dare. He didn't understand where she was headed, and until he did, he apparently planned to keep his guard up as high as it would go.

"Well, do you?"

"Of course I do."

"Good. I like you, too. I also love you."

"Jill, I—"

She clamped her hand over his mouth. "That love is without strings, Mason. I'm not asking you to love me back. Stop laying guilt on yourself because you don't share that feeling. I love you for the man you are. You're gentle, honest, kind and a fantastic lover."

He pulled her hand away. "You make me sound like a regular Prince Charming."

She shrugged. "Is that bad?"

His cheeks pinkened. Men didn't blush often. It struck her as kind of cute.

"Where are you going with this?"

"I told you. No strings. We're together at least until Claire is grown. That's a long time. I will love you for the rest of my life, whether you ever love me in return or not. We like each other, Bradshaw. We have developed a great deal in common. Enough, I think, to be happy even if your feelings never change."

"Do you have any idea the pressure you're putting on me?"

"Absolutely none. You're doing that to yourself. You're so afraid your emotions will lead you off a cliff again that you're trying to live by intellect alone. The head without the heart is only half alive."

"You're not in any position to throw rocks, Jill."

Having him turn the tables on her was no more than she expected or deserved. "Yeah, I know. But I'm reforming." She laid her hand along his cheek. To her surprise, he covered it with his own. "Just don't keep me at arm's length, Bradshaw, and we'll be okay."

Rather than wait for him to answer, she turned out the light and made herself at home in his arms. He held her stiffly, but he didn't push her away.

"Want to talk about our childhoods now?"

"No." She heard the frown in his voice. "Jill, I don't understand you," he said softly.

"Sure you do." She planted a kiss on his chest. "I'm just scaring you to death. Just like I used to." She kissed him again. This time on the mouth. "Good night, sweetheart. I love you."

Jill fell asleep long before the tension eased from Mason's body.

Chapter 13

For two days, Mason brooded about what she'd said. They hadn't made love again, although he knew beyond a doubt she'd be receptive. In a single conversation she'd stripped away all the protective walls between them. Mason felt as if a thousand prying eyes scrutinized him for shortcomings. Jill could see his inability to give freely of himself or to be as casual as other people. When he'd brought that up the day before, she had brushed everything aside.

"Bradshaw, you do give of yourself. You're just not gushy about it—except where Claire's concerned. And so what if you're more comfortable in a suit than jeans and a T-shirt?" Then she'd smiled at him. "You should like who you are. It's pretty special, and you're very good at it." She'd planted a noisy kiss on his mouth. "I love you." Then she turned and left him gaping after her.

Truthfully, he did like himself. He just hadn't been in any close relationships in which the other person accepted him that way. Jill smiled every time she saw him. If he didn't return the smile, the sadness he used to see didn't fill her eyes anymore. She had become a woman at peace with herself.

The next morning, Mason stood in the doorway of his office and watched her work. He remembered his first concerns about her when he bought the paper. He'd thought of her as the bookkeeper who'd pass judgment on his ability to keep the paper afloat. After over a year, he couldn't imagine anyone else in that capacity. Even before he'd learned that she carried Claire, Jill had become more partner than employee. Without conscious design, she'd also become friend and lover.

Today, she sat with her back to the door, unsnarling one of the endless budget problems. Claire happily played on her tummy in her mini-crib, chewing on a stuffed puppy. A mellow Travis Tritt ballad about foolish pride spilled from his old stereo on the file cabinet.

For the last two nights, he had searched for a trace of the distance that had existed between them, tried to find evidence that she might be hurting in any way. He honestly didn't see a thing. She had become a part of him now, always would be. But were they any closer to a true marriage? To love?

He stepped into the room. Without a backward glance, Jill reached up and changed radio stations to the classical one he preferred. Now that he thought about it, she'd done that a number of times in the past, and he hadn't really noticed.

"You don't have to do that," he said.

She gave him a puzzled frown over her shoulder, and he realized something else.

"I kind of like Tritt's music," he confessed. "Some of it, anyway. The less rowdy stuff."

The surprise underscored with amused disbelief on her face made him pull back. Then he remembered. *Jill loves me unconditionally. And it's okay.*

"Bradshaw, since when do you like my music?"

"I don't know. When did you start humming along to the classical station—not an easy feat, I might add."

Soft pink stained her cheeks. "When did you catch me doing that?"

"Last night while you cooked dinner."

"Oh."

Helen peeked around the corner. "Jill, I hate to bother you, but the vending machine is jammed again and you're the one with the magic touch. Do you mind?"

"'Course not. I know my niche in the scheme of life." She stood, planted a kiss on Mason's lips, then followed a laughing Helen toward the break room. "Nobody clobbers inanimate objects like I can."

Alone, Mason felt himself smile. Jill had such an easy camaraderie with everyone. She wasn't invincible—particularly pregnant, scared and feeling trapped—but in her element she shone like the finest diamond. *And she was his wife.* That reality didn't throw all his defenses into high alert like it once had. He tapped his pen on his desk, trying to decide what to do next.

"Hi, Mason. No one was out front, so I decided to look for you myself."

His gaze snapped to the open door. *Now* his defenses came alive. Karen stood there, wearing full war paint and a blue suit with a blouse beneath too translucent to be anything other than what it was—bait.

"What are you doing here?" he growled, coming to his feet.

She turned up the volume on her smile, and flipped her hair behind her shoulders. "I've been waiting for your call for weeks, hoping you'd explain that restraining order nonsense. That really hurt, you know." She took a step closer and glanced at Claire. "The baby's been born. Honor is satisfied. When are we going to sit down and discuss this situation like rational adults?"

Mason feared that if he showed any of the rage that boiled through him, he might physically throw her out onto the street. Getting arrested for assault wouldn't improve his mood.

Jill smacked the side of the machine a fourth time and shook her head. "Well, that's what one gets for being cocky."

"Come on, girlfriend," Vicki said over Helen's shoulder. "One more try. I have faith in you."

"Fine, but if it doesn't work, we're calling the vendor."

"Agreed."

Jill lined up her hand, then hit the panel again. The chocolate bar dropped into the tray. Helen and Vicki clapped in exaggerated approval, and Jill headed back to her office.

As she rounded the corner, her heart slammed into her throat and seemed to stop beating. Mason and Karen stood less than an arm's length apart. Karen looked to be the picture of confidence. Mason's face lacked any expression at all. Jill felt as if she'd intruded on an intimate conversation. Fear of getting hurt reared its head, but she squelched it. This was her first test of the absolute trust she'd committed to, and she didn't dare fail.

"Can anyone join the party?" she asked, forcing a smile.

Karen's eyes rounded. "You work here with him?"

"We own the paper *together*," Mason snarled, moving to Jill's side and slipping an arm around her.

Oh, so he's not as calm as he looks. His tone pleased her almost as much as did his holding her close.

"Karen was just telling me how she thought the restraining order threat was nonsense."

"Oh?" Jill ached to add her own two cents' worth, but Mason didn't seem to need any help.

"Would you like to call the paper's attorney and begin proceedings? Or shall I?"

Never before had Jill heard such ice in Mason's voice. Then she realized the extent of his anger. From the tension radiating from him, she half expected him to explode. "I'd be happy to."

Karen cocked her head in shock. "You're serious?"

"I was serious the night I went to your house," he growled. "You're just too vain to accept the truth. I plan on living the rest of my life without ever looking at your lying, deceitful face again. The restraining order will be a good start."

He motioned to Jill, and she left his side to hunt through his directory. After she'd located the number, she glanced up for confirmation. He nodded; Jill dialed.

The confident set to Karen's expression shattered. "I moved to this backwater pit for you, Mason."

"You moved here for your own vanity, and you know it. Now, you have thirty seconds to leave the premises."

Jill was acutely aware of the other woman's gaze as Jill made the appointment for the next morning. After she hung up, she faced her rival. "You can't have someone just because you want him."

The words held truth for Jill, too, but she knew she stood far closer to winning Mason's heart than Karen ever would again. The lost look in Karen's eyes struck her as that of a woman who saw reality for the first time and didn't know what to do with it.

"I see," she said faintly.

"It doesn't matter whether you do or not," Mason snapped. "We're taking out the restraining order, regardless. You've caused my wife enough pain and me enough aggravation." He checked his watch. "You're out of time—again."

With each word, Karen lost a little more color in her cheeks. She nodded, but Jill doubted she saw anything but her own defeat.

"I think I'll move back to L.A." Then with a ghost of her old defiance, she added, "I have people there who care about me."

"Sounds like a plan," Jill retorted, stepping back to Mason's side.

Pointedly, he wrapped an arm around her again. Karen stared at the sight a moment, then turned and left. Mason stepped out into the hallway, watching until she'd crossed through the reception area. Jill heard the front door open and close. Only then did the anger leach from his body.

"*Now* it's over," he said, relief claiming his face.

"Is it?"

He frowned.

"I look like her." She didn't intend to sound so bleak.

Vicki appeared in the doorway, eyes wide. "Who in the world was that!"

Mason's gaze flicked to her then back to Jill. "Just a cheap copy of someone special, someone who I used to think looks more like Jill than she does."

Vicki frowned. "You're going to explain all that later, right?"

They both nodded.

"Good, because this sounds like another story that's bigger than a bread box, and I need *serious* details." With that, she left.

"Did you mean what you said?" Jill asked him when they were alone again. "Do you really see Karen as a cheap copy? Of me?" She swallowed hard.

Mason took her hands, drew her close and brushed a lingering kiss on her cheek. The sheer tenderness of it made it more erotic than some of their bedroom adventures.

"Jill, she's nothing. When I look at you, I only see *you*. Always will. At first, the resemblance was very noticeable, and that was very hard."

"I can imagine," she said drily.

He ignored it. "That's over. I don't even think about it anymore. You and I have been through so much. We're building a life together. We have Claire."

The conviction in his eyes and in his voice made the truth self-evident. Even if Karen had another trick up her sleeve, she couldn't hurt them. His ex-wife and his life with her were dead to him.

His brows lowered. "You don't believe me?"

He sounded so worried that it offered a measure of comfort. "It's not you, Mason. It's me. I can't help but wonder if I'll think about it from time to time anyway."

A pained shadow darkened his eyes. "If the doubts start eating at you, would you talk to me about—"

She covered his lips with the tip of a finger, stopping him from saying more. "You have a good heart, Mason Bradshaw. Did you know that?"

His eyes twinkled, and he kissed her finger. "Come on, Mrs. Bradshaw. We've got a paper to run.

As they returned to the business of making a living, a silence descended between them, but it lacked the strain of before. Contentment was so new to Mason that he had a hard time accepting that it could possibly be real. He couldn't imagine his life without Jill. Putting his arm around her in front of Karen had been to make a point, but it felt so right. Yet…. "Jill, if Vicki can babysit tonight, would you go dancing with me?"

Her dark eyes bored into him, looking for truth. "Because you want to go out with *me,* or because you're a dinosaur who believes in hearth and home?"

"Both." He absolutely had to know if the walls had permanently vanished or if this was a temporary aberration that would disappear the moment he trusted it.

"Then you're on."

Jill couldn't decide if she was more puzzled or suspicious. Mason had asked her to wear her best dress. Until recently, her collection of militantly casual clothing offered nothing along those lines. Now it offered two—the gown she'd worn for the symphony and her wedding dress. Fortunately, neither looked like maternity wear when worn with a belt. She chose the black satin.

"You're not going to tell me what you're up to?"

He merely shook his head and helped her into the car. They headed onto the interstate, and her curiosity got the better of her. "I know. We're driving to the courthouse to see if our marriage license disintegrated."

"Very funny," he muttered, never taking his eyes from the road. "Besides, the courthouse is in the other direction."

"Minor detail, Bradshaw."

He glanced at her. "You're nervous."

She felt color stain her cheeks. "Why would you think that?"

"You're hiding behind your glib tongue again."

Jill settled back in the seat, feeling exposed. It didn't really bother her, though. Someone had to trust first, and she had elected herself. Whatever Mason intended, he had their best interests in mind. "Dinosaurs are like that."

"What?" he asked, frowning at her in confusion.

"Nothing."

He pulled into the parking lot of a calculatedly rustic-looking building. A simple marquee above the door proclaimed it Howard's.

"Mason, this is the most expensive restaurant in Stafford!"

"I think our budget will forgive us this once."

"I'm serious, Bradshaw."

He opened her car door and reached for her hand. "So am I."

Stunned, she let him lead her inside.

The maitre d' smiled graciously. "Good evening. The name of your party, sir?"

"Bradshaw," Mason answered.

The man's smile widened. "This way, please." He motioned them to follow and turned on his heel.

In the subdued lighting, Jill took in the rich decor. The linen-covered mahogany tables were adorned with fresh flowers and lead crystal, the chairs upholstered in brushed leather. She could have sworn she heard her checkbook cry.

As the maitre d' seated them, he said, "Giancarlo will be your waiter tonight if that meets with your approval?"

He arched a questioning glance at Mason, who nodded. "Very good, sir."

The moment he left, Jill leaned to Mason, convinced their finances had just gone into shocked convulsions. "The paper may actually be making a profit now, but the prices in this place—"

He quelled her with a steady look. "Having trouble trusting me?"

That hit rather close to the mark. "Aren't I entitled to backslide occasionally?"

His lips twitched. He saw right through her, knew how badly she hated unknowns, but it apparently didn't matter to him in the face of whatever he'd planned for tonight.

"Jill, the day I learned you were carrying our baby, you said I'd never taken you out on a date, that we had no interests in common. My sole intent then was to convince you to marry me."

"I remember," she said drily, not surprised that he changed the subject. "You were relentless."

His eyes sparkled with suppressed male satisfaction. Then they darkened with concern. "I want to start over."

She pulled back defensively. Before she could reply, he added, "And this isn't a charity date."

She visibly relaxed. "What is it then?"

He paused, weighing his words. Apparently, they had to be just right. "If we weren't married and I wanted to take you someplace where we could get to know each other—" his gaze swept their surroundings "—I'd take you someplace like this."

A part of Jill responded with a joyous cry. But the rest of her felt extremely off balance. "Because you're filet mignon and champagne, not barbecue and iced tea?"

"Something like that." His eyes twinkled.

"Okay, we're on a real date. What's the agenda, oh tyrannosaur mine?"

"Do you know what tonight is?"

She shrugged. "Thursday?"

He gave her a mock glare of disappointment. "When I first bought the paper, you fascinated me." Then he added from the side of his mouth, "You scared the hell out of me, too."

"I have that effect on people. So what's special about tonight?"

Giancarlo arrived with their menus, and Mason used the moment to avoid answering. Two could play at that game, she decided. Then her eye caught the prices. "Bradshaw, the cheapest thing here are the appetizers," she whispered, struggling not to gag. "And they're twenty bucks apiece."

He glanced up, amusement lighting his eyes. "Tonight's worth it."

She couldn't bring herself to order anything that cost that much, especially when she knew what the charge card bill would look like later. When the waiter returned, Mason ordered for them both.

"Out with it, Bradshaw. What's worth bankruptcy?"

He smirked. "We've come a long way in a year, Jill."

Frantically, she backtracked dates. When dawning struck, she drew in a long breath. "Your divorce was finalized a year ago today."

He shook his head. "More important than that, honey."

The aura of mystery he'd woven charged the air, making her feel a little breathless. "What?"

"Claire."

At his whispered answer, her blood fired. Few people knew the exact date a child had been conceived, but she and Mason did. And he'd wanted to celebrate it. His thoughtfulness brought a lump to her throat.

"You're something else, Bradshaw."

"Dinosaurs are like that."

Throughout the exquisite meal, Mason was a flawless date, attentive and every inch the gentleman. At eight, a quartet began singing romantic ballads in the lounge, and to her surprise, he took her out onto the dance floor. He held her tenderly, but she still felt a trace of reserve. Mason's body might be next to hers, but as always his heart belonged to him alone. Or did it?

She noticed a change in him, as if he were testing the stability of new ground before he put his full weight on it. By the time they left the restaurant, Jill was so turned on, she thought she might explode. Rather than taking her to Vicki's house to pick up Claire, they went home.

"What are we doing?" she asked, hoping he intended to head for the bedroom.

"Change into something western."

She blinked. "Something what?"

"You heard me." Grinning, he retrieved two huge shopping bags from the closet and disappeared into the bathroom.

Confused, she pulled on her favorite western-cut denim skirt with its matching blouse, and her tan boots. When Mason stepped out of the bathroom, her jaw sagged. He wore brand-new jeans, a body-hugging, blue-and-white striped western shirt and tobacco-brown cowboy boots.

"When did you buy all that?" she breathed.

"This afternoon when I took a long lunch." He stepped toward her—a bit tentatively, considering she doubted he had any idea how to walk in boots with an inch-and-a-half heel—then rested his hands at her waist. Their warmth permeated through the denim to her skin, easing a chill she hadn't noticed until that moment.

"You said we needed common interests. Companionship. The things that make a marriage last a lifetime."

The words were an eerie echo of what she'd told him when she'd turned down his first marriage proposal.

"It's time to see how much ground we've gained." He kissed her on the forehead.

Ten minutes later, they were parked in front of the North Forty Club. For the next two hours they danced and talked. A new line dance was introduced. Learning the intricate steps turned into a study of goofs and slipups that melted into relaxed laughter. Mason even struggled on bravely, long after mentioning his feet had begun to swell in the new boots.

"They're not like running shoes, Bradshaw," she said. "There's a getting-acquainted period with those things. No one just pulls them on and zooms off into the sunset."

He smiled at her. "Normal humor. It's not masking any defensiveness. Good."

Jill blushed, his observation making her unreasonably touchy. "What is this? Analyze Jill Night?"

"No," he said softly, then touched her cheek. "We created a child. Then we married and, *finally,* we're at the getting-to-know-each-other part. Like you said when I first found out about Claire, it's not the normal order of things, but I'm having a good time. Are you?"

Rendered mute, she could only stare at him in wonder. With effort she shook off the spell. "Bradshaw, why don't we go home and soak your feet?" Then a new thought struck her, and she giggled.

"What?"

"I was just wondering what your parents would say if they saw how you're dressed."

Mason snorted. "They'd probably have matching strokes."

Then Jill sobered. "They really need to see Claire. She'll only be little once."

He took her hands. "Let's give ourselves another month, then invite them up for a weekend. If they're civil, the invitation will be repeated in the future. If not...." He shrugged.

Jill took a deep breath. From the tone in his voice and from her limited experience with her in-laws, the relationship would never be anything other than what it was—an armed truce. She nodded in acceptance.

Jill didn't know what to make of Mason over the next few days. After she'd stirred things up between them, he'd been so quiet. To her disappointment, he hadn't wanted to do anything in bed except cuddle for a few minutes before going to sleep. Since then, he'd watched her constantly, making her feel like his pet science project.

At the end of a particularly long day, Jill nursed the baby before putting her down for the night. Mason had watched her feed Claire since the beginning, and she'd long ago dismissed the idea that he found it revolting. He never said anything, but sometimes, like now, his eyes burned with barely concealed sexual desire—a pleasant prospect.

Claire dozed off almost the moment she'd filled her tummy. Mason rose and took her in his arms. She burrowed beneath his chin and rubbed her eyes. As he carried her off to bed, he cast a look at Jill over his shoulder that rooted her to the couch. It wasn't just determination and male sex drive on his face. It went deeper. He didn't just want sex, he wanted *her,* and badly.

A lump formed in her throat, one she could hardly swallow around. Through the sexual haze, she became acutely aware of his quiet baritone as he tucked the baby in and shut the door. Reappearing in the hallway, he stood just outside the nursery, his head cocked, obviously listening for any crying. After a moment of absolute silence, he lifted his gaze. In the muted light, their eyes met across the distance and locked. Jill forgot how to breathe.

He approached slowly, his steps unhurried and sure. Jill didn't move, couldn't move. Then he reached out his hand to her. For an eternal moment, she could do nothing except stare in wonder. The long, well-formed fingers seemed somehow enchanted, Mason himself to be approached only after due consideration.

"You're still up to something, Bradshaw." Her voice trembled nearly as much as her insides.

"It would seem that journalists aren't the only ones prone to being suspicious." With torturous slowness, he pulled her to her feet and brushed his lips across hers, the contact light, its invitation more demanding than any open assault.

Jill squared her shoulders to keep from swaying into his arms.

Looking infinitely content, Mason framed her face with his hands, still studying her—the silence smothering, frightening.

"What am I up to?" He drew in a long, slow breath. "I'm preparing to take my wife to bed. Any objections?" Mason blinked with a lazy sensuality, a wealth of meaning within the gesture.

Their lovemaking had always rocked her world. But there had always been an afterward, a hollowness of knowing he'd only made love to her because he'd given his word to be her husband, not because she was his choice for a wife. This would be the first time since she rewrote the rules of their marriage. Would the emptiness ruin it like it had before? Could she be strong enough to get through it?

Jill swallowed hard and took his hand. Drawing her behind him down the hall toward the bedroom, he didn't say a word, didn't need to.

By the time they reached the bed, her pulse pounded so loudly in her ears that she could hear nothing else. Turning to her, he impaled her with a gaze that weakened her knees. She'd only thought she'd seen him aroused before. Jill opened her mouth to fire off a terse comment about still waters running deep, but no words came. Mason shut the door.

The soft click of the latch was the most erotic sound Jill had ever heard. She stood rooted in place as Mason unbuttoned his shirt. This man knew what he wanted and had no intention of wasting time. Finding herself the focus of such desire made her slightly drunk with power. He caught a glimpse of her from the corner of his eye.

"Are you okay with this?" he asked softly.

Beyond speech, she could only stare at him in wonder and nod weakly.

He straightened, still dressed in socks and Fruit Of The Looms, and absolutely gorgeous. Almost in slow motion, he cupped her face in his hands and lowered his head. Their lips touched, and pure lightning leapt between their bodies. In desperate need of support, she raised her hands and rested them against his naked chest. Seemingly of their own volition, her fingers slid across the smooth skin. The need in his eyes went soul deep.

Mason helped her slip from her clothes, then removed the remainder of his own. She stopped breathing under the weight of anticipation. He took her hands and gazed into her eyes, the distance between their nude bodies unbearable. Slowly, he pulled her close and kissed her hair. Jill sighed as sensations blurred together in a sparkling haze of passion.

His simple, almost distracted kisses turned into something more, and Jill stopped breathing again. Slowly, she lifted her head, and the smoldering desire in his eyes lowered her hormonal ignition point. In a searing proclamation of need, their lips met and left her limp and clinging to him.

Something playful flashed in his eyes, but before she could guess what he had in mind, he picked her up and carried her to the bed. The abrasiveness of his arm hair against her back and thighs emphasized the differences between their bodies. Her blood pressure rose and her pulse thudded in her ears. They'd done virtually nothing at all, but the heat radiating between them turned her into a mindless mass of clamoring nerve endings.

He laid her on the mattress and followed her down, pressing her deep into the fluffy bedding. His mouth slanted across hers in a demanding invasion and in a way she'd only dreamt he would. Mason seemed to touch her everywhere at once, stroking, driving her wild with need.

"I need you, Jill," he moaned as he gently bit her ear.

His sweet, hot breath against her skin set her on fire, and she wrapped her hand around his engorged flesh, groaning from satisfaction in knowing she was responsible for his physical state. Part of her wanted to draw out their loving, but the part that needed him *now* was stronger, and she guided him home.

He sucked in a harsh breath. "Honey, you'd better know what you're doing, because—"

Her delighted laughter cut off the harsh rasping words. "I'd like to think so," she purred, tunneling her fingers through his hair and drawing his face down to hers.

What little remaining self-control he had shattered, and she knew that this time he held nothing back. Their loving came hard and fast—two souls alone too long—and Jill gloried in the union. Deliberately, she asked herself no questions about the future, but loved him with every fiber of her being.

All rational thought spun away into mist as the wave of sensuality overtook them. It spun out into forever. Then again, it ended in a moment of timelessness, and she lay breathless in his arms, clinging to him as the only anchor in a world turned upside down. Only when she relaxed into the pillow did he begin to move again. Her eyes flew open and she saw the clenched-jawed control he'd exerted on his body's demands.

Spent, Jill almost recoiled from the power of his need, but in moments, her own body's inner voice picked up the rhythm anew. A sudden determination set in to satisfy him as completely as he had her.

Through the haze, she realized tonight was different than it ever had been between them. Before, all Mason had been able to give her was sex. This time he gave her a piece of himself. She felt it in every stroke of his lean body, and she raced to meet him, pushing them both over the precipice once more.

The magic hit with stunning force. The near-violent impact of his own climax sent her soaring through a world of shooting stars that slowly drifted to earth, carrying her and Mason with them. Spent and unable to move, they lay in a tangle of damp arms and legs, languorously sprinkling each other with weak kisses until even that required too much effort.

"Did I hurt you, honey?"

The endearment warmed her. She sighed, wanting to stretch like a contented cat, but she couldn't find the strength. "If that's pain, I'll be happy to become a masochist."

She felt rather than heard his rumbling chuckle against her sweat-slicked hair. Eventually, he rolled to his side, taking her with him. The effort it cost him was intensely gratifying. She'd never worn a man out before, and a smug giggle of her own slipped out.

"You have a mean streak, Jill," he groaned, tucking her in close.

"Thank you," she sighed. "That's the nicest thing anyone's ever said to me." With the tip of her tongue, she touched the salty moisture of the skin along his collarbone. He flinched.

"Stop that," he muttered, without releasing his hold on her.

Seeing her self-contained husband completely wrung out was a new experience, too. She liked it—a lot.

Mason propped himself up on one elbow. "Would you like to take a shower?"

Jill couldn't believe she'd heard right. "Not if it requires staying awake and hauling my body out of bed."

His gaze became oddly probing. "I'll scrub your back." The enticing note in his voice tempted her.

"I'm not the only one in this family with a mean streak, Bradshaw. Now go to sleep. I'm dead."

A low chuckle rumbled from his throat. "Come on. Get up. I want a shower." He drew a finger along her ribs. She wasn't particularly ticklish, but it did get her attention. "By myself won't do, either."

Groaning, she rolled over and hung her legs over the bed. "If you gotta, you gotta, I guess." She padded toward the bathroom. But he didn't move. He lay there watching her with an expression she couldn't identify. As near as she could tell, it was part distrust and part fearful hope. Whatever his thoughts, they had a lot to do with an unhealthy dose of Bradshaw reserve. Before she'd made the decision to trust him, seeing that would have depressed her—but not tonight. She had accepted what she couldn't change, and that made it okay. "All right, Bradshaw. Showering was your idea. Haul it out or let me go to sleep. Your choice."

Her comment swept away whatever he'd been thinking, and he climbed from bed. His body was magnificent, and she sighed in contentment.

"I don't think I'll ever get tired of looking at you."

His eyebrows lifted in surprise. "What if I stop running and get fat?"

"Love handles would just give me more to hang on to." She walked out the door.

Mason realized he still hadn't moved when he heard her turn on the water. He didn't want a shower. He just needed the two of them to stay awake long enough for him to see if the usual shadows were in her eyes after they'd made love. But the shadows were *gone*. She loved him enough to accept what he could give, and she wouldn't demand more.

For the first time in his life, his heart felt safe in another's care. Savoring the sensation, he followed Jill into the bathroom.

She was just pulling the curtain into place. At his approach, she cast a playful smile over her shoulder. "I'm awake now, Bradshaw, so you'd better make this good."

"I can't imagine anything between us being any other way."

Her huge brown eyes widened. "What do you mean?"

Absolute trust was so new that he needed a moment to absorb it undisturbed. "Nothing, honey." He followed her into the tub. "Where's the soap?"

She handed it to him and turned her back. The water

splashed over his shoulder and onto her body, and he ran the soap bar across her back, watching the sheets of water and bubbles drip down her skin. In silence, he washed every inch of her, wordlessly claiming her for his own. His heart opened as it never had before. Placing the soap in the tray, he turned her to face him.

"I love you, Jill."

At first, her face lit with joy—then darkened. Looking betrayed, she pushed against him, but he put his arms around her again, and pulled her close, resting his cheek against the side of her head.

"Listen to me, honey. It's true."

"No, it's not, Bradshaw. This is just the aftereffects of really great sex. I think we outdid ourselves tonight."

"You're wrong."

"Could be." She shrugged. "The other possibility is that you've started smoking funny cigarettes."

He hadn't known what to expect from his declaration, but her disbelief hadn't occurred to him. "Loving you didn't come in a blaze of fireworks, Jill. It came gently, on quiet feet. I don't even know how long it's been there."

With a mildly indulgent air, she reached up and touched his cheek. He covered her hand, then slid her palm across his lips so he could plant a kiss in its center.

She shuddered, then cleared her throat. "Mason, listen to me. If you think you love me, it's because you've done what I was afraid of all along. You worked so hard to feel something for me that you've conned yourself into believing it's real."

That bothered him, but her answer changed nothing. "We have a lifetime together for me to prove it to you. You'll see."

She shook her head sadly. "Just turn the water off, Bradshaw. We need to go to sleep or we'll never make it to work tomorrow."

The next morning, he tried again before breakfast to convince her he really did love her, and again after they ate, plus once more on the way to work. Her reaction was the same each time—a pitying smile and a slow shake of her head.

Mid-morning, he cornered Vicki. "Did you tell me once that you'd installed a banner-maker of some kind on your computer?"

She frowned at him. "I use it for my kids' birthdays. It makes greeting cards and all kinds of other things, too. Why?"

"Good. I need something I can put together quickly." He felt a determined grin claim his face. "May I borrow your desk for a while?"

"What's going on, Mason?"

"I have a wife who needs to see something."

Her eyes twinkled. "Do I need to keep her busy?"

"Please."

Jill fussed and fumed when Vicki dragged her and Claire out the door. "I've got work to do, Vicki. I can't go shopping at ten a.m."

"Girl, it's one of the perks of being the boss's wife. You can get away with all sorts of misbehavior."

"Mason, what is she doing?"

He waved goodbye to both women. "Have fun."

Once they were gone, he dropped into Vicki's chair and went to work.

Two hours later, Jill swung back into the office. "Vicki, you can't tell me you and Mason aren't cooking up something."

"I didn't say we weren't, girlfriend. I just said, I didn't know the specifics."

Jill shifted her hold on the baby. The reception area looked normal enough. So did the hallway and break room. But with each step she expected something to jump out and bite her. Then she went into the office she shared with Mason.

Jill sucked in her breath. The walls were covered with silly banners. One had hers and Mason's initials in the middle of a traditional heart with an arrow through it. In huge letters, another declared Mason Bradshaw Adores His Wife. Jill, Are You Listening?

Tears fogged her vision, and she had to blink several times before she could read the next one. The graphic was of a Barney-type dinosaur with a heart in his mouth. The soulful eyes said it all.

"What has come over you?" Sudden emotion choked her up so badly that she could hardly talk.

Mason looked determined. "You didn't believe me last night. Or this morning. So I'm trying another tactic. If this doesn't work, I'll try something else. You called me a tyrannosaur once or twice." He glanced at the purple dinosaur. "That's as close as that program had in its graphics collection."

She shook her head to clear it. "Bradshaw, what will you do if one of our advertisers comes in and sees this?"

He shrugged. "Tell him the truth. That I feel like a teenager with his first crush."

The man she adored was telling her everything she'd ever dreamed of hearing, but she was afraid to believe it. Her knees trembled, so she put Claire in her mini-crib, then sagged down at her desk. That's when she noticed the stack of computer-generated award certificates on her keyboard. Reverently, she picked them up. One entitled her to unlimited bubble baths. Another made her his invited guest as he picked out a mountain bike for him and a pair of running shoes for her. The others entitled her to activities both sexy and ridiculous—until she came to the last one.

"Certificate of Ownership," she read aloud. "This document constitutes legal notice to all interested parties that Jill Mathesin Bradshaw is sole owner and caretaker of Mason Bradshaw's heart. Paid for in full. No reversion rights, loopholes or exclusions." He'd signed it, then dated it the night before.

"Last night?"

He nodded. "That's when I figured it out."

Scanning the banners again, she said, "Mason, I've never seen you like this." Her voice was filled with a wonder she made no attempt to hide.

He placed his hands on her shoulders and gazed down into her face. Love radiated from him in peaceful waves. His was the expression of a man who knew he had everything he'd ever wanted. "It's brand-new."

Swallowing hard, she asked, "Are you *sure?*"

He pulled her close. "Why don't we give it forty or so years, and see if anything changes by then?"

He kissed her again, but she was still too stunned to return the gesture.

"I love you, Jill," he said. "I will love you for the rest of my life, whether you can ever love me in return or not." The words were an exact echo of what she'd told him the night she'd stripped away the walls between them.

With a glad cry, Jill flung her arms around his neck. Mason kissed her hard enough to make it a permanent memory. Plans began to form for a few certificates she could present *him* with after they put Claire to bed that night. By morning, Mason would have a few permanent memories of his own.

* * * * *

Take 2 bestselling love stories FREE

Plus get a FREE surprise gift!

Special Limited-Time Offer

Mail to Silhouette Reader Service™

3010 Walden Avenue
P.O. Box 1867
Buffalo, N.Y. 14240-1867

YES! Please send me 2 free Silhouette Intimate Moments® novels and my free surprise gift. Then send me 6 brand-new novels every month, which I will receive months before they appear in bookstores. Bill me at the low price of $3.57 each plus 25¢ delivery and applicable sales tax, if any.* That's the complete price, and a saving of over 10% off the cover prices—quite a bargain! I understand that accepting the books and gift places me under no obligation ever to buy any books. I can always return a shipment and cancel at any time. Even if I never buy another book from Silhouette, the 2 free books and the surprise gift are mine to keep forever.

245 SEN CH7Y

Name	(PLEASE PRINT)	
Address	Apt. No.	
City	State	Zip

This offer is limited to one order per household and not valid to present Silhouette Intimate Moments® subscribers. *Terms and prices are subject to change without notice.
Sales tax applicable in N.Y.

UIM-98   ©1990 Harlequin Enterprises Limited

Catch more great
HARLEQUIN™ Movies

featured on

Premiering July 11th
Another Woman
Starring Justine Bateman and
Peter Outerbridge
Based on the novel by Margot Dalton

Don't miss next month's movie!
Premiering August 8th
The Waiting Game
Based on the novel by *New York Times*
bestselling author Jayne Ann Krentz

If you are not currently a subscriber to
The Movie Channel, simply call your
local cable or satellite provider for more
details. Call today, and don't miss out
on the romance!

 HARLEQUIN®

Makes any time special ™

100% pure movies.
100% pure fun.

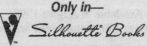

International bestselling author

JOAN JOHNSTON

**continues her wildly popular Hawk's Way
miniseries with an all-new, longer-length novel**

THE SUBSTITUTE GROOM

HAWK'S WAY

August 1998

Jennifer Wright's hopes and dreams had rested on her summer wedding—until a single moment changed everything. Including the *groom*. Suddenly Jennifer agreed to marry her fiancé's best friend, a darkly handsome Texan she needed—and desperately wanted—almost against her will. But U.S. Air Force Major Colt Whitelaw had sacrificed too much to settle for a marriage of convenience, and that made hiding her passion all the more difficult. And hiding her biggest secret downright impossible…

**"Joan Johnston does contemporary Westerns
to perfection."** —*Publishers Weekly*

Available in August 1998
wherever Silhouette books are sold.

Silhouette®

The World's Most Eligible Bachelors are about to be named! And Silhouette Books brings them to you in an all-new, original series....

World's Most Eligible Bachelors

Twelve of the sexiest, most sought-after men share every intimate detail of their lives in twelve never-before-published novels by the genre's top authors.

Don't miss these unforgettable stories by:

Dixie Browning

Marie Ferrarella

Jackie Merritt

Tracy Sinclair

BJ James

Rachel Lee

Suzanne Carey

Gina Wilkins

VICTORIA PADE

Susan Mallery

Maggie Shayne

Anne McAllister

Look for one new book each month in the
World's Most Eligible Bachelors series beginning
September 1998 from Silhouette Books.

V™ *Silhouette*®

Available at your favorite retail outlet.

Look us up on-line at: http://www.romance.net   PSWMEB

SILHOUETTE·INTIMATE·MOMENTS®
commemorates its

15th Anniversary

15 years of rugged, irresistible heroes!

15 years of warm, wonderful heroines!

15 years of exciting, emotion-filled romance!

In May, June and July 1998 join the celebration as Intimate Moments brings you new stories from some of your favorite authors—authors like:

Marie Ferrarella
Maggie Shayne
Sharon Sala
Beverly Barton
Rachel Lee
Merline Lovelace
and many more!

Don't miss this special event! Look for our distinctive anniversary covers during all three celebration months. Only from Silhouette Intimate Moments, committed to bringing you the best in romance fiction, today, tomorrow—always.

Available at your favorite retail outlet.

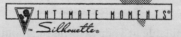

INTIMATE MOMENTS®
Silhouette®

Look us up on-line at: http://www.romance.net

SIM15YR